POWERS of INFLUENCE

POWERS of INFLUENCE

JORDAN AREY

PUBLISHED BY HOMEBOUND PUBLICATIONS

POWERS OF INFLUENCE
Copyright © 2012 by Jordan Arey

All Rights Reserved. Without limiting the rights under copyright reserved above, no part of this publication may be reproduced, stored in or introduced into a retrieval system or transmitted in any means (electronic, mechanical, photocopying, recording or otherwise) without the prior written permission of both the copyright owner and publisher, except for brief quotations embodied in critical articles and reviews. For bulk ordering information or permissions write:

Homebound Publications, PO Box 1442
Pawcatuck, Connecticut 06379 United States of America

All characters appearing in this work are fictitious. Any resemblance to real persons, living or dead, is purely coincidental. All occurrences in this work are fictitious. Any resemblance to actual events, past or present, is purely coincidental.

Visit our website: www.homeboundpublications
Visit the author at: www.powersofinfluence.com
and www.jordanarey.com

FIRST EDITION
ISBN 13: 978-1-938846-02-1 (pbk)

BOOK DESIGN
Front Cover Image Attribution: © Andreas Kermann | istock.com
Front Cover Image Attribution: © Jokerpro | Shuttershock.com
Interior and Cover Design: Leslie M. Browning

Library of Congress Cataloging-in-Publication Data

Arey, Jordan, 1983-
  Powers of influence / Jordan Arey. -- 1st ed.
     p. cm.
  ISBN 978-1-938846-02-1 (pbk.)
  1. Identity (Psychology)—Fiction. 2. Self-realization—Fiction. 3. Suspense fiction. 4. Fables. I. Title.
  PS3601.R466P69 2012
  813'.6--dc23
                                                                              2012035773

10 9 8 7 6 5 4 3 2 1

Chapter 1

At first it seemed as though it was all a dream, or some faint memory surfacing through the abyss of a deep sleep. Though it must have come only once, the voice echoed through my thoughts several times before I realized that it was borne from a world outside my own mind. It was a voice of pure innocence, and it came with a tone of child-like curiosity.

"Is he dead, Mommy?" I heard through the darkness. I slowly, almost involuntarily, opened my eyes to the light of the sun coming from behind the round face of a blue-eyed little girl. She had bright blond hair that was pulled to either side and fastened above her ears, and it glowed like gold with the aid of the piercing rays. She had a look of slight concern on her face while peering down at me, but she hovered over my head without the slightest reticence.

I tried to sit up but was unable to do so. I felt stiff and numb. I blinked repeatedly to ward off an immense fatigue that was hanging over me, and I noticed then that my whole body was nearly paralyzed. "Nope, he ain't dead at all. See, he's movin'!" the little girl exclaimed. Despite her excitement, I paid very little attention to her now. The strange circumstance in which I found myself commanded all my focus, and it was beginning to cause me to worry deeply.

The next thing that came to my realization was the feeling of sand beneath my hands and the sound of waves crashing a short distance from me. A slight breeze ruffled my clothes and carried a salty scent of ocean past my nose. I closed my eyes tightly and tilted my head to the side, straining to move my neck even the slightest degree. When I opened them, I saw another person running toward me from a distance.

"Susan, you come over here and give that man some room," her voice rang. "I told you not to run ahead of us, didn't I?" I watched as a matured yet pretty-looking woman came to her side. She appeared to be what I would consider middle-aged, but as far as looks could tell, she seemed to maintain in her demeanor some unrelenting hold on youth.

"Yes, Mommy," Susan whimpered as she turned her head to the ground. Soon a third individual came into view, shading my face from the sun with his broad shoulders. From what I could make through squinted eyes, he was rather tall and about the same age as the woman crouched at my side. His face looked callused and drawn as if from years of hard labor in the sun, but his eyes were kind and sympathetic.

"Is he moving at all?" he quickly asked. I slowly attempted to sit up again, trying to support my weary frame with outstretched arms, but all my efforts were to no avail. I blinked several times again to better focus on my surroundings. I attempted to speak but nothing came. "He looks as exhausted as all the others."

"Loot, he's tryin' to say sometin!" Susan shouted. My failure to talk was as unexpected as my impaired movement, and I was growing increasingly frustrated with my limitations. Though my mouth functioned, it only barely did so, and I was incapable of forming any sounds of articulate speech. Though my limbs moved, it was minimal. I wasn't able to direct them as I wished, nor was I able to summon any considerable strength from them.

CHAPTER 1 | 3

A sense of near panic started to well inside of me. I began to feel helpless in my motionless and speechless state. If this wasn't enough to cause desperation, the next realization was. Despite the two unfortunate facts that were presently causing such anxiety in my heart, there was an additional reality that struck me as far more unsettling. It was at that moment that I realized I had no idea where I was. Far worse than this was that I wasn't even sure of my own name. I couldn't picture in my mind any event, except what I had just seen, and I soon came to find that I had no recollection of anything at all.

"Are you alright, Son?" the man asked.

The woman gave him a strange look. "Thomas, you know he can't speak," she replied, a bit bewildered. "Besides, they never remember anyway," she added, "none that we have ever seen."

The man's expression took on a defeated look. "I know, but why not try? One day someone might show up that actually remembers something."

While listening intently to their conversation, I quickly tried again to conjure any memory I could, but my mind remained as blank as my stare into the clouds above me. Helplessness and frustration returned as I lay verbally and physically disabled in front of people I knew nothing about, without even a sense of my own identity to calm my pulsing anxiety.

"It's been a long time since any have washed ashore," the woman continued as she looked at me with concern.

"You're right, Martha, and it's a good thing we were here to find him," Thomas replied.

"Can we take'm home?" Susan asked, turning toward her mother. The woman expressed an immediate interest in what she had said, looking her in the eyes and then turning her gaze toward me.

"Yes, Dear, he certainly needs our help." She looked at me again and delivered a sympathetic expression. As her eyes met mine, something unexpected happened; peace filled my heart as suddenly as panic had filled it earlier. Something about her was comforting and helped to assure me that I was going to be alright.

"Come on, Son. We'll take care of you," Thomas affirmed, reaching down to scoop my languid frame off the sandy shores. My mind, which had once raced with anxiousness, was now beginning to feel calm after such seemingly-charitable individuals had come to my assistance. Though I knew nothing about them, I could easily sense that they were genuine and kind.

"Is he goin' to be my new brudder, Mommy?" Susan inquired as she skipped alongside her parents. Martha and Thomas returned a smile without saying anything more as we hurried from off the beach and into the rolling hills and tall grass that stood swaying in the ocean breeze.

A short time later, we came upon a small carriage that sat behind a large brown horse standing calm and still as we approached. Susan scurried up to the back of the carriage where her mother helped her into a pile of cloth that lined the base of the wooden frame. I soon found myself being wrapped snugly in a blanket next to her while her eyes remained fixed on my own.

"Do we have any water left?" Martha called. Without a word, Thomas reached for a leather bladder in the carriage and passed it to her. The water she offered was no longer cool but was enough to quench my thirst. "He needs something to eat, I'm sure. He looks famished."

"Let's not waste any time getting back then," Thomas said. With no delay, he and the woman took their seats and cautioned Susan to remain seated as well. Thomas made a clicking noise with his mouth while flicking the reins over the horse's back, prompting the animal into a steady gallop.

My eyes soon began to grow heavy again as I sat perched on the padding in the far corner of the bed. The exhaustion I felt when first I came to consciousness on the shore started to weigh on me once more while I watched my surroundings rock to and fro over the horizon of the carriage walls.

"Do you think he's alright?" I heard Martha ask.

"I hope so," Thomas replied. "Most others seem to end up just fine. I think he'll be much better after he gets some rest." After that, I heard nothing more.

I woke to the same eyes that had peered down at me on the shore, and they were very near my face again. They remained still and focused, so close that I could see my reflection in them. Susan said nothing for a while but just stared at me as if she was trying to place the first time she had met my familiar face.

"Whana see my shea shells?" she finally asked, holding up a small leather bag that was bulging at the seams. Next thing I knew, she was dumping its contents into a small pile in front of me amid the rumbling of the carriage. I looked upon a jumble of large and small shells mixed with several rocks of varying sizes. "Dese are my rocks fer my cllection," she said, picking them out of the cluster and placing them back into the bag. "I'm goin' to mate a netlace out of da shells."

My eyes scanned the variations in front of me. Some were very dull, while others were rather intricate in color and design. "Dat's a pretty netlace you got," Susan said, opening up a small white box that she held in her hand and pulling from inside it a brilliant shining band of white metal. "It was in yer potet, bout to fall out."

"Susan, please don't bother him," Martha pled as she turned around from facing the direction we were going. "He isn't feeling well. Please, let him be."

"I not bodderin' him. I jest lootin at his netlace." Martha's face moved toward her daughter's tiny hand where the necklace laid gripped between her fingers.

"Yes, it's pretty, isn't it?" she affirmed. "Can you put it back where you found it?" Susan lingered for a moment in indecision, then, almost as if she could feel her mother's glare, she yielded to her wishes.

"Yep, it jest goes right here," she replied, stuffing it back into a pocket in my shirt. "I still goin' to mate a shea shell netlace." I did all I could to smile in return, one of the few things I was able to do. Despite the rushing uncertainty of the passing moments, I felt at home around little Susan, and her adorable nature was endearing to me.

My mind thought back to the shore, my stupor, and my physical inabilities. Perhaps the owner of this necklace would have answers to my present situation, which also begged to question why I was in possession of it, being that it was clearly the necklace of a woman. I started again to feel overwhelmingly uneasy after this thought, and I began looking all around, hoping that some element of my surroundings might trigger a memory.

My heart began to race, and my face must have expressed my fears well, because Martha spoke to me as if she could sense all my worries. Her sympathetic stare met with my restless eyes, and she looked as though she was experiencing all my inner turmoil along with me. "It's alright, Dear; we're going to take care of you. It won't be long now." I got the feeling, by the way she spoke to me, that I was much younger than she was, which made her assuming role as a motherly influence seem all the more fitting.

Our course continued with a sense of urgency. We lumbered along an unpaved road that wound onward through clusters of large trees while at one point crossing over an old bridge that spanned the gap between the banks of a small river. All the while, Susan kept me occupied with a one-sided conversation about her mom and dad and brothers and sister, cheerfully informing me that I could be her newest brother.

I was glad to see that she was warming up to me so much, and her carefree tone helped to soothe my nerves. Martha turned back to check on me every so often and continued to advise Susan against bothering me, affirming that I needed to rest and be left alone.

Time seemed to move as rapidly as the ride itself. Before too long, we came upon an opening in the trees where the road rolled down a grassy hill toward a small house that sat in an open meadow. The carriage rumbled at a quicker rate than before, drawing nearer to the cottage with each sway and bump. Susan had taken to kneeling just behind Thomas and Martha, grinning from ear to ear as we moved down the slope toward her home.

"Dere, dat's my house, John," she said excitedly, pointing her small finger in the direction of our course. "You get to meet my brudders and zister!"

"John?" Martha asked from behind a smile that quickly melted away, as if she felt reproach for having allowed herself a moment of humor under the current circumstance.

"Yep, dat's his name," she said, gesturing toward me. "I named him John."

As we neared the house, two young children came into view. One of them appeared close to the age of Susan while the other seemed somewhat older. Upon seeing the carriage, the young girl turned to the little boy, and both started running toward us.

Chapter 2

Thomas came to a stop just before a barn as the two children ran past the horse and the little boy started tugging on Thomas's pant leg.

"Daddy, daddy," he said. "I got a toad in da pond," which well explained the water lines on his pants and shirt sleeves. "Wanta see um?"

"I picked you some flowers, Mom," the older girl said, holding up a bundle of stems laced with yellow petals.

"Well, thank you very much," she replied in a bit of a rush.

Before Thomas or Martha even had a chance to respond much further, the young boy chimed in with more to say. "Who's dat?" he sounded, looking up to me with questioning eyes.

"His name is John," Susan proclaimed, as if she was the only authority on the matter. "He goin' to be our new brudder." As she said it, a look of excitement came to the little boy's face.

"Wanta see da toad, John?"

"Maybe later, Timmy," Thomas answered, jumping down from his seat. "Our friend needs to be cared for right now."

"Where's Simon?" I heard Martha ask.

"He's feeding the horses," the older girl answered.

"Will you run and tell him we're back and that we found someone on the shores again?" I watched as the young one nodded her head and ran past the barn toward a fenced field.

A short moment later, Thomas was carrying me toward the door of the small home as all the others followed in line behind him. The door opened into a cozy and welcoming room. The sun peeked through the few windows there were and illuminated the place with a welcoming glow. In the center of the house was a table, and to the left of it was a humble set of furniture that partitioned the room from a bed that sat behind it in the corner. To the other side sat a pair of smaller beds that the children likely shared, and farther in the opposite corner lay a lone cot that seemed large enough for only one person. I was taken to where the cot stood and placed on its surprisingly-soft bedding while the two little children stood around me.

"Susan, Timmy, will you go and fetch some fresh vegetables for a soup?" Martha asked. "Get Mary and Simon to help you." Without a word, they ran to the front door, excitedly racing for position to be the first one outside.

Martha proceeded to wash my face with a cool cloth, which felt refreshing against my sandy warm skin. A short time after she had bathed my face and head, she offered me more water from a ladle the man had brought her, which on this occasion, was cold and fresh.

All three children came rushing back some time later. In their arms was a variety of vegetables that they must have picked from a nearby garden. They walked over to the far end of the cottage and placed them in a crude basin near an equally-modest stove.

"We got dem, Mommy. Dey're all set," Susan said, who now looked to be the youngest of the three when standing next to the other two.

"Thank you. You've all been very helpful. Now go and play while we take care of our visitor."

"Can John come wiff us?" Timmy asked.

"John needs to stay where he is right now, Son. You three go on and play," Thomas said.

"We see ya lader, John," Susan whispered while patting me on the head.

Suddenly, the door opened again, and a person I hadn't seen before walked through the entryway. He was a young man, similar in stature to the one who had carried me inside, only youth prevailed over his shoulders in a way it no longer did with Thomas. The hat which he wore on his head had been removed upon entering the home, along with his coat which he hung on a hook near a window. He had, in one hand, a bucket that he set on the floor after closing the door behind him, and in the other was a pair of gloves that appeared to be used for difficult labor.

"Mary said..." His words ended as he saw me lying on the cot. Thomas nodded in answer to the expression on his face. "From the shores?" Another nod followed, and Martha turned to the sound of his voice for the first time. "I was beginning to think that we weren't ever going to see another," he continued. The young man slowly took to his knees at Martha's side and, in a brotherly manner, placed his hand on my shoulder.

"It must be frustrating just laying here, can't say anything, can't hardly move." As he spoke, I could read empathy in his eyes. "Or is this time different?" he asked, turning toward Thomas with a degree of hope in his countenance.

"I'm afraid not. He's like all the others." If I could have voiced my frustration, I would have gladly done so, but I was only able to manage a haphazard jostling of my head.

"Here, see if he will take more water. I'm afraid he's severely parched," Martha insisted. He took from her hand the ladle that she had refilled from a bucket at her side and raised it to my mouth. Meanwhile, Martha walked toward her husband where she paused before moving toward the basin of vegetables. "I'm going to get started on something for him to eat," she said. "He must be hurting for some food."

The comfort and warmth of the cot and the blanket which had been draped over me brought relaxation to my tired frame, and I could feel sleep coming upon me again. I once more began to ponder on my situation. I still could not remember anything. Opening my eyes to the innocent face of Susan was my nearest recollection, but I began to worry less about what didn't seem to be changing and tried to rest my wearied mind.

The wonderful smell of a hearty soup soon began to fill the room with an appetizing scent, and though my stomach was almost as hungry as I was tired, my exhaustion seemed to be winning. My eyelids grew heavy, and I was soon viewing the room and the people around me through slowly-fluttering sight.

The time that passed accounted for bouts with drowsiness dispersed between long moments of sleep. With each occasion, even the limited memory I had seemed to flee all the more from me, and by the time I actually woke again, I noticed that the sun had not begun to set but to rise. At the very least, I could figure that a day must have already passed, but it could easily have been more.

I finally felt somewhat rested but still rather sluggish. My sight panned across the sunlit roof above me, one that was familiar but only slightly so. From the view I had lying on my back, the room appeared at first glance to be empty, but I remembered having seen very welcoming faces and hearing calm and comforting voices from before.

In attempting to move my legs, I was slowly able to do so, though they had what seemed to be limited coordination and strength. Through tedious and gradual efforts, I rolled my weakened limbs from off the cot and onto the wooden floor below me. My torso and arms seemed somewhat weaker and less coordinated, and I sat in a degree of discomfort as my feet

touched the ground and the rest of me still lay flat on the bed.
I tried to sit up and failed on several attempts. Finally, I was able to lift my back enough to move my arms underneath me. They strained under my weight as I held them for as long as I could. I leaned forward as much as my weary frame would allow, pushing with my arms and pulling with my stomach, until at last I sat up for the first time I could recall.

Despite my slowness to start, I had no interest in remaining where I was. I was ready to move off the cot and into the surroundings that I knew so little about. I braced my legs and summoned all the strength I could from my arms. They shook again under the weight of my body, and I pushed with all the force that I could muster. My arms propelled me forward, but my legs weren't ready to support me. Suddenly, they collapsed, and I found myself meeting the floor in a thud. Next, I heard the rustle of sheets and the patter of feet, which refuted my assumption that I had been alone.

"John felled out of bed!" a voice exclaimed. By the time I rolled from my stomach to my back, a man and woman hovered over me with expressions of surprise written on their faces. They looked most familiar, and it was no more than a brief moment before I recalled their names.

"Are you otay, John?" a little girl asked as she pushed between Thomas's legs and knelt at my side. It was Susan, and I immediately recalled the vaguest memory of seeing her eyes looking down at me from a sunny sky.

"Here, let's get him back in bed, Dear," Martha said as she reached down to help me onto the cot.

She and Thomas, with the help of the other man I remembered as Simon, placed me back in the bed and tucked me snugly into the covers. All the work I had exerted to free myself had only brought me back to the beginning. If only I could tell them I wanted to be up and going but lacked the strength to do it on my own.

"I...wa...," was all I could manage upon my attempt to speak.

"He said something!" an older girl shouted. It was Mary. Some of the small amount of memory I had was all coming back to me now.

"Oh, he's probably sick of lying around," Martha said.

"Don't worry, you'll be up and about soon enough," Thomas encouraged. I laid there moving my eyes from one person to the next. Each returned a smile that reminded me I was in good hands.

"JJJooohhhnnn..." I managed to say, though the remainder of what I hoped to speak eluded me.

"Dat's yer name!" Susan yelled in excitement. "My name's Susan, dis is Timmy, and dis is my zister, Mary," she added, pointing to both of them. The three smiled back at me as if to introduce themselves. I returned the same, hoping to say something more, but I was forced to yield to my only form of communication—a simple grin.

"Well, now that we're all up, we might as well get an early start on things," Thomas announced.

As I lay involuntarily in the bed, everyone else in the house attended to preparations for the day. Shortly, a small meal of what looked like dried fish and fruit was placed on the table while everyone took their seats and began eating.

I didn't feel hungry at first, but as I peered at the food, my appetite was soon enticed. Unfortunately, I was stuck in bed, snugly tucked in covers that were a less-than-welcome restraint. I attempted to free myself as discreetly as possible by turning side to side in the bed, hoping not to attract any attention as I did. I anticipated a possible escape from the quilted fortress once everyone was gone. I closed my eyes again in order to look asleep, all the while thinking back on the events that played through my mind.

I could recall eating soup from the bed I was in. I remembered talk and laughter and the quiet noise of the wind against the window to my right. I could recollect falling asleep a few times within these walls, but everything beyond that, whatever it might be, was blank. Before long, I could hear the shuffling of feet and the opening of the front door.

Eventually, the sounds of the children and their parents drifted into the background, and I was left to assume that I was alone in the small house. I slowly opened my eyes to confirm what I had just concluded, and sure enough, all of them had left. The room was still and quiet.

I was slowly able to sit up as before and look out the window that sat just above the bed. As I did, I could see Martha, Mary, and Susan pulling weeds from around the vegetables in the garden. Farther along, I could see Simon standing with Timmy on a slow-moving plow while a large brown horse pulled it along. As I lingered in my observations, I could see Thomas chopping firewood off by a stable that stood adjacent to the garden. I had so little recollection of anything, so I was left to assume that these kind people were my loving family. Yet, despite this fact, I was glad they were finally away, so that I might attend to my goals uninterrupted.

I decided to stage my progress. I kicked my legs to free them from the covers and leaned to my side to begin my exit from off the mattress. I rolled onto my stomach this time, hoping to avoid falling again, and slowly placed my knees on the floor. Next, I attempted to sit down, so that I might turn around and crawl to the table if need be. I moved while balancing my weight the best I could. However, I soon found myself involuntarily leaning toward the ground. I rocked backward in what seemed like slow motion, trying all I could to stay upright as I toppled toward the floor. Eventually, I met with another thud to the back of my head, which shot a stunning vibration through my whole body.

I lay still for a moment, frustrated with another failed attempt. But I soon determined that I wasn't really all that surprised with the outcome. I made it onto my stomach again and worked my knees and hands under me. It took a considerable amount of effort, but I was finally able to crawl my way to the table.

When I reached the closest chair, I pulled it out with one arm while balancing on the other. I accomplished the task only to fall on my side immediately after. I recouped what little strength I had and began to climb the chair. The effort was quite a struggle, but at long last I was able to get my upper frame onto the seat and pull the rest of my sluggish body into a sitting position.

Once I was steady, I leaned forward and rested my face and arms on the table in front of me. I felt very accomplished now, having left the bed to make it to the table where I had seen the others sitting. I lifted my head from off the wooden surface and surveyed my surroundings from a new perspective. Immediately, my eyes caught hold of something that I found somewhat intriguing.

About an arm's reach from where I sat was a book bound in a worn leather cover. I reached across the table and grasped hold of it, pulling it toward me with growing anticipation. It appeared as though it had seen many years of use, and yet one could tell that it had been cared for. The binding was rather faded on the edges, and the pages were raised and crumpled a small degree from numerous turns of the paper. Strangely, I felt drawn to this book I had never seen before, as if it contained something which I had long forgotten. Slowly and carefully, I folded back the leather flap and looked upon the first page, but what I saw next befuddled me to no small degree.

Chapter 3

I expected to view the beginnings of a story, or some personal account perhaps, but I saw nothing more than what appeared to be haphazard notes from some unknown person's random thoughts. I began to leaf through the middle of the book, moving the pages between my thumb and forefinger and scanning through the words. Nothing changed. The whole book was the same as what I saw in the first few pages. Eventually, I noticed the placement of words that seemed distantly linked:

> "...light, smiles, warm friendships...found myself in a peculiar building...beautiful and intricate."

I turned the page over, and a sheet of paper lay folded behind it. I opened it and saw what must have been an illustration of the last words I had just read. Before me was a detailed image of a building that looked like nothing I could remember having ever seen. A steady hand had obviously penned it out with great care.

Just then, the door was flung open. Thomas and Susan were the first ones through the entrance while the others followed quickly behind. "John's awake!" Susan exclaimed as she came running from behind her father.

"Yes, isn't that wonderful?" Martha remarked, closing the door behind her and the others. "Why don't you take a seat next to him, Dear," she added in a hurried tone while Thomas hastily drew the drapes shut. I fully expected them to be quite surprised about my location at the table, but Timmy and Susan seemed to be the only ones undeterred by whatever had gripped the others' focus.

"Whaaat's...go...going...on?" I managed. Their attention could no longer be suspended, and everyone was now drawn not only to the fact that I was awake and had made it to the table, but also to the fact that I had just spoken.

"You said sometin agin, John, dat's jest great," Susan said, patting me on the back as she knelt in the seat of the chair next to me.

Without saying anything, Thomas left the window, where he was peering through the cloth that covered it, and walked over to where I was sitting. In the brief moment that followed, we could hear the distant thundering of horses' hooves. He quickly returned to the window and peeked through the curtain again. "I was afraid this might happen," Thomas muttered. "It's a good thing that rider tipped us off. Martha, take everyone to the back room and stay there please. I'll tell you when all is clear."

Without a moment's hesitation, the children scurried to the back of the house where a rickety wooden door opened into a small cellar. As Martha and Simon assisted me in the same direction, I could hear the noise drawing closer. Thomas calmly took a seat at the table, where he grabbed from it the very same book with which I had just become acquainted and made himself to look comfortable.

I was quickly swung past the door into the damp cold room. Everyone, even the children, sat completely still and quiet in the darkened seclusion that the cellar provided. There was very little space to move about, if anyone even had the inclination, and even little Susan sat immovable and speechless.

Martha stood near the entrance, peeking through one of several gaps left between the butted panels of wood that formed the door. I made an attempt to crawl just below her to do the same, finding that I was more able to move with each passing moment.

I moved toward the door on my hands and knees until I was positioned in such a way that I could see Thomas sitting at the table just as he was when we left. Immediately after, we could all hear the faint sound of footsteps nearing the house.

Suddenly, the door to the home creaked on its hinges, and in walked a tall man with a white head of hair and a beard to match it. He wore a maroon cape with golden lace, which was draped over garb of a similar fashion. His polished black boots thudded on the wooden floor as he strutted his way toward the table.

Thomas, however, continued reading as if no one was even present. The white-haired man stopped behind one of the chairs and took from his waist a golden sheath that held a sword. He placed it on the table and slowly took a seat, all the while staring at Thomas.

"You barge in here as if you were invited, Henry," Thomas finally said, keeping his eyes glued to the book in his hand. Henry responded by kicking his feet up onto the table and leaning back in the chair.

"You forget, Thomas, I am a Pridion. Mind you, the leader of the Pridions. Invitations aren't really needed," he said arrogantly. "It appears as though your adorable little family is nowhere to be found, as usual."

"What is it you want?" Thomas replied, putting the book down for the first time and looking the intruder straight in the eyes.

"Rumor has it you've brought a traveler back from the shores." He picked at something in his teeth, only to rudely spit it on the floor. "If I remember right, it's been years since any washed up here."

"Word travels fast in these parts, even to those it shouldn't," Thomas said.

"We make it our business to know these things," Henry boasted, swinging his feet to the floor and leaning forward. "You would do well to teach him of our ways, Thomas."

"I would do much better to warn him of you."

Henry laughed maniacally at this response. "When are you going to learn, Thomas? Times aren't as they used to be."

"If only they were," Thomas said wishfully.

"What, you mean begging at the feet of the hill-dwellers simply to live our lives? They're tyrants, Thomas, and I'm through listening to them."

"They are a peaceful people," Thomas replied. "They do us no harm. Besides, I don't remember ever begging at their feet."

"You know what I mean. They're a greedy people; their only joy is to control everyone around them," Henry retorted.

"They merely have laws, laws that were in place long before we came here."

"Came here? I don't remember ever coming here," Henry insisted.

"The hill-dwellers have helped to keep order in the colony. I don't understand what the problem is."

"See, Thomas, this is where you and I differed from the start. I seek to shape my own destiny, and you are content with some strange and peculiar cult ruling over you," Henry snapped.

"I would hardly call them a cult."

"Really? They live in the hills in some secret city where no colonist is allowed to go. They never come to us unless it's to enact some law they've conjured up, or make sure we're keeping the ones they already have. They steal the bodies of our dead, and to top it all off, they claim it all to be some timeless and everlasting order," Henry said.

Thomas remained silent for a moment, as if he was considering his words with a degree of seriousness. "I don't understand why they do everything they do, but burying the dead is hardly stealing them."

"If they take them away from us, it is. Have you ever seen where they're buried? You're just lucky you've never lost someone."

"And you have?" Thomas questioned with a tone of sarcastic surprise.

"No, but if I had, I wouldn't let any mongrel from the mountains make some ceremony out of them. You see, it's things just like this that make them a threat."

"But they are a good people. Their laws protect and promote order and—"

"I won't be told what to do! That's the bottom line!" Henry thundered, pounding his fist on the table. Moments later, he leaned back in the chair and resumed a seemingly-calm demeanor. "Certain matters of particular importance will soon be upon us. You will want to make sure you are on the winning side."

"And what makes you so certain that yours will be it?" Thomas asked.

"We are leaders, my friend. We are the wings on which progress is borne."

"Says you," Thomas remarked.

Henry looked at him as if he'd said nothing and continued. "Soon, my forces will be enough to match the hill-dweller's, and the rest will soon be history, our history," he concluded.

"I hope you don't intend on starting a war over your illusions?"

"The war was started a long time ago, dear Thomas. We are merely going to finish it," Henry said with a tone of finality.

Thomas sat still, saying nothing for a time. He folded his arms across his chest and leaned back in his chair.

"You know, Thomas, you should consider yourself fortunate to have received my invitation, and on more than one occasion, I might add."

"Fortune is a matter of what side you're looking from."

"Very well," Henry responded. "But this may be your last chance," he added emphatically.

"Are you quite through then?" Thomas questioned in a tone of eagerness.

Henry said nothing but gradually rose from the table with an expression that seemed to speak his apparent discontent. He returned his sword to his belt and slowly began walking toward the door. "One day, Thomas, you'll realize how foolish you've been. The Pridions will rule this land, and you and your family will be left out of it all."

Thomas sat as still as before, picking up the book again while saying nothing in response to Henry. Fully annoyed at this, Henry turned on his heel, swung open the door, and slammed it shut behind him.

From the cellar we could hear Henry outside as he mounted his horse and began to ride away. Thomas remained where he was for a time before he stood up and walked to the window. He drew the drapes to the side and peered into the distance for what seemed to be a moment suspended in time. He then opened them completely, along with the drapes over the other windows, and the room was once again filled with the morning's light.

Upon completing the task, looking through every window for a short time, he quickly walked to the cellar door and pulled it open. "Alright, it's fine to come out now," he assured, gently taking Martha by the hand. Susan scurried after her mother while the others proceeded behind. I slowly began to make my way from the floor when suddenly I was hefted to my feet.

"I got ya, Buddy. It's troublesome labor getting up in your state," Simon said, wrapping my arm over his shoulder to help stabilize my still-somewhat-incapable frame. He placed me back in the same chair I was in earlier, making certain I was steady. I was thankful for his help, but most of all, I was grateful he had not put me back in the bed.

Susan took a seat next to me again, though for the present moment, she lacked her normal excitement and vibrancy. Rather than speaking with a look of child-like ecstasy on her face as she had earlier, she sat still in her seat, facing her father with a look of concern. Martha took to peering out the window as Thomas had earlier while the others paced about, almost as if uncertain as to the next action they should take.

"Who was that?" I said with improved articulation. Once again, my utterance commanded the attention of everyone in the room.

"Oh, it's good to hear you speak," Martha said, leaving her preoccupied thoughts and walking to the table. Susan's head turned my way, her face showing a half smile.

"Yer talkin' vaster now," she grinned.

"It seems a shame to trouble you with such matters so early," Martha continued. "You haven't really even had the chance to get to know everyone yet." She then exchanged a look with Thomas.

"Wha... what do you mean?" I asked.

"Well, John," Thomas answered, pushing in the chairs that had earlier been occupied. "You haven't been here with us for very long."

I remained silent for a time, trying to make sense of the seemingly-disconnected portions of memory that I had. With everyone around me calling me by name and acting as though my presence was expected, I had grown to assume that I was with my own family, whether I could remember them or not. As for the strangeness of my circumstances, I was in the dark.

Yet, the idea that I hadn't been with these people for very long created even greater confusion in my mind.

"You've been with us just over three days," Martha added.

Her words came as a shock to me. If I had only been here three days, there was naturally another question to follow. "Then where was I before?" I asked.

"We're not sure," Thomas replied. "We found you stranded on the shores."

"The shores?" I questioned.

Thomas took a seat in the chair next to me. "It often comes as somewhat of a surprise, as much to us as those we find. But the extent of your beginnings here trace back to the morning we found you lying on the shores of this place."

The shock continued. I dropped my head in my hands and ran my fingers through my hair. "How did I get here?" I managed.

"No one knows," Thomas said.

"You must be a survivor of some shipwreck," Martha injected. "Countless others have come to this island the same way."

"Why do I remember none of this?" I questioned, as much to myself as to anyone else.

"Well, that's the mystery, isn't it?" Simon added. I turned toward him and waited for him to say something else, but he remained silent.

"What do you mean?"

"You're not the only one who doesn't remember," he continued. There was a pause, as if those around me were letting the weight of Simon's words sink deep into my mind.

"Not a single soul that's ever washed up in this place ever remembers anything about where they came from," Thomas remarked. I said nothing in response to this but sat still and contemplative. I suddenly felt very lucky to be alive and well and in the presence of caring people.

"We're glad we happened to be there that morning," Martha added. I looked at her kind face and could sense deep sincerity in her tone.

"I imagine I have more to thank you for than I can even remember," I said.

"No need to be thanking us, Son. Anyone else would have done the same," Thomas replied.

"That's simply not true," Simon added. "What you two have done is noble, and there are some far less than noble and far less than decent. You're a fortunate fellow, John. You're lucky that Thomas and Martha found you before someone else did." No one seemed to want to talk about the person to whom he was alluding, and if my premonition served me well, I couldn't blame them.

"Do you mean the man who was just—?"

"I'm afraid so," Thomas interrupted. He turned back toward me after glaring at the floor for a moment. "Henry makes it his business to persuade any poor soul he can find to join his army."

"Persuasion? Coercion's what it is!" Martha exclaimed. All of a sudden, everyone seemed to want to add their opinions on the subject of this Henry.

"He's a mad man, always patrolling with his minions along the shoreline, preying on the shipwrecks. He takes them in and cares for them only so they can serve his ambitions later," Simon continued. "It's likely to be where he's headed now."

"No doubt it is," Thomas added. "Best thing to do is just avoid the man."

"Until he comes barging into your home?" I asked.

"Right. Well, there's only so much that can be done," Thomas affirmed.

I sat staring forward for a time with a look that must have expressed the many questions I had in my mind. Then Thomas broke the silence of my thoughts. "But you don't have anything to worry about now. We're glad we found you," he said. "You can live with us as our own, just like Simon."

I looked over at Simon, and he returned a smile. "That's right, John. And you wouldn't find a better home if you went looking for it," he boasted. "Thomas and Martha will take good care of you."

Once again, quietness followed before Thomas pushed away from the table and stood on his feet. "You'll have questions along the way, and we will answer them as best we can for you. In the meantime let me show you around the place." He reached out and placed his hand on my shoulder in a fatherly manner.

I pushed my chair back, the noise turning everyone's attention my way again. Before they could take any thought of rushing to my side, or before Thomas offered any assistance, I put my arms over the table and forced myself up onto my feet. The task proved easier than I expected, and I felt steady, unlike before. I slowly stepped forward with confidence at my new-found ability, and though I took longer than anyone else, I eventually made it to the door.

"You manage well," Thomas said. "You've recovered rather quickly, really." He placed a coat around my shoulders and gestured toward the door. "Let's show you all the places you haven't seen yet." I nodded my head in response. I hadn't ventured outside before now, at least not as far as I could remember, and though I was more than anxious and excited to do so, I wondered how far I could make it on my own.

The air outside of the small home was crisp and refreshing. I took in a hearty breath and savored the scent of the trees brought in on a gentle wind. The sun glared down from its lofty place in a rich-blue sky, and the grass of the fields danced to the tune of the morning breeze. The scenery that surrounded me was beautiful to behold, from the open fields of grain and garden, to the forest and hills that lay beyond it. The accommodations of the place, both inside and out, spoke of a simple but fulfilling life—one which I already longed to be a part of.

"We'd best be on our way now," I heard the next morning. "Mr. Foster will be expecting us soon. I promised to bring the mare by today," Thomas said.

"Come along Susan," Martha beckoned. The others rose from their chairs around the table and followed Thomas to a coat rack by the door, each fetching a jacket tailored to their respective size. I was still rather tired from the day before and must have slept much longer than the others.

"Where is everyone going?" I asked. They turned to me as if they were a bit surprised that I was awake.

"To the city," Simon replied. "Throw on your shoes and such and let's go." I hurriedly attended to matters as he suggested and then followed the others into the cool morning air. My trip to the carriage took some time, but I felt more assured of my capabilities after yesterday.

The children piled into the back with the giddiness of youth on their faces while Thomas and Martha took the seats in the front behind the reins. As soon as all were rested in the confines of the wooden carriage, Simon jumped amid Mary, Susan, and Timmy, wrestling a hug around their necks in the playful nature of an older brother.

"Come on, John," he said, offering his hand. "I'll help you in." I reached out and received a strong pull into the padded lining of the carriage floor. As soon as I was seated, Thomas softly whipped the reins over the horse's back, and we began to slowly move away from the home.

Before we continued the journey into town, Thomas brought the carriage to a stop in front of the barn that stood adjacent to the house. From where I sat, I could see into the dim confines of the structure. As I peered deeper toward the back, a beautiful horse slowly walked from out of the shadows.

"Here, Simon," he said, coaxing the animal up the rear of the carriage. "Would you mind tying Sophia down somewhere?"

The trip into town passed with moments of great interest and elation at being outside the house again. The path took us over a dirt road that the continual passage of horses and carriages had carved out of the landscape. Every now and again, we hit a rough patch that would send the children jostling about a bit with laughter following every occasion.

At times, we would find ourselves passing through wooded areas that later turned into spaces as open and broad as I had ever seen. This pattern continued until we moved through one final forest of trees and began descending down a small climb that led into a valley of sorts.

Amid a far-less-wooded glen stood the structures that composed the small city of Caprecia, which I was informed was the center of a settlement of people referred to as colonists. We were fortunate enough to live on our own in the countryside, according to Simon, but when it came to any real distinction, we were considered colonists as much as anyone else.

The road on which we had been traveling gradually merged into a street made of stone. The slabs of rock that composed our new path looked as though they had seen better days. Our travels now followed closely along the banks of the river that had snaked its way adjacent to our course the entire trip, and I could begin to see small thatched houses nestled amid the outlying surroundings that preceded the city.

I rose to my knees and turned in the direction of our movement, peering past Thomas and Martha toward the city in front of us. The path disappeared around each bend into the trees that lined its shoulders before it opened up again and one could see its winding protraction ahead once more.

"Thomas?" I asked.

"Yes?" he replied, turning for a moment to look at me.

"Does this Mr. Foster live in the city or in one of these homes along the way?" I had suddenly grown interested in knowing if we would actually be going through the city itself or not.

"Ernest lives on the other side of town, I'm afraid. We'll have to go through the city to get there," he said. Regardless of his impartial tone, I was excited to see the city for the first time. I wondered what the place might look like up close, what sorts of people we might meet, and what happenings might comprise the daily activities of the township.

I placed myself in a more advantageous position to obtain an optimal view of the city as we neared the outskirts. Gradually, the road became smoother and continued in much better repair than our course through the country.

"There it is," Simon sounded from the back of the cart, "the great city of Caprecia. But it's not as great as some would have you believe." Simon paused for a moment but continued staring forward into nothingness as it appeared, or else he looked as if he was peering into his own thoughts as they materialized in front of him. "You'll find a lot of confused people in this place, John. Don't pay them any mind," he added, turning to look at me.

Moments later I could hear a considerable noise and commotion coming from within the walls of the city. As we neared the beginnings of the town, the noise grew louder, and I began to make out a heated argument among a large group of people.

Chapter 4

As we came to the center of the city, it became apparent what had conjured all the clamor. Dispersed amid the town square were two separate groups, both attempting to obtain the greater attention of onlookers. One of the groups was adorned in gaudy apparel with golden lace and capes of maroon, and in their midst stood the man who had intruded upon us the day before.

He seemed to be the foremost speaker among them, contending with the words of the others who were apart from his own followers. There appeared also to be those who assumed the role of leadership coming forth from the opposing party to combat the words of Henry and issue their own dissertations. These others seemed to be dressed more like the common people and were easily distinguished from the first group and their elaborate garb.

Unfortunate as it appeared, there was no apparent way around the mess that had settled itself in the center of the main road. Though I searched the present sight, I couldn't see that there was any way in our course to avoid the tumultuous groups, and it seemed at that moment as though Thomas intended to pass right through it.

"Just don't pay them any attention," Simon said. The debates seemed even more heated up close as we neared a circular formation where the road wound about a large tree and garden in the center of all the traffic.

As we carried on with the movement of other carts and horses around the right side of the roundabout, I noticed Henry walking with a sway of pomp and arrogance toward the stone border that enclosed the garden. He jumped onto the small stone wall and began speaking in a voice loud enough for everyone around to hear.

"Fellow citizens!" he roared. "The time is at hand for every colonist to choose his side. Do not be swayed by the foolish imaginations of those who would have you believe that a complacent continuation in our plight is the only way to ensure peace. The answer to our problem with tyranny is obvious, and the Pridions hold that answer in our ever-capable hands. We will yet govern ourselves!" he raged.

His words, though they seemed to catch only brief attention from some of the townspeople, appeared to greatly annoy and provoke the individuals of the other grouping to considerable anger, and an even greater commotion was now brewing among them. I peered into the storming crowds of people and marveled at the disorderly sight of it all. Soon after, my stare met with Henry. He looked directly at me, as if he knew very well who I was. His eyes seemed to harbor a great deal of conceit, and he stared at me as if to inform me of the unfortunate reality that I would be seeing more of him.

Thankfully, we were out of the mess in a short amount of time, and once past it all, the city took on a much more welcoming and quaint ambiance. I could hear again the sound of the wheels knocking on the cobbles of the road beneath us, a sound that had altogether disappeared amid the noise of the crowd. Surprisingly, no one in my company had anything to say about what we had just witnessed. Not even Simon spoke a word, and I was left to imagine that they had so often been exposed to such happenstance that it had become a usual expectation when visiting this place.

A seemingly short time elapsed before we had journeyed outside the bounds of the city and began to roll along a country road similar to the one we had taken into town. The layout was extremely peaceful compared to the tumult of the city, and I felt relaxed again to be amid the quiet sounds that surrounded us.

Some distance down the road, I could see the outline of homes that appeared to be larger in size than those that preceded the city. The pathway itself was also in better repair, and the cobbles were neat and evenly placed as they were through town. Soon after traveling toward the neighborhood and coming upon one of the first few houses, Thomas brought the cart to a stop. "Ernest!" he yelled, waving to a man that stood just outside a wooden archway that spanned the entrance to an adjacent shop of sorts.

Jumping down from the carriage and walking toward him, the two greeted with a hearty hand shake. "Thomas, good friend," the other said.

"You look as young as ever, Ernest."

"Young? Very funny, but to be quite serious, I've never felt so old," Ernest said.

"What do you mean?" Thomas asked.

"Well, you might guess." Thomas didn't say anything after this but began to look a bit concerned.

"Wait, now who is this?" Ernest questioned as they both stepped toward the carriage.

"Dis is my new brudder, John!" Susan exclaimed, leaning over the side of the wagon as if she expected Ernest to catch her mid-air.

"Ah, and how's my little Susan?" Ernest charmed as he swept her into his arms.

"John's gonna stay wiff us. He can talk now, and walk, jest a little." When she said this, Ernest turned to Thomas and offered a surprised look.

"From the shores?" he asked.

"Yes, Martha and I found him four days ago," Thomas answered. Ernest turned to me next and, with a smile on his face, offered a kind response.

"Welcome, John is it?"

"I suppose so," I said.

"I imagine you're still feeling awfully confused about where you are and how you got here. I'm afraid we're all in a rather peculiar place, you know," Ernest continued. "I'm assuming you know now that you aren't the only one."

"That's what I've been told," I replied.

"Well, all of you will come inside for a moment, won't you?" Ernest looked around at everyone and exchanged another smile with Martha and Thomas. Suddenly, a woman walked out from inside the shop and came to his side. She had a bright complexion and made a kindly approach toward him as a wife would do.

"Sarah, meet John," Ernest said. I nodded once again, feeling still a little timid in my circumstance. "John's new here."

"You mean…?"

"That's right," Ernest confirmed.

"You are fortunate to be in the company of such good people, John." Sarah said. "You won't meet a finer family." She was older than I supposed myself to be, about the age of Thomas and Martha, and looked to be just as nice.

"You're too kind, Sarah," Martha replied.

Ernest slapped his hand atop the wall of the carriage to offer a finalization to the small talk. "Well, follow me, everyone."

"Where would you like me to put Sophia?" Simon questioned.

"Oh, she'll be just fine over here by the shop for now." Simon followed closely after Ernest while pulling the horse by the reins. "Have you had any run-ins with Henry lately?" I heard Ernest ask as they walked away. By the time Simon began to answer, his voice was already droned into incoherence by their increasing distance. I was able to manage getting down from the carriage on my own to follow after the others behind Mrs. Sarah, but I was still a bit slow to start.

"Do make yourselves at home," she said as we entered the house. The place was larger than the residence I had been living in, and by the sight of it, I would guess that Sarah and Ernest were doing just fine for themselves. I followed the others and took a seat on a bench padded with a blue cloth and pillow. Shortly after we were all comfortable and a casual conversation arose between Sarah and Martha, Ernest and Simon walked through the door.

"Simon's been telling me about your recent meeting with Henry," Ernest remarked while hanging up his coat on a nearby hook.

"Yes, I'm afraid he made another uninvited visit to our home yesterday," Thomas replied.

"That might be a bit of an understatement," Martha added.

"You're a patient man, Thomas. I wouldn't have acted so passive under the same circumstance," Ernest said. "I'll tell you this much, these Pridions are getting out of hand. I should welcome the day Henry shows his face around my home again." As he said this, his hand rested on the handle of a small sword which hung at his side. "He wouldn't get away with both arms if I had my way."

"Might he be why you're feeling so old, Ernest?" Thomas asked.

"That man has caused more trouble than good all these years, and now he thinks he can wage war against the hill-dwellers. Did you have any idea, Thomas? He plans to march on the East Mountains."

"Yes, I know. I'm afraid he was creating quite the riot in town as we were passing through."

"Was he speaking of it there to everyone? Oh, he moves fast, as fast as any snake can."

"Actually, it just sounded like his usual rantings and ravings, the kind he speaks to gain followers. I imagine he is keeping the idea pretty secretive still. He doesn't have enough of an army yet, does he?" Thomas asked.

"I don't know, Thomas, but he has to be stopped before he does."

"But there's nothing we can do to stop him," Thomas insisted.

"But there is," Ernest concluded, walking over to a table that stood in the middle of the adjoining room. He pulled from its center some weathered paper and binding that he stopped and looked over before returning to his seat. "Do you know what this is, Thomas?" After asking the question, Ernest chuckled. "Of course you don't, because I've never shown you, but this is the answer right here."

"What is it?" Thomas questioned.

"I've been doing a bit of petitioning myself, you see, and this is a list of my followers."

"Your followers?"

"Yes, here are the names of everyone as enraged with Henry as I am. Should he wage war, I will be prepared to meet him." No one said anything for a moment long enough to create a sense of awkwardness.

"It all sounds so dreadful," Martha replied. Ernest's wife seemed to share her opinion in silence as her face showed very little joy.

"I was hoping to add you to the list, Thomas."

"War only worries me, Ernest."

"It worries me too, Friend, but what are we to do, sit around while Henry attempts to disrupt what's already an unstable settlement?"

"Perhaps we should merely warn the hill-dwellers, let

them deal with Henry," Thomas answered.

"If they hear word of insurrection, they're likely to consider every colonist a threat. Who's to say what would happen? We have to stop Henry before he starts. It's up to us, no one else."

Thomas sat for a good while, contemplating Ernest's words. "Maybe you're right," he finally said.

"I know it's what has to be done, but I don't like it any more than you."

"And how do you propose we begin such a feat?" Thomas asked.

"It's already been started," Ernest answered, holding up the book in his hand. "For you, it starts with putting your name in here." Suddenly, Simon rose to his feet and walked over to Ernest.

"I'm in," he said, taking the book from his hand. "Where's a quill?"

"Simon, you don't have to feel obligated, you've only been among us a short time," Sarah said from her seat. "You're still so young."

"It's my fight as much as yours," he replied. "And I'm not going to sit around and watch Henry make things worse."

Ernest's face was equally surprised. "Son, you're good to offer, but really—" Before he could finish what he was saying, Simon walked over to the table and snatched a pen from a small pot of ink. Throwing the book down, he quickly signed his name.

"It's done, count me in." Afterward, Simon brought the book and pen to Thomas. He hesitated for a moment before taking it from him, but eventually rested it in his lap and stared upon the place where Simon had ambitiously inscribed his name. The whole room was still and quiet while all eyes rested on Thomas.

"Surely this isn't the only answer," Martha exclaimed after

a long moment of speechless tension. All eyes now turned to her. "Leave it between Henry and the hill-dwellers. Let them punish him."

"Dear Martha," Ernest spoke. "You must think that this whole matter only involves them. But it doesn't." As he was speaking, Ernest made his way to a nearby window, which he peered out of in a thoughtful daze. Again, silence fell on the room. "Their harassment is growing worse," he continued. "They came through here not two days ago and scattered my flocks all over the hillside. It took a long time and help from our neighboring friends to round them back up. Of course, there were many dead and missing in the end."

"I'm sorry, Ernest, I didn't know," Thomas said. Martha's face expressed the same sympathy, but she remained silent.

"And do you know what they dared to leave on my door?" he continued, snatching a crumpled parchment from the same nearby table. "This," he added, handing it over to Thomas. "They already think that they are the government, and they think they can harass anyone who gets in their way. *Remember who's in charge*, it says. Thomas, it's enough to drive a man to rage." As he spoke, his wife seemed to quiver and fret over the matter. "Do what needs to be done, good friend."

The remainder of our visit consisted of such conversations between the two families. Though I wished to have been able to participate, there wasn't much I could have said on the subject. Most of the time, I found myself merely listening and learning a considerable amount about the unrest within the colony.

Friends parted at length, and our travels back home passed quickly. I didn't take as much notice of my surroundings as before. Rather, I thought upon the concern I could see in the eyes of Thomas when he was finally persuaded to sign alongside Simon's name. It was that same concern that had now transformed into his present silence.

Several nights later, I lay sleepless, thinking about all I had learned since waking in the home of Thomas and Martha. Questions regarding the Pridions and the hill-dwellers, and all that had been said about them, danced through my mind and gave rise to many more. I determined to find out as much as I could about the mysterious people that lived in the East Mountains, who governed the colonists under a strict order.

The first and most common source to consult was a certain decree that Thomas and Martha had by their front door. I had read the document once before, and as I lay in my bed that night, I began to recall what it said. I remembered Thomas informing me that the hill-dwellers required it to be kept in plain view in every home in the colony. Afterward, I recalled what I had read from the decree and thought upon the peculiarity of anyone fighting against it.

The statutes outlined within it were sensible and apparent in their necessity for sustaining a civilized society, so I found it strange that someone would try to undermine its moral code. It seemed evident that every human soul should be accepting of such a constitution, and when I thought that Henry was intent on freeing himself from its obligations, I was angry toward the man.

Many more moments passed before I was able to put my thoughts to rest. Yet, as I did, my mind turned to another matter. Despite the generosity that Thomas and Martha had so consistently offered, and the deep friendships that had already begun with the whole family, there were moments I felt rather lonely, as if my heart still remembered people my mind could not. I reached for the stand next to my cot and grabbed hold of the brilliant white necklace that Martha had placed there. I remembered her telling me how it was mine, how they found it with me the day they took me in.

I held it in my hand with great care, and while I knew nothing of its significance, some undefined sentiment endeared it to me. The light from the moon, which peeked through the slit between the curtains behind me, multiplied its brilliance as fragments of sparkling reflections glimmered from its silver-like casing.

As I admired its beauty, I again felt the loneliness that was impartial to the fact that I knew no reason for feeling lonely, and yet it was present in my heart and very real. I laid my hands on my chest with the necklace still wrapped between my fingers and pondered on the emotion for a time.

I felt a great deal of affection toward the source of these stirrings. I felt that certain and special love that a man has for a woman well inside my chest, as it seemed, and yet I knew not why, nor had I the face of any woman to attribute it to. It was at that moment, under whatever influence it was that compelled me, that I determined to never part with the necklace but to always carry it with me.

I placed it back on the small wooden nightstand then rolled on my back and began staring at the ceiling overhead. I thought about it all again and began to dream of the elusive affection that had enlivened my soul. I imagined what my life would be like when coupled with the admiration and love of a woman, and I began to vividly picture in my mind a most beautiful girl.

Her smile was captivating, her hair, a dark rich silk that seemed to caress the ridges of her face with every move she made. Her eyes were more beautiful than the finest pearl the markets of the colony had ever seen, and her lips were like the petals of a red rose I had seen on a morning when the dews had rested gently on its soft exterior.

Strangely, even though I was the proprietor of these imagined circumstances, the dream soon began to take on a life of its own. The woman I saw remained still for a time but soon started walking toward me and drawing ever closer. It appeared as though we were on the peak of some beautiful mountain, standing next to a pool of crystal-clear water. Tall grass swayed around us while the blissful but distant splashing of a waterfall echoed through the air.

    I reached out in my thoughts upon her approach and drew her into my arms, embracing the warmth of her imagined presence. While once her features were apparent to me at a distance, I could not, as much as I tried, conjure any memory of her face, though I could see it in all its beauty. For whatever reason, she remained unidentifiable to me, and shortly, our surroundings blurred into incoherence as well.

    The dream soon faded, but the impressions remained as I woke from a slight sleep. I was almost surprised to find myself where I was. The experience had seemed so real. However, it wasn't long before my eyes slowly began to close under the weight of dreariness, and somewhere between consciousness and sleep, I was awakened again to the sound of footsteps creeping past my bed.

Chapter 5

I sat up just in time to see the door closing slowly behind a blur of black. My eyes panned the room and found Simon's bed empty. I turned in my cot toward the window behind me and peered out into the moon-lit night. When I did, I saw him dressed in a black coat and hood walking toward the barn. As to where he was going at this hour, I had no idea. I was filled with intrigue, however, and decided to investigate his departure, anonymously if possible. I put on the boots I kept at the side of my bed and swung on my coat as quietly as I could. I slowly peeked out the entrance to see if I would be able to exit unnoticed, and upon finding that Simon was out of sight, I slipped out the door into the night.

I wasn't sure of my next course of action at this point. There was nothing between the house and the barn that would offer concealment should Simon walk out into the open at that moment. So I rushed to my left and hid behind the woodpile against the far wall. From here I was able to view the entrance to the barn fairly well, and my eyes remained fixed on the opening, waiting to spot Simon's next move.

Just then, I saw him with Thomas and Martha's horse, Claudia. He walked her over to the carriage that sat just outside the door to the stables and began to fasten the reins over her shoulders. He petted her nose time and again in attempts to keep her quiet and still, and when he completed the task, he disappeared into the barn again. I realized immediately that if I was going to make it to the carriage bed unnoticed, now was my only chance.

I bolted through the open yard between the house and stable in hopes that Claudia wouldn't make a noise and give me away. As I neared my destination, I stumbled over a rock that lay above the surface of the ground and fell flat on my face. I lay prostrate and still on the cold grass that covered the fields around me, hoping I hadn't been discovered. I slowly raised my head and waited for a moment to make certain I hadn't brought my presence to Simon's attention.

Once I determined that I had remained unseen, I quickly got up and continued my course to the carriage. When I reached the back, I quietly slid into the bed, covering myself with the blankets that were used to the line the interior. The shift in weight caused Claudia to shuffle on her feet and neigh in response.

I gritted my teeth, fearing I had blown my chance. I heard quickened steps from the barn and then their abrupt ceasing alongside the carriage. "Shhh...shhh...shhh," I heard Simon calmly whisper. "Let's not wake anybody up," he said. I could then hear Claudia munching on some hay that had been offered to calm her down. "There you go, see everything's alright."

The night air was cool and would have added a chill to the bones of anyone left uncovered. Yet, under the weight of the cloth that concealed me, along with the coat I had brought as a covering, I was beginning to grow quite warm. Beads of perspiration started to form on my forehead, and I began to hope that our destination wasn't very far.

Aside from the sound of Claudia feeding, all had fallen silent again. Then I heard the shuffle of Simon's feet, and moments later, the thumping of several glass bottles in the bed, one of which hit me directly on the head. I bit my tongue, holding back my initial shock while Simon climbed behind the reins.

The carriage rocked from side to side and creaked in a small degree as he situated himself in the seat. I was close enough to hear his every move and was reminded that he, in turn, would be able to hear me if I was to shuffle the slightest. A sigh escaped his chest, he quietly flicked the reins over Claudia's back, and the carriage started into a steady roll.

Before long, I was completely unaware as to where I was in relation to anything. After a short moment, I began formulating theories in my mind as to how far we were from the house and which direction we might be going. The wood pallets of the carriage bed were quite uncomfortable without the blankets to pad me from the bumps and jars of the road beneath us. This, along with the fact that it was growing increasingly hot under the covering, made for a rather disquieting experience.

How long it had been and how far we had traveled, I can't say, considering that my discomforted perspective made it seem far too distant, but the first inkling that the trip might be coming to its end came when I began to hear the faint sound of crashing waves. Not a moment too soon, Claudia came to a stop, and I heard Simon climb down from his place behind her. Next, he gathered the bottles from the bed, and I waited until I could be sure he had ventured far enough away for me to exit the carriage without him knowing.

At length, I slowly removed the cloth from over my head. I looked around from my left to my right. All appeared to be clear, so I continued. I then began to gradually sit up, and as I turned to my side, I saw Simon walking toward some nearby shore that lay shimmering beneath the moonlight. I quickly flung off the rest of the blankets and hopped down from the carriage bed. I began to follow him with a plan to fall behind one of the dunes near the beach as I grew closer.

As I tiptoed my way from the carriage toward the shore,

Simon suddenly stopped. Before he could turn around, I slid as stealthily as possible behind the nearest sandy knoll. I remained perfectly motionless and silent, hoping he hadn't caught sight of me.

Eventually, I raised my head again to see where he had gone in the short moment I spent crouching on the coarse surface beneath me. I saw him now, standing near the water's edge gazing out over the ocean in front of him. He stood as still as the night itself, and for what seemed to be a very long time, he didn't move the slightest.

I remained where I was and watched him patiently, trying to see whatever there was to see that might have compelled him to sojourn to this beach tonight. Soon after, I determined that if I was to know why he had come here, I was going to have to ask him myself. I rose with confidence from my hiding place, and for the first time since the beginning of my endeavor, I walked with normal steps.

As I continued, my feet made very little noise passing over the white sands of the beach. I tried to decide what I would say and how I would explain myself when I reached him. I took my final steps softly, so as not to startle him, and slowly began reaching forward to place my hand on his shoulder.

"Why did you follow me?" He loudly questioned. I jerked in response and ended up pushing him rather than applying an acknowledging nudge.

"Sorry, I didn't mean to..." I swallowed my last word. "You startled me."

"And you might have startled me right out of my mind coming up behind me like that," he said in an unenforced tone.

"I assure you that wasn't my intention."

"I know," he replied with a smile. "So why did you follow?"

"Well, I wanted to see where you might be going, and besides, how did you know I had come along?" This whole time, I thought I had operated completely undetected.

"Well, let's just say that the bedding of the carriage was a little lumpy looking. The funniest part was tossing the bottle at your head. You did really well at not making a sound," he chuckled. "Did you really think I wouldn't notice?"

Something about him bringing it up made me rub my head a little. To think, the drudgery and ill-comfort I had endured for the entire trip might have been altogether avoided if I had known that Simon already knew I was there.

"So you knew all along...?" I asked.

"Afraid so," he replied, turning toward the shore again.

"You're not upset, are you?"

"Upset? Good heavens, no. Why would I be upset? I was just like you when Martha and Thomas took me in, wanting to know all about everything going on around me."

"Why did you come out here then?" I questioned.

"Because, from what I'm told, this is where I came from. For you and me, and every other colonist you'll meet, life started here on these shores. At least, if life started anywhere else, we know nothing about it." His thoughts protracted off in the distance across the ocean and on as far as he could see.

I had never seen these shores, but I remembered how Thomas and Martha had told me of a place like this and how they found me there. I had assumed by the way they spoke of the matter that there were others under the same circumstance as myself, Simon being one, but I never thought to consider there being as many as Simon had just said. I had always felt as though my situation was a bit unique.

"All the colonists are shipwrecks then?"

"Let me put it this way; you haven't met a single person that hasn't wound up here just like you and me, or else they are the son or daughter of someone who has."

"You mean like Thomas and Martha?"

"That's right. Of course, for them it was some time ago," he said.

This knowledge placed things in an entirely different perspective for me. All of a sudden, I didn't feel so alone. "Are these the shores they found me on?" I asked.

"The very same." My eyes joined Simon's in peering off into the distance.

"What's on the other side?" He turned and looked at me in silence.

"I don't know," he answered. "No one does, no one like us at least. I come here every now and then hoping to find out, hoping someday to find answers or to find some poor soul stranded here who remembers something." Simon slowly reached for the ground and picked up the last remaining bottle. He held it carefully in his hands, switching it from one to the other.

"By the way, what's that all about?" I asked.

"This, John, this is a cry for answers." With that said, he took two quick steps forward and hurled the bottle beyond the breaking waves. "Maybe there's someone out there that knows," he concluded.

Without another word, he turned around and started walking back to the carriage. I stood in a spell of thoughtfulness at what he had said. I wondered how often he had employed this same pattern. Most of all, I began to wonder what it was about this ocean that enabled so many people to come from it, or how many dead bodies lay at the bottom. Surely there were those who never made it here at all.

"How many bottles have you thrown in?" I inquired as I joined Simon again.

"Seven."

"No, I mean altogether."

"Oh, I can't remember. I lost track a long time ago," he said. "Let's face it; most of them don't end up going anywhere. I've found a lot washed back up on the shore."

"Do you think anyone will ever find one of your bottles?"

After I asked him this, he remained speechless for a time, staring forward as if he was trying to determine whether he should answer me.

"Well, when I said that I didn't know what was out there, I meant I don't know for sure. There is a rumor that an island exists a day's travel from here. Many have gone looking for it in the past, but no one who has gone ever comes back. Now most people are sure it's a myth and are convinced that those who left died in an open ocean."

"But what if it is there?"

"Look, chances are the rumor is just that, a rumor. I don't know that throwing bottles in the ocean is ever going to amount to anything, but it can't hurt," he said.

"No one's ever found one?" I assumed.

"Well, if they had would I still be throwing them in?" he chuckled.

"I guess not."

Simon grew quiet for a moment after this. "But really, someone did find one of my bottles once," He added. "It just wasn't anyone I ever expected would."

Chapter 6

"Who was it?" I asked with great interest.

"About the worst possible person who could have found it."

"Who?"

"Henry, that's who. Ever since, he has treated me like someone that needs to be disposed of," Simon responded.

"Why?"

"Henry gave up on the idea of anything existing beyond these shores a long time ago, so Thomas tells me. It's like he's forgotten that he was here himself once. All he focuses on now is gaining followers that will humor his delusions."

"But he comes back to the shores to find people. Surely he questions where they come from?" I asked.

"Actually, I think the fact is that he doesn't care."

I thought for a moment after this. "Or maybe he doesn't want anyone finding out," I said.

"Finding out what?" Simon questioned.

"Well, anything. Think about it. If he's trying to take advantage of our crazy situation here in order to subject everyone around him, he's not going to want anyone getting assistance from beyond these shores. He's not going to want any interference."

Simon looked at me with a degree of surprise written on

his face. "You know something, John? You have a good head on your shoulders. You're no dummy."

"Thanks," I said as we approached the carriage.

"Now, let's get back home before Thomas and Martha wonder what's happened to us," Simon returned.

The proceeding days accounted for much learning at the hand of Thomas and Martha, as well as a considerable amount from Simon. I had begun to feel a great kinship to the entire family, and I had learned to look to Simon specifically as a role model and a friend. I patterned my actions after him and Thomas, taking occasion as often as I found it to glean understanding from their examples.

Thomas and Martha had become like parents to me. I learned kindness and virtue at the hand of Martha, wisdom and courage from the example of Thomas. The children brought great joy to my daily affairs. Mary, Timmy, and of course, little Susan were for lack of a better word, adorable. And Susan never ceased to amaze me with the words that came from her tiny mouth.

I also learned that Susan wasn't any younger than Timmy but was, rather, his twin. Chance had taken her fair share away from her and left Susan as the runt of the two. After Martha had told me about it, I began to take notice of things I didn't before. Susan couldn't keep up with Timmy as they were running and playing, and she was easily taken to feeling sick when everyone else was fine, despite her brilliant personality that never seemed to wane.

Many days passed with the blessing of these fine people's company. The seasons changed, the little ones grew, and the time that passed soon amounted to an entire year. I had found my place within the family and gained a sense of purpose and cause. Tending to the fields, the animals, planting, and more such duties were my privilege along with everyone else. The life my new family lived was one of hard work and self reliance.

I had learned much more about my situation from Thomas. He taught me his theories of our plight and purpose in this strange place. He told me what he knew of the hill-dwellers and his concerns for what was developing between Henry and Ernest. It seemed that very little had changed since the conversation we had at the Foster's home, but Thomas was convinced that it was a, calm before the storm.

I visited the shore with him on several occasions. He told me of his own story and how he and Martha met and shared with me his pity for everyone in our situation. He returned to the shores often, he said, to see if he might be able to help anyone else ease into this peculiar place.

He mentioned more than once that his greatest suspicions were surrounding the nature of our lives, as he put it. How peculiar it was that, with so many people shipwrecking on this place, none ever remembered anything about where they came from. There was never a ship or boat beached on the sands, and there was never any trace of water or the smell of ocean on any of the incapacitated individuals that were discovered. He told me how, when they found me, I was dry as a bone and my clothes only smelled of the sand I had been lying on.

From conversations such as this, I discovered early on that Thomas was a very observant man, and Simon seemed to follow in his footsteps in many ways. Others I had met in town, however, seemed more content with merely making a life with what knowledge they had and seemed to almost forget that they had lost any identity at all. And yet, I was obliged to follow after the same suspicions as Thomas.

When I asked him about the rumor of the island, he told me that he thought there could be one. However, he was sure that if there was, it wouldn't be inhabited. His reasoning came from the fact that if there was anyone living on it, they would have visited the mainland of Caprecia by now. People are naturally curious, and if for no other reason, they would have come to see what was here, he had told me.

Still the same, I employed my mind in thinking about the possibility of the island often. Ever since Simon had told me of the rumor that existed, it lingered in the forefront of my thoughts. I talked about it with him a couple of times since then, but for the most part, I kept the matter to myself, wondering whether I should add my name to the history of those that went looking for it.

On a particular night, long after the work for the day had been completed, I spent my time looking over another interest of mine, the book I had discovered during my first days here. It was the same book I saw Thomas studying on many occasions. I had read over it several times and revisited certain passages with frequency, but on this occasion as I read it, I was inclined toward thinking about the woman I had seen in my dreams. Suddenly, I found myself raising my head from the table at the sound of Thomas's voice.

"You should go to bed if you're that tired," he said.

I shook my head to wake myself further. "How long have I been asleep?"

"Only a short time, I think." He pulled out a chair and took a seat across from me. "You've always been rather interested in that book. Why is that?" he asked.

"I don't know," I answered. "It intrigues me for some reason."

"Have I ever told you where it came from?"

I sat up in my seat and looked directly at him. "No, I've asked you before but you've always managed to change the subject."

Thomas sighed deeply and slowly. "Well, that's probably because I'm not very certain that anything in there is worthwhile."

"What do you mean?"

"It could be just a bunch of unimportant fluff," he said.

"What makes you say that? I mean, I guess it could be, but I think there are some patterns here."

"You do?" Thomas questioned.

"Yes, I´ve noticed a few similarities at least."

"Well, just don´t spend too much time in it. It may not get you anywhere," he concluded.

"Perhaps," I said. Thomas slowly began to rise from his seat as I continued. "Where did you find it?"

"I didn´t," he said as he pushed in the chair. "I wrote everything in there."

"These are your words?" I asked in complete surprise.

"Indeed."

"Well, what does it all mean?"

"Don´t you think I would have put that in there if I knew?" he laughed. He took his seat again and looked at me from across the table. "Several years ago, I started having dreams. They were vivid but uncertain. Dreams can be strange and, most of the time, entirely irrelevant, but these dreams were different. They came during the day and night. Anyway, I started writing down what I could remember of them, so that I could look back on it all later."

"Did you ever stop to think that they could be…you know… memories?"

"Of course," he said. "But it´s all too 'here and there' to make much of it."

I didn´t say anything about the visions I had of the woman, but rather decided to do just as Thomas had. If I found a pattern in my own dreams, if ever they produced something similar to Thomas´s, then maybe it could shed light on the words he had written. Perhaps it could prove a window into our beginnings.

I lay awake that night thinking on the matter time and again until I had settled on a plan that combined the two subjects I thought on most often. If there were answers to be had for us, they must exist beyond the shores. And despite Thomas's assumption, I was intent on settling the question conclusively. After mulling the idea over in my mind, I determined that I would leave in search of the island as soon as possible.

The first obstacle I faced, however, was the fact that I knew of no one who could loan me a ship or even a small boat to make a journey across the ocean. This posed a troubling dilemma, but I was determined not to let it stop me from accomplishing what I had set my mind to do. Even if I had to build my own ship, I was going to find what others had rumored.

I would begin my efforts to procure a boat tomorrow, and I would start by asking Thomas. I was pretty sure he didn't have one himself, but he might know of someone who did. Afterward, I would be able to find my way home and bring answers back to my new friends. It seemed simple enough, and I wondered what had kept others from doing the same. Perhaps there was no island at all, so I determined to take enough provisions to last me two days travel, and if it proved to be a rumor, I would come back and debunk the myth for everyone else. However, I was convinced in my mind that there was a reason that no one ever returned, and it was because they found what they were looking for.

These thoughts were enough to calm my mind sufficiently to begin falling asleep. I postponed the plans of my future endeavor, and the dreariness I had left unattended started to bring my eyelids to a close. Soon after, I drifted into a deep and well-needed sleep.

In the morning, I woke to the sound of the clanking of plates and things around the table. I slowly rose to a sitting position and rubbed my eyes open to see all my friends sitting amid a spread of the usual morning meal. "Well, look who's finally awake," Simon said in a jesting tone. The eyes of everyone turned my way.

"Why, Dear, you haven't slept this late since you were first with us," Martha sounded in a loving manner.

"I'm afraid I didn't fall asleep until late last night," I explained, rising to my feet and starting toward the table. I took the last open chair next to Timmy and rested my head in my hands. "Do you know of anyone with a boat?" I asked, looking at Thomas for an answer. He returned an expressionless gaze while continuing to cut the apple in his hand.

"Why do you need a boat?" Martha asked.

Thomas placed the apple aside and folded his arms. "I have a boat of sorts, but it isn't in good repair. It will take some work to make it useful again. What is it you need it for?"

My jaw hung in anticipation of what I should say. "Never mind, I..."

Then Thomas went on. "I used to fish in that boat some years back. It would be good to get it going again."

Simon shot an inquisitive stare across the table as if he was wondering what I might be up to. Then he offered a change in expression. "I can get it repaired for you," he volunteered, still staring at me as if he expected my face to soon divulge my plans. "There should be time enough today."

"Good, and I'm sure John would love to help," Thomas replied.

I was delighted to see that my search for a boat didn't take me as far as I had feared it might, but I also couldn't think where Thomas could have been keeping it.

Only the most necessary tasks were attended to that morning in order that we might have time enough to work on the boat. As midday came upon us, I found myself following Simon and Thomas over to the barn. On the far side sat a small object under a sandy dirt-colored cloth that kept it not only concealed but also very inconspicuous. If indeed this covering harbored the boat Thomas spoke of, I couldn't imagine that it would hold anything more than one single person.

"Here it is," Thomas said, lifting the dusty cover from off the small craft. The needed repairs that Thomas had mentioned earlier were immediately apparent. In the base of the boat was a fair-sized hole. Along the left side was a crack that was large enough to cause concern, and the hull of the craft was splitting in two separate directions at the very front. Aside from these obvious inadequacies, it appeared to have seen some great wear over time. The panels and joints seemed rather weathered, though most still held their intended form. I was left to venture that, by the looks of it, the boat must have been through a wreck of sorts.

"It will take some time, but we can finish it today I think." After saying this, Thomas left us for a moment to walk back to the barn.

"It used to be a rather nice little boat," Simon remarked.

"What happened to it?" I asked.

"I don't know. Thomas came back one day with it looking like this and didn't want to say anything about it."

"What do you think it was?"

"Well, Thomas used to do a lot of fishing with it," Simon said. "He would spend hours on the water, long into the night sometimes. It's how he used to support the family, but then this happened. Anyway, I think he ran it too close to the rocks or something." Once Simon had said this, we spotted Thomas returning from the barn with some tools and wood.

"Alright boys, let's get this boat working again," he said as he dropped it all at our feet.

Our tasks of repairing the vessel took the remainder of the day and, like Thomas had supposed, it was a considerable amount of work, more than I had expected at first sight. We first had to make a sealant and adhesive of sorts by brewing the stems and roots of a certain plant. Once this was done, a considerable amount of time was spent in the process of shaping the pieces of wood meant to repair the holes and gaps in the body of the boat.

Filler, wood, and the crude plant-derived sealer were added in the needed areas, and by the end of it all, the craft was ready to dry and soon take to the water again. It didn´t look as good as I imagined its original appearance had. It was, nonetheless, a welcoming sight, considering that I was now a good deal closer to setting sail, or in the case of this craft, it looked as though I might be rowing.

Afterward, Thomas showed me a small cart that he said was used to carry the boat to the shores. The end of it had an attachment that hooked to the harness of a horse in order to pull the craft behind like a carriage. "Well, Son, you´re set," he said. "Whatever it is you plan to use it for, you can now. If you're going fishing, I have some netting you can use just don't go at night."

"Why's that?" I asked.

Thomas hesitated for a moment as if he didn´t want to tell me, but after a brief pause, he began answering me anyway. "Something ran under this boat when I was fishing past dark one night. Or maybe I was the one that ran over the top of it. I can´t say what it was. It was too dark. But that's why it's in the poor shape it is," he said, pointing to the boat. "Anyway, I was fishing in an area I wasn't that familiar with. It was south of here, by the shores of the forest."

"What do you think it was?"

"I probably ran up on some reef or a large rock. If I could have seen where I was going, I would have avoided whatever it was," he reasoned. "Just don´t go out past dark. You´ll have no problems then."

"I'll be sure to be careful," I returned. Thomas merely nodded and smiled.

I was glad that he was under the impression I was going

fishing. After all, I was, only mine was a different type of fishing. I was fishing for answers, and I was determined to keep my intentions to myself for as long as possible. I certainly planned to return the ship as soon as I was finished with it, but I wasn't sure when that would be. It would work much better to merely leave a note and explain everything when I returned.

However, Simon was sure to have some insight into my interest, due to our conversation on the shores a year ago. For this reason, I had cause to expect questions from him. He was likely to believe that my endeavors were related to what was discussed that night. But ultimately, I gleaned confidence from Thomas's unquestionable trust in me and planned to use it to my advantage.

"Thank you, Thomas, very much," I replied.

I determined that evening to leave first thing the next morning. Simon, sensing my plans for an expedition, told me that he would let Thomas and Martha know where I was if they should ask, but he also said that he couldn't promise that they would like the news. Already he was assuming he knew where I was going, and his confidence in his assumption began to be somewhat intimidating.

Shortly before we all retired to bed, Simon shuffled to his feet in front of the fire place and began walking toward the door. He stopped at the coat rack and proceeded to wrap a cloak around himself. Afterward, he shot a glance my way. "Follow me," he said. I sat up and immediately realized that no one else seemed to take any notice of his departure, as sudden and unexpected as it seemed. Thomas and Martha sat on their bed reading some story to the children, who had snuggled up next to them. I swung on my coat and slid past the door, hoping to remain as inconspicuous as Simon had.

Just outside, leaning against the wall of the house under the shadow of a still night, was Simon. "Look, I'm not going to try and stop you, but you have to understand that once I tell Thomas and Martha what you've done, they're bound to worry themselves sick." He stopped for a moment. "They care about you, John, like they would their own son."

"I have to go, Simon. Something inside of me is pressing on my mind. I can't stop thinking about it."

"Some would call that curiosity."

"No, it's more than that."

He said nothing for a moment and began to pace about. "Let's just say that you and I are a lot alike," he replied. "But I have to look out for this family. They took me in as their own, just like you. They've done more for me than I can repay. Thomas is getting older, and he's not going to be able to handle everything any more. If Martha and the kids were ever left alone, there's no telling what would happen to them in this crazy place."

His words left me feeling a little selfish, but they still could not deter the focus of my thoughts. The matter on which I pondered took a supreme priority in my heart, and it was clear to me that leaving Caprecia was the thing I must do.

"I know how you feel, but I can't silence what's inside of me. The conviction that creates such loyalty in you is the same force urging me to leave. I must have come from somewhere beyond these shores—you, me, and Thomas and Martha for that matter. Surely others plan to keep looking for the island."

"Maybe, but the risks seem to outweigh the payoff of finding some island that may or may not have anything to do with us," Simon said.

I remained silent for a brief spell of thought. "What do you mean?"

"A lot of others have tried to do what you're about to, but remember, they never came back—not a single one of them."

I wasn't sure at first how to react to what he said. As I stood silently in the chill of the night, I reasoned that my situation would be different. "Well," I finally replied. "Those who left before me probably didn't borrow a boat they would have to return. I'll be back, you'll see. Besides, the reason they stayed gone is likely because they found what they were looking for. They probably found our home."

Simon's face was still somewhat stern. "Or maybe they're all dead, sharing an ocean grave."

Something kept me feeling very optimistic about the trip, despite Simon's concern. If anything, it made me wonder even more about those before me who had ventured back to the sea. Surely, we weren't so far from civilization, not with so many ending up stranded on our shores. There had to be some sign or some people beyond here that could answer the riddle.

"There is something waiting for us, Simon, something away from this place, and I intend to find it." He turned from me and started walking toward the door. Once there, he stopped and looked back.

"If that's true, I only hope that I get to hear about it somehow."

Chapter 7

The following morning found me well rested and eager to embark on my quest. I thought about the conversation Simon and I had the night before. I couldn't help feeling a slight degree of timidity as I recalled his words of caution. As I lingered in these thoughts, however, my faculties were awakened, my resolve returned, and despite the uncertainty of danger, I was intent on leaving still the same. Whether courage or stubbornness prompted me to action, or else a more pure motivation caused by the visions in my dreams, I was holding to it with all I had.

The early hours of the day brought with them a chill in the air and sparkling dew that covered the ground. The sun had only just begun to rise over the horizon I would soon be traveling toward, and I stopped to admire its beauty for a moment before heading to the barn.

I decided to take Amos with me instead of Claudia. He was the strange white stallion that Thomas and Martha kept and the one which I had learned to ride as of late. Thomas had found him on the fringe of the southern forest several years ago, and though he appeared to be a wild horse, he was the most tame of any Thomas had ever seen. This is what he told me at least. The other matter of his nature that was peculiar to us all was the fact that he never stayed around for very long.

Even though Thomas and Martha kept him in a corral, he always managed to get out somehow and traipse off for days at a time, only to return back to the corral afterward.

Amos was waiting with an anxiousness that almost seemed to suggest he had an idea as to where we were going. I saddled and bridled him to the cart that pulled the craft and swung on after without any further delay.

By the time we reached the shores, the sun was well into the sky and had already warmed the air around us considerably. I brought Amos to a stop just before the grassy meadows merged into the sandy white beaches in front of us. The sight was serene, but my blissful indulgence of the scenery soon played into my earlier thoughts of what might lie ahead of me.

I brought us close enough to the water so that the distance left to push the craft on my own would be minimal. I jumped down from Amos and quickly untied the boat from the small carriage. Once it was on the sand, I turned the craft to face the water and began to push it in the direction of the small breaking waves.

As I stopped for a moment to turn around and unhook Amos from the carriage, I saw him stoop down and, butting his snout against the back of the boat, begin to push it the remainder of the way into the water. "Wait," I yelled, afraid he might nudge it too far and leave me wading in the ocean in attempts to catch it. I grabbed hold of the side just as he was bringing it to a halt in a perfect position for launching into the surf.

"Thanks pal," I said, a little surprised. I looked into his eyes until they met mine. "You know you can't come with me, right? You're free to go home now," I continued, standing up and coaxing him to where I could remove the cart from his back. "I appreciate all your help, really I do, but you couldn't even fit in the boat." For some reason, I was insistent that he could understand everything I was telling him. I slid the harness off his shoulders and gave him a pat on the back.

I brushed the hair on his head and neck and gave him a scratch on the shoulder before directing him to find his way back to the corral where he would be expecting a meal soon enough. I took from the saddle the bag I had brought with me, containing as much water, dried fruits, and fish as I could manage to pack, and looked to Amos one final time. He nodded, snorted at me as if to say good luck, and then turned to run out of sight beyond the small grassy dunes.

I wasted no time in pushing the boat the remaining distance into the churning water. Once I was knee deep, I jumped into the craft and quickly readied the oars on either side of me. I paddled with as much might as I could muster to get the boat past the waves and into more settled water as soon as possible.

There wasn't a cloud in the sky, and the air had warmed to a comfortable degree after a few hours had passed. It was a day as beautiful as my hopes of discovery, with the weather a perfect match for my mood.

After a good deal of effort and some considerable time, I found myself far enough away from the shore that its line amid the horizon was noticeably smaller. The water of the ocean tossed the small boat to and fro in a systematic sway, and I began to feel as though I was in the hands of a steady and kind sea. When I looked behind me, I couldn't yet see any sign of land, and the sight of only more ocean stretching beyond my view was enough to dishearten me a little.

I rested from my efforts for a spell and looked around and above me at a sky that harbored no threat of storm. It was amazingly clear and welcoming, and I felt almost as if I could glean strength merely from the beauty that surrounded me. I made a determination to find a rhythm that I could maintain for a good while and go to it with as much endurance as I could manage before looking behind me again. Afterward, I hoped to be able to see shores or some sign of something.

I fixed on a spot in front of me where the land formed a cove that I could distinguish well enough and use as a mark for my travels. I had learned from Thomas how to plow a straight line by doing the same thing, and after employing the technique, I found that my rows were often quite straight. Surely, this same concentration would ensure that my course remained a straight line, and I hoped that a straight line is what I needed.

The continuation of the journey appeared to pass slowly at first, but later it seemed that the time it took to cover the same distance was diminished. I found that I began to count in my mind one hundred strokes, only to start over again to count one hundred more.

Eventually, I found that I needed more rest after every hundred. I could feel my arms beginning to ache more deeply with every occasion I dipped the oars in the water. The thought came more than once as to how sore my arms and chest were bound to be the next morning, but on every occurrence, I shook such thoughts from my mind as quickly as I could and tried not to be discouraged.

I had kept with my promise to row on without looking behind, and as the day drew out, the shore in front of me grew dimmer from my view. After a time, I could no longer make out the mark I had earlier set, but by this point, I was content with the belief that I was pulling equally with each exhausted arm and, therefore, should be maintaining my intended course.

The time eventually came where I was in need of an extended break. I lay down in the bottom of the boat and stared at the sky overhead. When I had first begun, there wasn't a cloud in sight, but now several billowing plumes passed before me. The sun peaked out from between them on occasion and caused me to roll over on my side to avoid the bright and stinging presence of its rays.

After I had lain motionless for a long while, or so it felt, I began to greatly wonder how much closer I was to anything, or if I had merely distanced myself from the only home and refuge I knew. I began to hope that I could turn around and see land on the near horizon. I pulled from the side of the boat the bladder I had submerged beneath the surface with a rope in order to keep the drink from growing tastelessly warm. The water was cool enough to offer some refreshment, and after drinking a few gulps, I felt ready to begin again.

The strong inkling I had to turn about and see what lay behind me became all the stronger with the passing moments. Nonetheless, I pressed on, determined to go a good distance before looking. I began to view the desire as a self-imposed challenge, and I continually told myself that I could go just a little farther before giving in to my own mental pressure.

As slowly as time had seemed to pass with the difficulty of the present task, the late afternoon was upon me sooner than I had hoped. I looked at the sun as it fell in the sky and wondered how much longer it would be before its setting. I again started to sense the pulls of reason, as it would seem, and wondered whether I should turn back while I still had the chance. However, as chance would have it, my stubborn nature took over, and I brushed these thoughts from my mind before they could cause me to relinquish my zeal. I knew better than to let them linger. If I was going to remain out here, I would have to stay positive. I would have to remain calm and not let any pessimistic possibility creep into my mind.

Somehow, I had made it out here, despite the concern that Simon expressed for my safety, and while it was likely to be nothing more than the fact I was desperate to find answers, it was enough for me to take the chance. This present realization gave me new-found strength in my hopes, and I took to the oars with the vigor I had lost earlier in the day.

By the time the sun had touched the horizon in front of

me, I determined that I'd better take the opportunity to gauge my progress before it was too late to do so. I brought the oars into the boat and sat in anticipation, in a self-imposed postponement of the inevitable. Would I be turning back, hoping to reach Caprecia before I became unable to do so, or would there be a reason to move on? I slowly turned around, delaying the revelation even in my attempts to settle it. As I looked into the distant ocean, I saw, to my great surprise, the faint outline of a jagged landscape.

There was still some considerable distance to cover, but this reality wasn't enough to dim my elations. I had seen what I had so longed to see, and I relished in it. My hope had not been in vain. It was now that I only wished I had never allowed doubt to surface at all. However, along with my excitement came a stark realization. How could the presence of an island so close to us be merely a rumor? It wasn't visible from the shores, but surely others had come looking and would have seen what I saw.

Then I thought about what Simon had told me, how those who left never returned. I began to wonder what could be on the island and whether my interest in finding something beyond the colony was wise or not. Perhaps there was danger on the shores to which I was heading. Perhaps there was something that kept any colonist from returning with news of it. How else could its existence be such a mystery?

For a second time, I thought more about my ambitions from the stand point of someone like Simon. I wondered whether turning back would be a good idea, whether failing to do so would cause me to suffer an unfavorable fate. I closed my eyes and searched my thoughts, determining beforehand that I would go with my gut feeling. Despite the growing concern that had initiated my meditation, I suddenly began to feel at ease over continuing toward the island.

A new thought took over in my mind, one that played off

of Thomas's opinion. What if those looking for answers, like me, had found nothing on the island and had carried on past its shores to try and find something more? If this were the case, there would be no harm in taking a look around.

As I drew nearer to the place, I realized that it was a very small island and looked rather unlikely to harbor any civilization, which only supported my most recent theory. The closer I got to it, the more it looked like the peaks of a submerged mountain that had shot itself out of the water. There appeared to be very little flat ground anywhere.

My arms ached, and I was ready to collapse, but I eventually came to rest the boat on a beach that was, thankfully, much bigger than it looked at a distance. Night had since fallen, and the sand cast the faintest glimmer beneath the moonlight while the remainder of my surroundings formed a shadowy backdrop.

I beached the craft far enough past the waves to insure it would be there when I came back, and then I fell flat on my face on the cool ground. I couldn't remember ever being more tired, thirsty, or hungry in my life. My water had grown tastelessly warm before I reached the shore, and the dried fish and fruit I carried with me soon became the only real comfort I had for my pains.

After eating a small amount, I lay on the ground and began to feel most fortunate that I had made it. Before falling completely asleep where I lay, I was aroused by the realization that I needed to obtain some shelter for the night. I took from the boat the covers and clothes I had brought with me and summoned the remaining strength I had to pull the boat farther onto shore for an added measure of precaution. I did all I could to keep myself from falling to the ground in exhaustion afterward and then staggered toward the trees and growth that moved so subtly in the wind.

As I traveled farther away from the noise of the crashing

waves, a much more delightful sound filled my ears. I could hear, ever so softly, the babbling music of a brook or stream. Never had a sound sent so much relief to my heart. I ran in the direction of it and soon lost it under the trampling noise of my feet. I stopped and listened again, reassessed my bearings, and ran toward the welcoming sound once more.

After following this pattern several times, I finally arrived at the banks of a stream that coursed its way through the thick covering of trees and brush. I quickly dropped my luggage and fell on my knees before the rippling current. I lost count of how many times I plunged my hands into the cold water to send gulp after gulp of quenching refreshment down my parched throat.

I soon felt bloated with satiety as I lay down on the soft grass that covered the banks, ready to fall asleep for the entire night. I reached over and grabbed hold of the covers I had brought with me. As I did, a sharp but faint sound pierced the night.

I hurried to my feet and heard it again, the snapping of a twig and the rustling of footsteps. I turned around, trying to determine the direction of the movement, but all fell silent too quickly. I heard something snap again, and then a more ominous sound followed it, the clinking of metal. I spun around but failed to spot any source for the noise. I tried to calm myself and gather my belongings.

I walked carefully and slowly, alert and attentive to my surroundings. I moved cautiously back toward the shores where it felt safer, and where I would be afforded an open view to all around me. Suddenly, I heard the metallic sound again, and I felt an arm wrap around my neck and throw me to the ground. A boot stomped on my chest and held me pinned in place as a bright light flashed from above.

Chapter 8

The weight of the foot on my chest made it difficult to breathe, and though I tried to free myself, the force was too great. The light shone directly on my face, and I was blind to all my surroundings. I could hear feet shuffling around me and knew immediately that I was out numbered. I shut my eyes tightly and tried to breathe deeply enough to attempt another effort to free myself, and then I heard a voice.

"What are you doing here?" a man said.

Another voice followed right after his. "Wait a minute. Is he the one we've been told about? He looks like the picture."

"You're right. He does," the other said. "You two hold his arms, and you, knock him out." After he said this, four forceful hands grabbed each of my arms and anchored them to the ground. I struggled, but it was no use. A cloth with a strange smell on it was placed over my nose and mouth, and I suddenly felt overwhelmingly drowsy and weak.

When I woke later, it was morning. I could see the sun peeking through a small window above me, and I could hear the procession of footsteps to my right. I turned my head and found myself in a strangely-empty room. Four gray walls with nothing on them enclosed me in a cold shell. The crude bed on which I was laying was the only object in the place, and the door that sat a few paces from me seemed to be made of a material that looked like fine-plated metal.

It had a small opening in its center that could pass as a window, only on a technicality, and the rest of it was solid and gray like the walls that surrounded me. This door, and the other window that sat above the bed, were the only sources for light in the room. I swung my legs toward the door and placed my bare feet on a cold stone floor.

When I reached the entrance to the room, I pasted my face against the glass to see out of the tiny window in the door. It fogged under the presence of my exhalation, and I had to move back to wipe it away with my hand. I then leaned in again with my breath held in my chest in order to get a better look.

What I saw was an equally-empty hall with the same peculiar lights illuminating it from behind long squares of glass that were fastened to the ceiling. If candles were harbored inside, I couldn't figure how anyone would have lit them, since the whole thing was completely encased without any opening. Aside from this fact, the light didn't have the same effect as that of a fire, but rather, it looked a bit like the sun does at midday.

As I stood looking to my left and my right, I heard footsteps again. I saw, coming around the far corner, a man dressed in black with a red hooded cloak. I continued to watch him until he came to my door where his eyes met mine. I stepped away from the window and heard him speaking on the other side, although I wasn't sure who he would have been talking to.

"He's awake," he said. A pause followed before he spoke again. "Right away."

Slowly the door opened, and the man stood in the entrance with a glaring stare. "Come with me," he said.

"Where am I?" I demanded.

The man said nothing at first but just looked back at me. "Come with me and maybe your question will be answered." I was hesitant at first, but I quickly decided that whatever was out there was probably better than sitting in a cold and lifeless room. As we walked through the doorway, I was met with the same flooring, and my bare feet on its cool surface made the hallway feel just as cold.

The man that ushered me through the corridors of the building was silent and never looked anywhere but forward. We walked fast enough that his cloak danced behind him in the air, and I could see around his waist a strange looking contraption that was secured in a holster of some sort. It looked like nothing I had seen before, but I was left assuming that it was a weapon, though it didn't look as though it could inflict much damage.

After walking only a short distance, we stopped at a large pair of doors. They appeared to be as tightly shut as the one to the room we just left. They had no windows and no handles and made me wonder how anyone was supposed to get through them. The man walked over to a square box that sat on the wall and placed his hand on it. After a faint blue light emanated from the box, the doors suddenly opened with a strange sound, as if they were releasing trapped air.

There was nothing on the other side but another empty hallway, only this one was much more inviting. The floor was covered in a deep blue rug-type material, and the walls were very white. The lights from the ceiling were similar to but much brighter than the others, and at the end of the corridor was another pair of large doors.

As we walked, my feet felt much warmer, and the floor covering added some cushion to my step. The air around us was also far warmer and more pleasant, and I began to feel a bit relaxed. When we reached the doors, the man at my side grabbed a hold of his shirt collar and then did something most peculiar by speaking into it.

"We're here," he said. Suddenly, the doors opened as the others had, and a room that was even brighter than the hallway was extended before my view.

In the center of the room was a large table at which sat several men and women. Each man was dressed just like the one who stood alongside me while the women wore red-colored gowns of some type. The man at the head of the table waved his arm to invite us in. As we stepped into the room, the doors closed behind us just as the previous pair had opened, without any manual assistance. I found this strange, but there were matters of greater priority which kept me from dwelling on the mystery for long.

"Have a seat," I was told by the man who had just motioned to us. I took my place in the only chair available, which happened to sit directly in the middle of the room. Everyone remained silent for an uncomfortable amount of time while those at the table looked over something in front of them. They whispered amongst themselves and nodded their heads ever so slightly, stopping long enough to cast a glance at me and then return to their whispers.

"How did you learn of this island, and why have you come?" one of the women asked.

"I came looking for answers, you see—"

"But how did you know that we were here?" she interrupted.

"Well, I didn't actually. I merely hoped to find something or someone. I come from a place not far from here, a colony called—"

"We know," the man answered. I paused briefly.

"You do?"

"Yes," he returned before I could ask anymore. "And I'm afraid that is why we had to deal with you as we did the night before. We have no reason to trust your kind, unless we're told otherwise."

"My kind?"

"Yes, but fortunately, we've been told that we can trust

you. I would apologize for your treatment thus far, but we were merely exercising the needed precautions."

"What precautions are needed against someone like me? I'm no threat."

"Maybe not," the man returned. "But others are. This island must remain a secret, and if you are to return to your home, you must promise us, as we've been told you would, that you will speak of it to no one."

"Who told you this? I would like to talk with them," I said. "You must understand that I don't know who I am. I can't remember anything."

"Right, but they aren't here," he said.

"Then where are they?" I need answers. I've gone far too long without them."

"If you receive your answers, it won't be here. You must return to the colony and tell no one of this place or anything you have seen here."

"What's the big secret? Why is it that you seem to know who I am, and yet you'll tell me nothing? I can't leave here content under these conditions."

"Then we will have to deal with you as we did the others," the man replied. Suddenly, the conversation Simon and I had two nights ago came to mind. I knew now why no one who had ventured out here ever returned. They must have been as stubborn as I was, and I quickly became convinced that continuing in stubbornness would not serve me well in the current situation.

"Very well," I conceded. "Show me to my boat, and I will be on my way."

"You won't be taking your boat back. It has already been destroyed."

"What? But it didn't even belong to me. How am I going to explain—"

"No matter," the man interrupted; "a small sacrifice, and

I think you will soon agree with me." It took all that I had to keep from lashing out with the words that passed through my mind. Ultimately, I had nothing more I could say. I was angry more than anything. To come this far to be dealt with in this way was more than I cared to endure. The sooner I left the better.

"Don't think to go back on your promise, young man. We have eyes amid the colony, and we will be watching you."

I decided that silence would send a better message than any words could, and as I was escorted from the room I began to feel happy that I was leaving the place. Who was to tell me what I could or couldn't say? If they wanted to keep the place a secret, then they should have been kinder to me.

When we walked outside, the sight that awaited me was something that I didn't expect. The building we exited was situated deep within the dense growth of the island. There was no sign of the ocean anywhere, and even its sound was too distant to reach us. Everywhere I turned, I saw people dressed just as all the others. The island that I thought looked lifeless from a distance was crawling with crimson-laden individuals.

Several more buildings that were otherwise hidden amid the trees and growth soon came into view as I was shown down a pathway made of solid rock. Farther in our course, we approached a structure that looked far more appealing in its outer appearance than the stone-like fortress we had just left. I was ushered to its door without a word spoken, and once we entered, there was a man and woman standing to greet me.

"Come with us," the woman spoke with a tone a bit more pleasant than the others. I followed her and the man down a hallway of tall windows that cascaded sunlight on the white walls and smooth gold-tinted flooring. We walked in silence as before and soon reached a room built of glass walls with an equally-amazing atrium overhead.

"This is where you will stay," the man spoke.

"What is this? I thought I was going home."

"You are," he said, "but not until nightfall. It's of the greatest importance that we travel to the colony undetected."

I was left in the room alone, but my accommodations were far better than I could have expected. On a large table was a spread of the most appetizing food I had ever seen. I was immediately reminded of the hunger I had endured, and I began to fill a plate.

When there was no room left for me to pile on anything else, I walked over to a soft and plush chair that sat facing out of the room. It was the most comfortable seat I had ever taken, and I sunk into the cushions when I sat. I began to wonder what I might have thought of these people had I received this treatment from the beginning, but now I was merely left to wonder why their mood had suddenly changed.

I looked out the window and took a bite of a savory slice of bread, admiring the view as I did. People moved below me on the strange roads that wound their way through the trees and around the buildings. As my eyes traveled farther into the distance, however, I saw something that nearly made me choke on the food in my mouth. Standing in the middle of all the structures that were surrounding it, was the same building I had seen as a drawing in Thomas's book.

Chapter 9

By the time I was summoned from my room that night, I had decided not to mention the connection I had with the strange building. However, I wondered all day how it was that Thomas had seen such a thing in his dreams and whether he had been here before. I was sure that mentioning it might only make matters worse for me. Whether or not I could trust these people was something I had yet to settle in my mind. For now, all I was focused on was getting off the island.

"It's time for you to leave," a man told me as he opened the door. "Follow me." I got up from the comfortable chair I had been resting in and followed the man, along with another, out into the night.

Despite the fact that the evening was a dark and moonless one, our surroundings were visible. The same strange lights that were in the buildings I had been in lit the area around us with a sufficient glow. All along the road we walked, these spheres of light that sat atop metal-looking posts illuminated our path and made our surroundings clear to us. Our course took us directly toward the mysterious building that Thomas had drawn, only at the last moment to turn on another road that pointed us away from it. Regardless of my earlier determination, I couldn't keep from drawing attention to its presence and decided that all I needed to do was act casual about it.

"What is that building over there?" I asked, breaking the silence. "It looks much different than all the others, doesn't seem to fit in." The two men looked at me with serious eyes, only to turn back to peering forward again without a word. "Really, it's a pretty simple question," I continued. "It looks, well…peculiar. What makes it so special?"

"What makes you think it's special?" the man on the right said.

I paused for a moment, uncertain as to what I should say next, fearing now that I might have asked too much. "It just looks like it would be, that's all." Silence fell between the three of us again, and it was a long walk after that. At length, we came to stop at a small station, and sitting just outside the door of the building was a strange-looking carriage.

This particular carriage had four wheels and no top, like most, but the wheels had a thick black casing around them with small grooves woven on the surface. Inside the carriage were two rows of seats, but above one of the foremost was a large wheel that would be directly in front of anyone who sat there. There didn't appear to be anywhere to attach a horse to it, and there were no reins present either. Aside from these anomalies, it sat far too close to the ground for a horse to pull it anyway.

"Get in," one of the men said, opening a door on the side and directing me into the back. I took a seat on the black leather-looking bench and noticed that it was much softer than it looked. Immediately afterward, the two men took the seats in front of me, and the one that sat behind the wheel put his hands on it as if he planned to use it for something.

Suddenly, a faint humming noise resonated from beneath the carriage. A very subtle vibration traveled through everything around me and startled me a great deal in the process. Before I could pinpoint the exact source of the noise, it grew in amplitude, and the contraption began to move forward rather quickly. Soon enough, our speed was greater than any carriage could go, and the mystery behind it's propulsion left me astonished.

In a short time, the shore was in sight. The road ran parallel to its outline and wound us toward the far side of the island. The darkened shapes of trees whizzed past us on either side, and the wind caused a howling noise as it found its way through the crevices and nooks of the horseless carriage. I had never gone so fast in my life, and the exhilaration of the air flowing with such force past my face and through my hair was a moment worth relishing.

I had mixed emotions when the thing came to a stop. In many ways, I was rather enjoying the experience and found it one of the few brief moments of relaxation I had since being in this strange place. Yet, on the other hand, I was glad to be one step closer to leaving. The speed came to an end, and the motion that rocked through the contraption stopped along with the humming from inside.

Immediately after this, another individual began approaching us from a distant shadow that obscured the coastline. He was like all the others—no smile, no allusion to mood, just plain and commanding in appearance and communication. When he came within a few feet of us, he placed his hand on the front of the carriage and stared at me.

"They're certain he's the one?" he asked the others.

"Yes," the man behind the wheel announced. "He was reviewed before the panel."

"Very well, I'll take him from here." My door was opened, and I was commanded to follow him. The horizon was dark, but the large object toward which we walked was outlined amid the sky with a degree of clarity. As we approached it, I got a better look and realized that it protracted itself out of the ocean like a huge metal fish with a tall fin on its back. I hadn't any idea what it was, but I assumed that I was soon to find out, because there was no time wasted before I was taken directly to it.

"I'm sure you've been told many times how important it is that you speak nothing of what you've seen here," the man said.

"Yes, but I've never been told why."

"And you won't, not by us at least. We are merely following orders."

"Orders?"

"That's right," he replied, saying nothing more. As we drew close to the strange half-submerged thing, I could hear a similar but louder humming noise coming directly from it. I was shown to a dock that protruded from the banks and ended at the side of the interesting ship of sorts. I assumed it was something of the like at least, because as I walked the distance toward it, an individual appeared from inside.

"Are we ready then?" he asked as we approached.

"Yes, we're right on schedule if we leave immediately," the other responded.

"Very good, let's go then." I followed the man and stepped onto a small metal ladder that brought me to the top of the ship where we continued to a round opening that cast a light similar to the others I had seen. I hesitated a degree as the man before me crawled down another ladder into the belly of the metal beast. Meanwhile, the one behind me put forth his hand as a gesture for me to follow.

I did so, and as the other man shut the opening behind us, it made a loud metallic clank, and then a noise that sounded like wind being sucked through along tube followed it. Upon our descent, I was met with a narrow corridor and blue lights that outlined its edges and ran along the ceiling and floor. At the end of this passageway was a door into a small room that bustled with noise and the movement of several others. I was taken to the end of the hallway and into the room I had seen at a distance.

Taking a seat in a nearby chair, much like the bench on which I sat in the interesting carriage, my eyes panned the view of intriguing lights and instruments that surrounded me. The man whom I had followed into the ship sat down at the far end where he began operating some system of buttons. He spoke some broken language of words into a device of sorts and was answered with an equally broken response that seemed to come from the walls. The others around him sat at similar stations and tinkered with more blinking lights and instrumentations.

After this, I felt the ship move and quickly gain momentum. I clutched the arms of my chair in response and immediately wondered where we would be going without the ability to see anything. I looked at the face of the others and saw nothing but calm expressions.

"Are we moving? Under the water?" I asked. "It feels like we just fell a good distance."

"Yes, we are," one of the men replied. "Just sit back and relax."

"How can I do that when I can't even see where I'm going?"

"I can see where we're going," he said, "and that's all that matters." The man was insane. I was sure of it. There was no way to see anything. All he was looking at was a flashing light on some glass in front of him that, on occasion, would flash another light.

I sat back and closed my eyes, trying to think what I was going to say to Thomas about his boat, if indeed I ever made it back alive. I tried to determine what I was going to do about all that had happened to me. Most of all, I began to wonder if somehow I came from this place, if some decree of banishment had sent me to the shores of Caprecia. They seemed to know who I was and didn't appear to like me either.

"Why was I sent to the colony?" I asked. "I came from

this island, didn't I?" They all remained silent, not one of them so much as turned to look at me. I'd had enough, and I couldn't hide my frustration any longer. "I came all this way for answers, and I'm not leaving this ship without them!" I exclaimed. Finally, the man that had brought me to the ship from the strange carriage turned and looked at me with a face that was calm and collected.

"I already told you," he said. "You won't get any answers from us."

"And why not? You appear to know who I am, but I don't even have that luxury. What is the matter with you people anyway?" By this point, my voice had risen all the more, and my anger was apparent in my tone. Suddenly, the man who had just spoken to me looked at the others and gave a nod. Before I could figure out what was going on, my arms were pinned to the chair, and a rag with the same smell as before was forced over my nose and mouth.

I woke again, after what seemed like only a brief moment, to a smell even worse than the first. It seemed to burn through my nostrils and out my eyes. I stammered into consciousness in time to see one of the red-cloaked men waving a vial of something in my face. "Help him to his feet," he commanded, while two others grabbed my arms and supported me as we walked toward the ladder. With the assistance of those around me, I was hoisted into the night air above. Waves sprayed against the side of the ship, and the wind blew with more force than when we left the island.

I assumed that we were near the shores of the colony, but they were not the same I had seen before. The landscape was more elevated and rough than the soft sands that lay east of Thomas and Martha's, and the ground was shrouded in forest.

As I stood peering toward the darkened shoreline, I saw a boat approaching the ship from the mainland, and it was moving very quickly. Only a short time passed before it reached us, and no time was spared before the vessel's operator climbed on board.

After ascending the ladder, I could see that the man wasn't clothed in the common red garb the others were. In fact, he was dressed plainly, but nonetheless, he was extremely neat in his appearance. His apparel seemed, as much as could be discerned in the dark, to be of a conservative blue, and the coat that he wore over it was the same in color. His face appeared youthful in expression, but his eyes seemed to convey an age of wisdom and experience. As he greeted the men standing to meet him, he turned to me and smiled. It was the first smile I had seen for over two days, and it surprised me to say the least.

"I'm afraid we had to apply a knock out on the way over," one of the red-clothed men said, who seemed foremost among the others and likely the captain. "He was beginning to prove insubordinate." The visitor from the boat looked at him, and his smile ebbed. "Are you sure about this one?" the captain continued.

"Yes, definitely," the visitor answered.

"Very well. We'll support you as always," he replied.

"Thank you," the visitor returned. "I'll take it from here." As he said this, he looked at me again and waved a beckoning hand. "Come with me, John." It was the first time I had been called such sense leaving Caprecia,, and of course, I was very intrigued as to how this man knew that John was my given name. I had never met him before, but then, I didn't remember ever meeting the people of the island either, and somehow they knew who I was.

"Any further orders?" the captain asked.

"No, that will be all," the visitor replied. After this, I was helped toward the boat that sat at the base of the long metal ladder. By now, my strength had returned, and I was able to manage my way into the small boat with minimal assistance. Once I found a seat, the man took his place behind a wheel similar to the one that was part of the four wheeled contraption on the island, and we began to pull away from the large metal boat.

The water craft also made a humming noise, only the source of it seemed more apparent. Behind us, water churned as if some huge and powerful oar was rapidly stirring beneath us, and it was here that the sound was most pronounced.

"How do you know my name?" I asked.

"You mean, John? Well, it's not your real name, of course."

"What do you know about me?" I questioned in a tone of urgency.

"A lot," he replied.

"I just spent more time than I cared to with people who also seemed to know a lot about me, and they did nothing to clue me in. I'm getting a bit fed up with it. I don't remember—"

"I know," he interrupted.

"Know what?"

"That you don't remember who you are, and Thomas and Martha found you on the shores."

This astonished me. "How could you know all of that? I've never met you before in my life."

"Well, that's not true, but even still, we've been watching you, waiting for you to prove that you're ready."

"Ready for what?"

"I will answer that question one step at a time," he said. "I take it that you didn't enjoy your stay much with the hill-dwellers, or so they're called."

"Is that who those people were?" I asked. "I thought the hill-dwellers lived in the mountains west of Caprecia."

"Yes, they do. That's where they come from, but a small number of them occupy the island for a specific reason." From what I had seen, small was not the word I would have used to describe their numbers, and his comment made me wonder how large they're numbers must be in the hills beyond the colony.

"Let's just say I've heard certain things about them, and after my experience, I'm inclined to believe them," I said.

"Yes, well, they are a cold and calculating people, but they aren't what some have made them out to be. If nothing else, they are fair and equitable."

"Fair? How could the way they treated me be fair? They acted as though I was a criminal."

"They have reason to take extreme precautions, and all of it will make sense soon enough."

Somehow, though I didn't know why, I felt as if he was right, and I was able to relax the frustration that had built inside. "Good, because I have some questions. I've seen some crazy things in the last two days."

"What, you mean like this boat we're traveling in?"

"Right, how does it move, and why have I never seen anything like it?"

"Actually, you've seen far greater, but of course you don't remember," the man said.

"Who are you anyway?"

"My name is Delvarus. Consider me a mediator between the colonists and the hill-dwellers. My aim is to keep the peace."

"Delvarus? That's an interesting name. It's not like any I've heard around here," I said.

"Yes, well, it's not so uncommon where I come from," he replied.

"So you aren't a hill-dweller?"

He just smiled and continued looking forward. "No, I'm not."

"Where do you come from then, and what reason do you have for dealing with me?"

"You are the one we have chosen to undertake an extremely important assignment."

"And what would that be?"

"It's a bit of a loaded question, I'm afraid, and the answers will start first thing in the morning." As strange as the whole conversation was, and as vague and allusive as his answers to my questions had been, for some reason, I felt as though I could trust the man.

"Where are we going now? I've never been to this side of the mainland before."

"Well, we're a considerable distance from Caprecia right now, but we are headed back to your home inevitably."

"Then why are we so far away?"

"We can't afford to be detected. The island that you came from must remain a secret."

All of a sudden, I was reminded of the frustration that arose when first I was told this. "And why is that, why all the secrets? What are you people trying to hide?"

"Something very important resides on the island, the knowledge of which shouldn't be privy to just anyone. That's why you mustn't speak of the island or anything you have seen there to anyone back on the mainland, not yet at least."

"Why is it that I'm expected to obey these hill-dwellers without any question as to why? They act as if I'm of no consequence to them, as if I can just be pushed around. I'm not so sure I should even keep their secret. Perhaps they're the reason I wound up nearly dead on some shore with no idea of who I am. Can you tell me that? You seem to know."

"No, they aren't the reason." Delvarus replied.

"Then who is?" I asked. He didn't answer at first but turned to look at me with a serious glare, as if he was assessing whether or not I was fit to receive the knowledge I longed for.

"How much do you want to know?" he asked.

"I've risked everything to know, including my life. Who's the reason?" I inquired again.

Delvarus brought the small boat to a slow crawl, and the noise which it produced was reduced to an even softer humming. He turned to me and placed his hand on my shoulder then looked me straight in the eye. "The reason you're here is because someone wants you to be here."

"Who?" I asked.

"The man we call Father," he said.

Chapter 10

The answer came as nothing less than a shock. In fact, I sat for a while, trying to process what he had said, trying to make sense of it in some way. And yet, somehow, I knew it was true. He must have sensed that I would react in this manner, because he said nothing to me for the duration of my silence, leaving me alone to my contemplations.

"Did our father disapprove of me?" I finally asked as he pulled the boat into a small and secluded cove.

"No, quite the contrary actually. He loves you more than you know."

"Then why would he leave me for dead on some distant shore, and why do I remember nothing about how I got there?"

"I know it all seems very strange right now, but it will make perfect sense in the end. Be assured, John, that you are here because our father cares deeply for you."

"Yeah, but why—?"

"Remember," he interrupted, "the answers start tomorrow. Right now, my time is short. I have to leave very soon." He stepped out of the boat onto the dock we had coasted alongside and beckoned me to follow. We walked into the trees toward a barn and cottage that stood quiet in the still night. Twigs and leaves crunched beneath our feet as we moved over a road that looked as if it never saw frequent travelers.

As we approached the door to the house, Delvarus walked right in without knocking or offering a summons of any sort. I followed after him and saw that the one room of which it consisted was totally unoccupied, aside from the essential accommodations for anyone who might be lodging in it.

"Here is where you'll stay for the night. In the morning, you can take Amos back to Thomas and Martha's. He knows the way very well."

"Amos?"

"That's right. If you've ever wondered where he goes when he disappears on his own for days at a time, you know now. He's out in the stall by the barn. We'll meet again tomorrow," he said. "Until then try and get some rest."

"Where am I supposed to meet you?"

"I'll let you know," he said. "But please, remember, you mustn't say anything about the island or what you've seen, not yet. The hill-dwellers aren't keeping it secret for themselves. Our father asked them to." He didn't linger for more than a moment after saying this before he disappeared out the door and into the night.

This statement caused further questions to arise, and as I thought about it all, I was left to determine that if I wanted answers, it was in my best interest to listen to what Delvarus was telling me. If for no other reason, I felt obliged to listen to him merely because he seemed to be a very wise and honest man. And in addition to this, he was family.

I had a hard time sleeping at first. Questions raced through my mind, and the events of the last few days played through my thoughts time and again. However, the bed I was lying in was comfortable enough that I was confident I would soon be able to rest. I pulled the covers up to my neck and tucked them around my shoulders. The night was cold, but being bundled in the warmth of the sheets offered a deep and peaceful comfort to my tired body.

As I rested my hands on my chest, I felt the object I always carried with me fold inside the pocket in which I kept it. It was the necklace that I had promised myself I would never part with. In those quiet moments of the night, the matters of the previous day and my conversation with Delvarus should have been pressing on the forefront of my mind. Yet, my attention to the necklace almost silenced it all. It had an astonishing influence on me every time I stopped to consider its forgotten significance.

I left it in my pocket and tried to think more about what Delvarus had told me. Why was I here, and why did he show up all of a sudden? Why would my own dad have nothing to do with me? I thought on this for some time, and as I did, I began to sense the same loneliness I had before when first I arrived in the colony, only now it was more intense. I had met my brother and that was something to be glad for, but I began yearning to know who else was lost to my failing memory. Inevitably, my mind turned back to the necklace, and I began to picture the same beautiful face I had many times since that night over a year ago.

Her smile was as captivating as ever, and I could almost feel the soft touch of her face against mine. Her eyes glimmered like a blue pool of water in the moonlight, and her dark silky hair blanketed her soft skin with a gentle touch. Then her lips spoke words of love.

I had seen her often when I slept. Sometimes, I would retire for the day, hoping she would appear in the restful hours of the night, only to find that she would elude me altogether. There was no real pattern to her existence, no real cause for her presence in my thoughts, except for the necklace. It somehow connected me to her, and I had assumed a long time ago that it had to be hers.

As I lingered in these contemplations, I felt at peace, as I often did when I thought of her. I breathed a deep sigh that seemed to relieve the stress of the last few days in one simple effort. Imagining her at my side soothed me, and I began to wish she was near me in reality, so that I might tell her of all that had happened.

"Of course I will," she said as she fell to the ground and threw her arms around my neck. "With all my heart I will." As she pulled back a little, I could see a slight welling of tears in her deep blue eyes.

"Don't cry," I said.

"I can't help it. I'm so happy," she replied. I took her soft and slender hand in mine and carefully applied the shining band to her finger. She looked at me again and then her smooth lips touched my own. "I love you," she whispered.

"I love you too," I returned. We rose to our feet and walked to a nearby cliff that looked out over a beautiful valley. Below us, basking in the morning sun, was a city that shimmered in the light. We stood there in silence for a moment as I held her in my arms. When I looked at her face, the tears were present again, but it was apparent that they weren't tears of joy any longer.

"What's the matter?" I asked.

"You know," she said. "I'm just worried."

"You mean about...?"

"Yes."

I turned to face her, and I looked deeper into her eyes. The moment lasted for what seemed like hours. Then a bright light began to burn, and I woke to the sun piercing through the window of the cottage.

I shot up in the bed, looking around me in hopes to find her sitting near my side, but like every time before, she wasn't there. I gathered my things slowly, musing on the dream with as much attention as I could devote. She was lost to me again, and there seemed to be nothing I could do to bring her back.

Amos was excited to see me as I approached the small fenced stable in which he was kept. He reared his legs and shook his head a little when I slid the wooden gate open. While Amos galloped about as if he had been penned up for days, I walked into the small shack of a barn to look for a saddle.

The place was dark and dusty with a hovering stale smell to it, just like I might have expected. I hadn't been able to shake the dream from my mind ever since I had woken. Its presence was so real that it helped to affirm my earliest notion that it was impossible for the occurrences to be part of my imagination. After learning what I had from my brother, I was more certain than ever before that this was the residue of some lost memory. The woman must be real, and my heart was still very tied to her.

As I stood amid my surroundings, I did nothing to search for the saddle at first. Rather, I stared into the space ahead of me and began to imagine her by my side again. Once I did, the tender emotions I felt for her in my subconscious mind came to life again. Shortly after, I could feel a tear touch my cheek and roll from off my face. I watched as it hit the ground and sent a small plume of dust into the beams of sunlight peeking through the door. My life seemed empty to me, as though I came to an awareness more certain than before of all that I had lost. Yet all I knew was that she was no longer with me.

I placed my hand on my chest and felt the necklace again. I held it there and thought back to the dream. When I took it out and ran its smooth surface through my fingers, I thought of how it once had draped on her soft and silk-like skin. I saw her smile in my contemplations, but inevitably, my last recollection was of her tears.

As the mind has a way of doing sometimes, I came to ponder the worst possibility, and it seemed strange that it wasn't until now that I had considered it. What if she hadn't made it? What if I had survived some sea-borne tragedy with only this necklace as a reminder of her? What if the woman for whom my heart ached, was lost to me forever? I fell to my knees and began to weep like a child. Though I was putting pieces of a fragmented memory together without knowing all the facts, my heart was intent on leaving it to this conclusion. I gripped the necklace in my fist and longed for a comfort that was never afforded me.

If I had known her name, it would have groaned inside of me. I dropped my head in my hands to muffle the sound of my sobs, as if I might hide their existence from myself, but it was no use. I almost wished the dreams had never started, that I might have never remembered the anguish of losing her. But then the pain was too sweet. Though it pulled my heart in pieces, I never wanted to forget it.

Suddenly, a snorting sound came from behind me. I turned to look and found Amos's snout casting a shadow in the doorway. I rose to my feet and dried my eyes, looking around me in an attempt to spot a saddle. I found it perched in the far corner of the room and reached to pick it up. "I suppose we better be on our way," I said. "Thomas and Martha are probably worried sick, don't you think?" Amos snorted again as if in response and moved his head up and down.

The forest through which we traveled was as quiet and somber as my mood and made dwelling on the thoughts that brought me to the current disposition a natural course to take. Amos sauntered in a methodical stride, as if he was trying to match the pace of my subdued mind while I stared ahead of us with no real consideration for where we were going.

Amos, on the other hand, was alert but calm. There didn't seem to be any real need for me to pay attention to our course, considering he seemed to know exactly where we were going and how to get there. It occurred to me that he must have made this journey on so many occasions that the details and directions of the route were of a second nature to him.

The forest was massive, and the time it took to get through it must have been significant. However, with my thoughts on such deep subjects as they were, my lack of attention to everything around me made it seem as though very little time had passed before the trees came to an end. As we moved into the open meadows that preceded the fields of Thomas and Martha's, Amos seemed to quicken his steps a little.

It was morning when we left, but by now, the sun was several degrees past its high point in the sky. The view of familiar grounds was the first thing capable of directing my mind away from the melancholy I was experiencing, and I soon began to feel very at home again, just like Amos.

Off in the distance, I saw Thomas standing alone in the fields, reaping wheat in the same systematic movement I had learned to employ at his hand. Seeing him at work somewhere and in some fashion was a sight I was used to. It was an observation I had experienced every day since I arrived in the colony, and witnessing it again made me miss being in his exemplary company for the first time since my absence.

When he finally saw me approaching, he dropped the reaper to the ground. Staring at me, he wiped at his eyes and brow, as if he was trying to determine whether he was indeed seeing what he saw. Eventually, a smile came to his weathered face as we came near enough to speak.

"You're back," he said in a tone of disbelief.

"Yes," I replied as I swung to the ground. Then Thomas did something I didn't expect. He embraced me in his fatherly arms and stood in silence for a moment.

"When Simon told us where you had gone, we were sure that you were lost to us for good."

"Well, I'm glad to be home," I said.

"You're like a son to us, you know," Thomas replied through his squinted and aged eyes.

"And you're the only father I know," I returned. I paused

for a moment and dropped my head toward the ground.

"No one who's left the shores has ever come back," he remarked. "Where did you go?"

"Thomas, I'm so sorry."

"It's alright, I understand why you left," he said.

"No, I mean about the boat. It's gone, destroyed." I braced myself for his disappointment, and when he placed his hand on my shoulder I expected the worst.

"I imagine there is some story behind it all but don't worry," he said. "I already know about the boat."

Chapter 11

"How could you know about the boat?" I asked. Thomas wrapped his arm around my shoulder and directed me toward the house.

"One of the hill-dwellers came to our door yesterday. He said that his people had found you on the shore and that the boat was destroyed."

"He did?"

"The hill-dwellers come to the colony periodically, John, but they had never come to our home before. They only ever show up for two reasons, either because there is some matter of government that needs addressing, or else it's because someone has died. Martha and I have always adhered to their laws, so naturally we didn't think they would have any reason such as this to visit us. Instead, we feared that they had found you dead somewhere and that we would never see you again."

"What all did he tell you?" I asked with great interest.

"Only what I've just said," Thomas replied. "But now another man has shown up, and he doesn't dress like the hill-dwellers."

"Where is he?" I asked.

"He's waiting in the house, and he's been there for a while now. I've never seen him before, but he was asking for you, said he had some business to discuss." I could feel him stare at me from the side as I turned to look toward the house. "What's going on, John?"

"I don't know," I said.

We walked in the door, and sitting on the floor, playfully engaged with the kids in a game of some sort, was none other than Delvarus. "Ah, John, it's good to see you again," he said as we approached. Once he was on his feet, he clasped his hand in mine and offered a smile. "I've been telling Martha and Thomas about our concerns," he continued with a now less-joyful face.

"Our concerns?"

"Yes, our concerns about the unrest."

"Right," I replied with reticence in my tone. "The unrest."

"He says that you've agreed to help him," Thomas spoke.

"It's true, and we must act fast, John. You will need to come with me if we are to stay a step ahead of the others."

"Why did you not tell us that you were a part of all this, whatever it is, or that you were leaving?" Martha implored.

"I didn't know," I spoke, confused about what I should have said.

"Didn't know what?" she asked.

"I mean, I didn't know how involved I was." The whole situation was intimidating. I wasn't sure what I should say or what I shouldn't. "And, I didn't want to worry you with my plans of leaving," I added.

"Well, you've worried us even more by not telling us," she reproached.

"Are you working with Ernest on this?" Thomas asked.

"I...The thing is—"

"John will have much more to tell you soon enough," Delvarus offered, "and you may find yourselves quite involved in it all. But for now, he needs to attend to his promise." I had no idea what he was talking about, and I assumed he knew that. Even still, I was rather befuddled about what was going to happen next. "We will be gone for a spell but will return with good news when all has been accomplished."

"Where is it you're going?" Simon asked with considerable interest.

"I'm afraid he can't say for now," Delvarus answered for me. "But soon enough, all will be known. I'll wait for you outside John, but do hurry; there is no time to waste." After this, Delvarus swung the door closed and everyone else in the room began staring at me.

"He seems a trustworthy man, but who is he?" Thomas whispered.

"We've never seen him before," Martha added. "What is it you're getting involved in?"

If only they knew. If only they understood that I was as confused as they were. Perhaps then they wouldn't press me with questions I didn't know the answers to. I wished I could tell them everything. I wished they could have known all that I had been through; but in the end, prudence of some sort advised against it.

"I would tell you the details if I could," I said. "But frankly, I don't know much of them myself. As for the man, yes, I've learned he can be trusted. He's my brother."

"Your brother?" Thomas questioned. "Where did he come from?" All of a sudden, I wondered if I should have even mentioned this fact; it was sure to only incite more questioning from everyone.

"Apparently, I need to be going. I'll tell you all that I can when I get back."

"This all seems very peculiar," Simon added. "I don't know what to make of it. Maybe the real question is whether we can trust you anymore."

"Simon!" Martha gasped.

"Think about it," he said. "What is he not telling us? For all we know, he could be in league with Henry's lot." I wasn't sure how to react to Simon at first, but I was surprised that he would even consider that I might associate myself with the likes of Henry.

"I'm no Pridion," I defended. "After all you taught me, you think I would so much as speak to the man?" I was offended, and it was showing in my voice. I wondered why one of my closest friends was acting the way he was; it was about all that I could handle.

"Well, you've gone very secretive on us, John, and that's a lot like Henry."

"It's not like that," I insisted. "Not at all."

"Then what is it like?" he yelled.

"Stop it, both of you!" Thomas reproached. "I won't have it!" He turned to me with a stern face. "I'm concerned for you, John. What is it you aren't telling us? Tell me Simon's assumptions aren't true."

"Not even close," I said.

"Then what is it?" Martha pled.

"I can't say. I was told not to."

"By who, your long lost brother?" Simon asked. For the first time since I had known the man, he was beginning to greatly upset me.

"Yes, if you must know. I can't tell you why I must keep such things secret. I just feel that I must for now. Please, trust me on this." Silence fell for a moment, and Simon's face relaxed a small degree.

Thomas looked to the ground and then at Martha who returned his gaze before looking at me intently. "We don't believe you would do anything to put our family in harm's way, but we are concerned for you," she said.

"I understand," I replied. "But I'm on my way to some answers. I'm closer now than ever before to knowing where I came from." Everyone looked at me in silence again, and I could sense that they were less than satisfied with my devotion to something I knew very little about.

"You have to go," Thomas finally said. "I believe you, but don't do anything rash. Don't hasten a war into existence."

"This might not have anything to do with that," I said. "Why are we assuming it's about this war that hasn't even started?"

"Because, your brother said it was," Thomas replied.

I didn't understand why I should go, beyond the fact that I knew it was the only way to have my questions answered. I didn't feel like saying much when we first left, and apparently Delvarus didn't either. I simply listened to the jingling sound of the horses' bridles and the clopping noise of their hooves pounding the road beneath us. By the time we had ventured beyond the sight of Thomas and Martha's, however, I suddenly felt it appropriate to voice my opinion. "Well, the only friends I have are against me now."

"They aren't against you, John."

"Perhaps you would feel otherwise if you had heard our conversation."

"Oh, I heard it alright. They are merely concerned, not mad."

"I don't know," I said, letting my head droop and stare at the passing road beneath me. "Simon used to be one of my closest friends, and now he thinks I'm working for Henry."

"Don't worry, he and the others will soon realize that Henry is the very person we are working against." This was the first real detail he had told me about the purpose of our departure, and as much as I might have guessed it based on his earlier comments about the unrest, it still came as an unwelcome surprise.

"What exactly are we going to do?" I asked, wondering what I had gotten myself into.

"I need you to inform the hill-dwellers about Henry's intentions of rebellion."

"Me? Why me? I thought no one from the colony was even allowed in their city."

"Well, it wasn't always that way."

"Why don't you tell them? Wouldn't they listen to you if you're some mediator as you say?"

"Of course they will listen to me, but they need to see proof that there are many in the colony against Henry. If you don't do this before Henry makes his first move, the hill-dwellers will assume all the colony has turned against them. After that, destruction is inevitable."

"And you can't convince them of that?"

"Tell me, what would be more convincing to you, hearing it from me, or hearing it from a colonist? Besides, you still need to add your name to the list before you take it to them."

"The list?"

"Yes, the one that a Mr. Ernest Foster started."

Chapter 12

When I knocked on the Foster's door, Sarah was the one to answer. She opened it only a crack at first, as if she didn't feel safe in her own home. She peered out at me and seemed to study my face before she was convinced that it was indeed me. "John is that you?"

"Hello, Sarah, is Mr. Ernest home?" I asked.

"We haven't seen you around here for a while. Come in, come in." I walked into the home, looking back at Delvarus who remained on his horse without any sign of following. "I'm afraid Ernest is in town at the moment, but what can I help you with?"

"Well, I came to add my name to the list."

"The list?"

"Yes, Ernest's petition against the Pridions."

"Oh, that list. Well, I don't want you to feel as though you need to, Dear."

"Don't worry, I want to," I said.

"Well, alright, but I know Ernest would have liked to have been here to see you. I'll have to tell him you stopped by." She walked over to the shelf where Ernest kept it and brought it to rest open on the table. I dipped the quill in the ink pot and inscribed my name alongside all the others. "Ernest will be proud to know you share in his passion for peace. I only hope it doesn't come to war," she said.

"You and me both," I replied. "There's just one more thing," I continued as I folded the leather flap over the parchment and held the document in my hand. "I need to take this with me."

"Take it with you? Whatever for?" she inquired.

"I need to use it to convince some people."

"I can't let you take it without Ernest's permission," she insisted. "He is always so careful about anyone even knowing about it."

I don't know what I expected, but I guess I didn't anticipate that she would disagree with my request. "It's really quite important that I have this. I'll bring it back when I have finished. I promise," I said.

"Ernest might be back within the hour. If you would like to wait, you can ask him when he returns." Just then, there was a knock on the door. Sarah exchanged a quick look with me before walking toward the sound.

"Excuse me," she said. I watched as she moved quickly to the front of the house and peeked through the small opening she created between the door and the paneling.

"Sarah is it?" I heard as a familiar voice spoke from the other side.

"Yes, and who are you?" she returned.

"My name is Delvarus. Word has it you have a petition that I need."

"I don't know what you're talking about?" she said. "I'm afraid I can't help you."

"Sarah, trust me. I'm here to help," Delvarus said.

"How do you know my name?" I heard her ask.

"Oh, I know more about you than your name," he said. "I know about what Henry has done to harass you and your husband, and I imagine that you lay awake at night scared that he may come again and do worse things. I want to help put a stop to all that. I'm here to stop Henry." While Delvarus was speaking, Sarah had allowed the door to open farther, until I could see him standing on the other side.

"It's alright Sarah," I called from the table. "He's telling the truth." She turned to me and offered a look of slight confusion, but somewhere deeper in her eyes I could sense hope.

"Let John take the list," Delvarus said. "He will put it to good use. There is no other way to spare the lives of the names written on it. If you don't let him take it, the colonists will have no chance of survival." Everything he was saying wasn't new to me, but I began to hope that Sarah felt as convinced as I did.

"What are you talking about?" she said in a nervous tone.

"The situation the colonists find themselves in is a grave one. Henry, the man you fear, is about to march an army against the hill-dwellers," Delvarus said. "If he does, not only will they destroy him and his people, but they will assume the whole colony a threat and will retaliate against everyone else. John and this list are what we need to convince them that there are many against Henry, many who are still loyal to their order."

Sarah's face was very concerned but accepting. "Ernest will be so worried when he finds out."

"Remember, Sarah, we're doing to this to protect you and Ernest," Delvarus said.

"I'm glad you were able to convince her," I remarked as we rode away, "but how do you know so much about her?"

"I have my ways," Delvarus said.

"I don't suppose you could elaborate on what those ways are?" I asked. He just answered with a smile and said nothing more for quite some time.

We followed a path that wound us through the wooded wilderness that lay past the outlying areas of Caprecia and soon came upon the small hills that bordered the colony on the west. I had never been beyond them, but Delvarus seemed familiar with the terrain. I found it strange that while my own brother was leading me on this trip, there was very little spoken between us. And it seemed especially odd when considering that I was in the dark on so many matters left unexplained. Eventually, I could stand the silence no longer. "I remember you telling me that today would be the day I got my answers," I said.

"Right," he returned, "one step at a time."

"What is that supposed to mean? Why can't you just start at the beginning and tell me everything you know?"

"What beginning?" he asked.

I rode up alongside him and looked at him intently. "Is that supposed to be a trick question or something? The only beginning there is, of course."

"Well, I'm afraid it's not that simple, really."

"Why wouldn't it be that simple?" I asked.

"Why don't you start by asking a question?" He said.

"Must it always start with a question?" I replied in a somewhat-frustrated tone. Besides, I did just ask a question.

"What if I were to give you the answer to a question that you've never considered before? Would you be ready for it? Would it make sense, or would it only confuse you more?" Delvarus questioned.

I wasn't sure how to answer. "I don't know."

"You see, John, the situation your mind is in right now is a tricky one. Matters regarding your past must be addressed with care, one step at a time, just like I said."

I reached in my chest pocket and pulled out the necklace. "Maybe you could start by telling me what happened to my wife," I spoke.

Delvarus pulled on the reins and brought his horse to a sudden stop. He turned in the saddle and looked back at me with a long stare. "Tell me what you mean," he said.

"There is a woman I left behind. I've seen her in my dream."

"You're dreaming already?" he questioned in a surprised

tone.

"What do you mean, already?"

"Never mind for now," he said. "Anyway, Janaea is her name, but she's not your wife."

"What do you mean? I happen to know that I proposed to her."

"It's best that you try to forget and move on, little brother."

"Move on? How can I move on? She's the one thing I have to hold to. She accepted. We got married," I insisted.

Delvarus remained speechless for a time, and the look on his face seemed sympathetic. "You two were going to get married, but then you left."

"I left? Why would I do such a thing? I loved her."

"Yes, but you also trusted our father," Delvarus replied.

"Trusted him about what?" I asked in frustration.

"About coming here."

I couldn't believe it. Why would I leave the woman I cared for so much to come to a strange place like this? "Then I must go back home to her now," I said.

"Like I said," Delvarus replied. "It's best if you move on, try to forget her."

"No, I can't. I have to get back to her. You have to show me how to get home," I pled. "After we take this list to the hill-dwellers show me the way back."

"You have to move on, John."

"Why should I?" I exclaimed. "Why should I forget the woman I love?" By now, my emotions were getting the better of me, and I could feel tears begin to well in my eyes.

"Because," he answered, "she's not waiting at home for you."

Up until now, I had been willing to postpone the somber conclusion I had arrived at that morning, but Delvarus's words caused the deep pain to course through me again. "What do you mean she's not waiting for me?" I asked. "Is she really dead?"

Delvarus remained silent, but he looked at me with sympathy written on his face. "She's gone, John."

"Then she's dead." I concluded.

"Not dead," he continued, "just gone. She's moved on, John, and you need to as well."

It was then I realized what he had been trying to tell me. I had been gone now for over a year, at least. She had moved on. She was now married to another man, and a lucky man he was. Whatever foolishness had caused me to leave her, I now regretted it. In my state of failing memory, wisdom had finally visited me. And yet, I wished I had allowed it to do so when we were still together. Now, the reality of her fate pained me more than my imagination of her death had.

I had nothing more to say about the matter now, and I wondered what more I had to hope for. My life felt empty again. Janaea was completely lost to me, and any further thoughts of her would only seem a haunting presence of all that I had left behind. As much as it hurt, I realized that Delvarus was right; I had to learn to move on.

As we wound our way through a canyon floor that a small river had carved out of the landscape, the spectacular beauty of the region began to engulf us on every side. Aside from the sound of the water, the place was quiet and very serene. The trees swayed to the breeze that rushed through the canyon walls. The air was cool and fresh, and yet, it all seemed sad and void of purpose to me now.

A good deal of time passed before the growth began to thin and open to the setting rays of the sun. As we came to the end of the canyon, we continued away from the path toward the river where we stopped to fill with water and take a brief rest.

"I know what's on your mind, Brother." Delvarus said as he returned to his horse. "Trust me when I say that Janaea would want you to move on."

I leaned on my saddle for a brief moment before remounting and thought about what he'd just said. "I realize that now," I replied, "but has she really so soon forgotten me?"

"To keep the answer simple, yes, she has." Delvarus swung into the saddle and looked down at me. "I know it's not easy, but you would be much better off if you learned to do the same."

I followed after him and gave what he said a considerable amount of meditation, despite how painful it was to do so. Upon leaving the foothills, we came upon a large plateau-like plain that preceded the mountains in which the hill-dwellers lived. We made camp as nightfall approached, and before long, I felt the exhaustion of the day's toils beckoning me to sleep amid the warmth of the fire and the comfort of a cloudless sky. Soon afterward, I found myself dreaming of Janaea by the side of a slowly flickering flame.

Chapter 13

"I love you," she said, staring deep into my eyes as if she were looking to the center of my soul. I wrapped my arms around the small of her back and pulled her close.

"I love you too," I replied. We stood in each other's arms for a moment that consumed my attention with every feature of her gorgeous complexion. Her eyes pierced the fondest regions of my heart, and her porcelain skin radiated a golden glow in the morning sun. Never had I seen anything more beautiful in my life.

"Before we go, I have something I want to show you," she said as she turned toward a door in the distance.

"What is it?"

"It's a surprise."

"Well, I suppose we have time for a surprise," I jested.

"Come on in then," she beckoned, walking toward the door with a slight skip in her step while her blue dress swayed in the light morning breeze.

Once we were inside, she took me by the hand and walked us through her foyer, down the hall, and into the dining area where we stopped at a table on which sat a small white box wrapped with a blue ribbon. She took two steps from me and, picking up the box from the table, spun back to face me with a smile of anticipation.

"I have a little something for you," she said, reaching out and handing it over. I looked back at her with uncertainty. "Go ahead, open it."

I held it in one hand and unwrapped the small ribbon from its casing, wondering the whole time what it might be. As I slowly lifted the lid from atop the box, my eyes caught hold of quite the surprise. Nestled amid a neatly-placed blue-silk handkerchief was a beautiful white-gold necklace.

"I don't understand," I said slowly.

"I can't help but feel the time is getting closer, very close," she said. "I wanted you to have something to take with you, something that might help you remember me." She folded her arms across her chest and raised her hand to hold back a tear.

I stepped toward her. "I will always keep it with me," I whispered in her ear.

The next thing I knew, I was hearing my brother's voice. "Wake up, John. We'll need to be on our way soon."

I opened my eyes to the fading embers of a dying fire with the smell of fish and the sight of fruit to accompany it. "When did you get all of this?" I asked as I slowly sat up into the chill of the morning air.

"This morning, while you were still dreaming," he said, taking the fish from the skewer he had fashioned over the fire. He placed it on a plate he took from his saddle bag, along with a cluster of wild grapes, and handed it over to me. "You dreamt of her again, didn't you?"

I really didn't feel like answering the question, especially if it was going to turn into another conversation on how I should forget about Janaea. "I'm afraid so," I finally consented.

"I'm sorry, John. I know it's a difficult thing to bear," Delvarus replied. After this he said nothing more.

I was somewhat surprised to find that he didn't have some admonition to add, but rather, he sat down quietly and poured a cup of water over the smoldering flames. The smoke billowed around us and then subsided to leave nothing between us but silence. Suddenly, I felt unsettled about the matter just as I had yesterday, and despite my initial mood, I was intent on talking about it until I reached some resolution.

"What would've compelled me to leave her?" I asked.

Delvarus poked at the fire with a stick to ensure that the flames were entirely out. "You made a promise," he answered.

"Who did I make a promise with?"

"Our father," he said. "You promised to come here and do what he asked you to."

I remembered then how he told me earlier that I was here because I trusted my father, but I still didn't know why, nor did I know what he was talking about regarding my fulfillment of our father's wishes. "And what did he ask me to do?"

"He asked you to come here to learn."

"To learn? Learn what?" I begged to know.

"Everything you already have and more."

I followed with a pause. "None of this answers my biggest question," I finally said. Delvarus looked at me with an expression that prompted me to go on. "Why don't I remember any of it?" I asked.

"That certainly is the mystery, isn't it?" he answered. "But it also happens to be another reason we're heading for those hills," he continued, motioning to his right. "The answer lies within the East Mountains. By the time you return to Thomas and Martha's, your life in the colony will never be the same."

I was eager to leave after our conversation and wasted no time or effort in anything but moving toward the peaks in the distance. By the time we had traversed the wind-swept plateau, it was midday, and the sun cast a radiant glow on the emerald foothills of the East Mountains. The air was cooler at their base, but the wind seemed to subside as we drew nearer.

Eventually, we came to stop at the mouth of another canyon that separated the two largest summits within view.

I stared upward at the majestic nature that surrounded me. The massive walls of rock that towered over us were an amazing sight up close. The growth that populated the mountain side reminded me of the woods that surrounded the colony, but the trees here seemed even taller and wider. "These aren't what I would call hills," I said.

"What do you mean?" Delvarus asked.

"I learned to refer to them as the hill-dwellers, but we left the hills behind us a long time ago. These are mountains."

"Yes, well, it's a matter of semantics I suppose. Truth is, they go by a much different name among themselves."

"What's their real name?" I asked.

"They call themselves the Justiton. Although, this distinction was lost to the colonists a long time ago, along with the peace that once existed between them."

"What happened?"

"Insurrection," he said. "The colonists used to live within these hills alongside the Justiton, but when the colonists turned against one another and began to kill, the Justiton drove them out. The Justiton were intent on destroying all those who were responsible for starting the war, but there were a few who escaped."

"When did this all happen?" I asked.

"It was a long time ago, but I'm afraid the effects still remain. Ever since, the Justiton have allowed no colonist within the East Mountains. They patrol the region frequently in order to keep any from returning."

"If that's the case, how am I going to get in?"

"Because, you're with me."

We weren't far into the valley before I could see an outline that ran along the canyon floor and up both peaks on either side. It was a light-colored wall that appeared to look something like the buildings I had seen on the island. "What's on the other side?" I asked as we came upon it.

"A city, and a grand one at that," Delvarus returned. As we came to the end of the path on which we traveled, we could see two guards dressed in the same type of apparel as the people on the island, standing just outside the massive wall. They stood tall and still with faces absent of emotion, remaining speechless until we came within several paces of them.

"Delvarus, we've been expecting you," one of the guards said. His face, though it remained as straight as it was before, seemed glad. "The governor is waiting for you in the place of records. He has a car prepared to take you there."

"Thank you," my brother replied. "John, you can leave Amos here. We won't be needing him any longer. These men will watch after him until you return." As we dismounted our horses, a section of the wall began to open slowly, like the doors in the strange buildings I had occupied on the island. Only, rather than opening inward, it swung upward in one solid mass.

On the other side, the path transformed into a solid slab of stone, much like what I had seen before when walking amid the buildings of the island. However, this path was considerably bigger, as if someone had taken a giant rock and rolled it flat like a ball of dough. It protracted in the distance farther than my eyes could see, disappearing into the horizon, and I began to become very interested to know where it would take us.

A few steps from where we entered was a four-wheeled contraption similar to the one I had ridden in before, but this one looked even more spectacular. It sat low to the ground and took on a sleek appearance, like the fletching of an arrow, as if it would slice through the air in the same fashion. Its exterior was black but cast a glistening glow off its surface, almost as if it was covered in a perpetual layer of water.

CHAPTER 13 | 111

"I trust you've been in something like this before," Delvarus said as we approached it.

"Yes, but this one's a little different."

"All the same, there's no need for an introduction."

As I sat in the soft interior, I noticed one particular difference. Though this vehicle had a wheel like the others, there was no crimson-clad individual behind it to turn it about as we moved. Then, suddenly, Delvarus took a seat in the unoccupied space. He turned around and looked at me as if to assess my reaction.

"What exactly are you doing?" I asked.

"Taking you to deliver the list, just as I said."

"You know how to manage one of these?" I inquired.

"Naturally." Soon after he said this, there followed a familiar humming noise. In a moment's time, we were flying down the road at a speed I didn't think was possible. I looked out the windows and watched as the landscape whizzed by in a blur. We soon crested a hill that dropped us down the other side into a large valley glowing in the sunlight, its rays cascading off structures of gray stone and glass.

The extent of the city's expanse seemed to reach beyond the wall of mountains that stood as a far-distant border for the valley's opposite side, and the roads that wound from one end to the next seemed to be alive with the passage of vehicles. I had never seen anything like it, and I sat in astonishment for a time before I was able to ask the question on my mind. "What is this place? And why is it that such things don't exist within the colony?"

"This is Litovia." Delvarus replied. "This is the city of the Justiton, and the Justiton don't share their secrets."

We soon found ourselves in the center of the city where the most magnificent buildings surrounded us on every side. Yet, despite the appearance and wonder of it all, I felt that greater life and love could be found in a simple place like the home of Thomas and Martha. When we came to a stop, it was in front of a structure that appeared to be the very heart of the entire city. Delvarus turned to look at me again and offered a reassuring nod.

"Are you ready?" he asked.

"As ready as anyone who doesn't know what to expect," I said.

"That's the spirit," he replied with a grin.

I followed Delvarus up the large marble steps outside the most prodigious edifice I had ever seen and watched as everyone we passed stopped to look at him. It was as if he was a man of great reputation among the people of Litovia.

"Why do they look at you like that?" I asked.

"Who?"

"All these people around us, who else?"

"It's because they know who I am."

"What do you mean?" I questioned.

"You'll find out later," he replied.

"Of course," I said. "So, why am I here then?"

"You're about to find out."

As we came to the door, we were ushered into a large foyer of sorts where a man that looked like all the others was waiting for us. "Delvarus, I heard you were returning, but who is this?" he asked. He managed to look at me afterward for the briefest moment before turning his attention to Delvarus again.

"I'm here to mediate, Josesh," he remarked, "on behalf of this man and many others."

"I don't follow you," Josesh returned.

"Perhaps we should sit down," Delvarus answered.

Shortly, we were shown to a room with a big table and chairs, where the purpose of a large meeting might be easily accommodated. I sat on the right side of my brother across from Josesh, another man, and a woman who had joined him. The door was closed and Josesh leaned forward in his chair.

"So, what's this all about?" he asked in a subdued tone.

"A certain man's lust for power, I'm afraid," Delvarus said.

"Henry?"

"Yes, and a significant army too."

"I might have guessed. He doesn't realize what he is doing, does he?" Josesh questioned. Delvarus shook his head in response. "I have no reason to fear anything for my people, but I don't take joy in killing colonists," he continued.

"I know," Delvarus said. "We will do what we can to convince him otherwise, but should he fail to listen, you must know that he plans to march against your city."

"The fools will be slaughtered like animals," Josesh said.

"Certainly, but you mustn't retaliate against the rest," Delvarus replied.

"But how can I be assured they won't try the same?"

Delvarus took the petition from my hand and slid it across the table to Josesh. "Because of this."

Chapter 14

"I know you make it a point to concern yourselves with every matter of business in the colony, so I trust you recognize these names," Delvarus added.

Josesh looked over the list for a time before answering. "I do, most of them at least. The rest can be looked up in our directories."

"All of these and their families are set against Henry?" the woman asked.

"That's right, Sovia" Delvarus replied, "every last one of them."

"Do they intend to wage war against Henry for his tyranny?" Josesh inquired.

"That is the very thing I'm trying to avoid," Delvarus answered. "You know these people are precious to me."

"Yes of course."

"Master Delvarus, do you intend for us to fight the battle for them?" the other man offered.

"I intend for your people to support my efforts, Karesh." Karesh returned a simple nod and nothing more, but it didn't seem as though he quite understood Delvarus's answer. I found it odd that my brother was addressed as a master among such domineering people, but I felt comfort over the idea that he was the one in charge.

"Very well, then. We will wait for your orders," Josesh concluded.

"Just remember," Delvarus added, "if you hear nothing from me before Henry makes his first move, deal only with his followers and him."

"As you wish," Josesh returned as he began to rise from his chair. "Thank you for coming."

"Actually, there's another matter of business that needs to be addressed," Delvarus continued.

"Go on," Josesh replied.

"It involves my brother, John," he said as he placed his hand on my shoulder. "I want you to tell him your story, the one involving us."

"You mean he's the one you've been telling us about?" Josesh asked.

"The very same."

Karesh, Sovia, and Josesh all looked at me with a different consideration now. "Welcome to Litovia," Sovia said. "Any friend of Delvarus is a friend of ours." With that, all three stood up and looked to Delvarus.

"How much does he know?" Josesh asked.

"Some, but not very much. I must be on my way, but show him to the chart room. It's the best setting you have to tell him what he needs to know."

"Certainly," Josesh returned.

Delvarus stood up and bid me do the same. Then he embraced me in a brotherly hug, afterward stepping back to look me in the eyes. "I'm proud of you, Brother. You've come so far in a short amount of time, and everything is about to make a lot more sense. They will take care of you here, and you'll soon be back to Thomas and Martha's where the real work will begin."

"The real work?"

"I'll see you seven days from now," he told me as he walked to the door. "And I will tell you more then."

"Where am I supposed to find you this time?" I asked.

"Don't worry about that," he replied. "I'll find you." The door shut behind him with a quiet latching sound, and I stood in the midst of complete strangers again for the first time since the island.

"You must feel privileged to have Delvarus as a brother," Sovia said.

I wasn't sure whether or not she was alluding to something specific that I might not know about him, but I was beginning to genuinely respect my brother. "I do, yes."

"There is no other person more like your father than Delvarus," Josesh added.

"My father?" I asked.

"That's right. He's his spitting image, and a duplicate in character, I might add."

"That's why everyone respects him so much," Karesh added. He looked at me with an inquisitive stare. "Delvarus tells us that you have some favorable similarities to your father as well."

I stood in silence, not sure how I should answer. "I don't remember anything about my father," I finally said.

"Well then, why don't we tell you what we know?" Josesh returned.

I followed the three of them down the main hall of the massive building. Our boots thudded on the marble floor like the percussion of drums in an otherwise silent parade. The walls were a bare white that reflected beams from overhanging lights and the rays of sun that coursed through the tall paned windows above us.

CHAPTER 14

We stopped in front of a large singular door that looked as though it was made of solid metal. The walls on either side of it had a noticeable curvature to them, as if the room they created took the form of a sphere. As the door was opened, nothing but blackness stood to greet us. I stepped inside along with the others, and the door was shut tightly behind me.

Suddenly, a faint blue light emanated from the base of the walls and outlined the floor on which we stood. In the center of the circular room was an enormous round table of glass that glowed with the same blue light as the walls and floor. Above it all was a dome-shaped ceiling that was populated with constellations and illustrations of larger objects that looked like moons and planets.

"What is this place?" I asked.

"This is the chart room," Josesh replied. "Come here, let me show you something." Soon, all four of us surrounded the transparent table and looked upon a sea of blue light. A moment later, Josesh pushed a bottom-like lever on the edge of its surface. The blue light immediately disappeared and was replaced with blackness. As I lingered in observation, however, small lights of white and then spheres of varying colors began to emerge from within the glass. Eventually, a scene very similar to the picture above me on the ceiling appeared vividly before me.

"It's quite amazing," I said, "but what is it?"

"This is our home," Sovia answered, pointing to a sapphire orb toward the center of the image, "the same world on which you are now standing."

"Everything else around it is what you see when you look into the night's sky," Karesh added.

I looked closer at the glowing lights on the table. "The world you say?"

"Yes, have you ever considered what it might look like from above?" Josesh asked.

"Not really," I replied, "but it all seems sensible—this picture I see."

"Well, it happens to be entirely accurate," Josesh continued. "You see, John, this is no mere painting or drawing of any sort like you may have seen in the colony. This is no one's imagination of what it might look like. This is an actual picture of what it is, the same thing your eye would see if you were to look down on it yourself."

"What do you mean?" I asked. "How's that even possible?"

"It's possible because we have created something of an artificial human eye, and we sent that eye into the space above us to see our surroundings."

"How did you make such a thing?" I asked.

"That's not really important. We've done even greater things with the sciences we've discovered. Some of the lesser inventions of ours you've already seen, the motor carriage that brought you here, the underwater ship from the island, and now this. But you were sent here to learn the greatest of our discoveries."

As he said this, I heard a humming noise coming from behind me. Soon after, a chair appeared by the side of each of us on a track that came to an end at the table. I was motioned to take a seat. I did so and waited for the conversation to commence.

"Our people have forever been interested in the world that surrounds them," Josesh continued. "For eons, we have searched to comprehend our existence in the physical environments we inhabit. We have settled and civilized every region of our world, we have visited the moon that orbits around us, and we have probed far into the stars and planets beyond our own. From it all, we have discovered that we are a lonely isolated island in a vast and seemingly-lifeless space," he concluded.

"However, by the time of my generation, a new science had long been underway. One century ago, our people turned to an interest in the matters of the unseen."

"The unseen? I'm afraid I don't follow you," I said.

"Of course you don't," he replied. "That's why I'm going to show it to you." Josesh reached for another lever on the edge of the table, and when he flipped it, the image we had been viewing disappeared and a new one replaced it. In the center of the table appeared a large picture of three concentric circles, all of equal size, that shared, not only a center, but also an axis. "What I'm about to explain is difficult to envision, but perhaps this illustration can help."

"I hope so," I said without any idea where he was going next.

"The science behind it all is complicated, so I will spare you the details," Josesh continued. "It should be sufficient to say, at least, that our people discovered evidence of life beyond our own universe. This illustration here," he said while pointing at the image in the table, "is a symbol of what they found. The circles represent three separate spheres existing within the same space. If there are more than these, we aren't certain of it, but there are at least three," he said.

"You mean three worlds?" I asked, feeling as though I understood what he was getting at.

"Not just worlds, John, but entire cosmoses," Sovia said.

"That's right," Karesh added. "All around us exists other galaxies, stars, and planets apart from our own."

"Around us? How can they be around us and we not see them?" I asked.

"Not only can we not see them, but we can't interact with them either," Josesh said. "This is because they're composed of substance different than that which exists here, and in the case of your home, the substance is more refined, and the physical laws that govern it are higher than our own." As he said this, he touched one of the circles whose outline was brighter than the rest.

I moved my hand through the space in front of me, imagining that it was passing through additional invisible space. "That's awfully interesting, but how can you prove it?" I dared to ask.

"You know, it's very fitting that you should ask that question. Let me tell you how it was proved." Josesh leaned on the table and folded his arms in front of him. "When the idea was proposed, it was pretty revolutionary, even for us. We live in a three dimensional world, John, and it's difficult to conceive of anything beyond that. But, there were many devoted to the idea, and they went to work to try and procure evidence from the other side. It took years of research, but they were finally able to communicate across the void."

"What do you mean, 'void'?"

"It's the term we use to refer to the space between our universe and another," Karesh offered.

"But what space is there between objects that exist in the same space?"

"That's a good question," Josesh replied. "We've learned that it is really no space at all but, rather, a question of frequency."

"Frequency?" I asked. "What does that mean?"

"Let me try to explain it like this." He took a small black box from inside his chest pocket. "This is something called a radio. I'm sure you have devices far better than this where you come from, but you won't remember anything you may have known about them. Even still, if you knew it before, you will probably grasp it again." He set the radio on the table and beckoned across from him. "Karesh, take yours out." He did so and placed it on the table as well.

"These devices communicate by means of frequency through something called an electro-magnetic current. It's a wavelength of energy that you can't see, kind of like the waves that travel through the air when you clap your hands," Josesh continued. "There are an innumerable amount of frequencies that these little devices can send, but they can only pick up, or discern, one at a time.

"As it is, radio waves are traveling all through the air around Litovia, but each is at a different frequency, so that one receiver can communicate with another without interference from a third, or fourth, or fifth, and so on. Now watch. Karesh, switch yours to the external speaker." After he said this, he turned his head and spoke into the collar of his shirt. "Testing, testing."

I heard the sound of his words come from across the table, but I also heard it from within the small box in front of Karesh. "That's interesting," I said.

"Well, existence in the physical world operates on a similar principle. When considering the composition of matter, down to its most basic building blocks, we're merely talking about small packs of pulsing energy moving at different frequencies, if you will. A different frequency can mean either a different type of building block for our world, or else an entirely different kind of element, something unseen to us here."

"So you mean the matter, as you call it, that makes up these other worlds exists at a different frequency, and that's why we can't see them or interact with them?" I asked.

"Exactly," Josesh answered. "I was hoping your mind would pick back up on it. You must have learned it all before."

"I don't know that I would say I quite get it yet," I returned.

"Perhaps you will later," Josesh replied. "Just remember this," he continued while pointing to the image in the table. "All realms of existence share a connection with the same origin, and it's from here that life is created."

"That's right," Sovia added, "and our people were very intrigued about the idea of life existing in other realms. Eventually, they were able to send messages by means of light."

"Yes, but it was a million-in-one shot or more that they would ever receive any communication back," Josesh said. "Not only would there have to be someone on the other side of the origin, but they would also have to be able to see our signals, so to speak. All metaphors aside, they would have to possess the same mechanism we had built in order to receive our attempt at communication. One might as well throw a bottled message into a raging ocean," he said.

"That's why our people were so surprised when they received an immediate reply," Sovia added.

"Someone was there?" I asked with great interest.

"Yes," she answered.

"Who was it?" I begged.

All three of them looked at each other and then at me. "It was your father," Josesh replied.

Chapter 15

"My father?" I asked. "But what does that mean—?"
"What does that mean about you?" Josesh interrupted. "Well, to understand your story, you must first understand his, so let me tell it to you." Josesh cleared the image in the table with the flip of a switch and then rested his elbows and hands on its edge. "One thing that greatly astonished our people about the response they received from your father was that it came back so quickly. You see, the nature of their communication was complicated."

"How so?" I asked.

"They sent our language across the void," Sovia answered. "But, of course, for anyone to reply, they would have to learn it first."

"So the messages included images and symbols to conceptualize the meanings of our words," Karesh added.

"That's right," Josesh continued. "Our people's hope was that anyone who could have received the message would also be able to learn it and, thus, communicate with us. However, your father not only responded more quickly than they could have expected, but what he said in his response greatly surprised them."

"What did he say?" I questioned.

Josesh flipped on the imaging beneath the glass again, and there appeared words in bold lettering. "This was the original response they received from him."

"I'm glad to finally hear from you. Now on to greater things,"

"I don't understand. I thought they hadn't spoken with him before."

"They hadn't," Josesh replied, "and that's what surprised them. They soon learned that your father had known about their existence long before they had even conceived of his."

"Then why did he not attempt to communicate with them first?" I asked.

"Maybe he did, but they wouldn't have been able to pick any of it up until they built a transmitter capable of receiving it," Josesh answered. "It didn't take long for the Justiton to learn that your father was far more intelligent than any one of us, or even a combination of our greatest minds. As they continued in communications with him, they realized that our greatest achievements and discoveries in science were mere fundamentals to him. He understood matters beyond our comprehension."

"Like what?"

"Like how to send life across the void," Sovia chimed in.

"Life, you mean—?"

"Yes, life like you," she answered. "Your father figured out how to change the frequency of matter in one realm in order for it to exist in a new one."

"That's right. You are a stranger to our world, John," Josesh said. "You come from an entirely different one, from a different universe altogether; one far better than where you are now, I might add."

"You mean, that's how I ended up here when I was beached on the shores like a shipwreck?"

"Well, there's more to it than that," Karesh added.

"Yes, much more." Josesh continued. "You see, John, like I've said, the idea of discovery has always intrigued my people. They have always wanted to know more. But what they learned from your father, they could only have dreamed of."

"So that's why I'm here?" I asked. "And so many others? We're some experiment?"

"Not a chance," Josesh answered. "Before you came here, your father had to."

"My father's been here?"

"He has, a long time ago. He and our people had planned to unite our two worlds, but before it could be done, there had to be a means to send life from our realm to his," Josesh said. "He had the ability to come here, but there was no way for us to get there. He tried to explain his methods, in hopes that we would catch on, but the science was beyond us. We were unable to comprehend it. So, he proposed a plan that our people considered uncertain."

"What was it?" I inquired.

"It was then he decided to be the first to come here and show us how to build our way to his world, but there was an element of risk to it."

"Go on."

Josesh turned a switch on the table again, and there appeared the same three circles he had spoken of earlier. "Look here," he said. "The connection between these two circles and the third is what imposed the risk. The third is that origin I told you of. Your father taught our people that the mind exists within its own realm, in the realm of origin, the realm that influences all others. Its existence is immortal, and it is its connection with the physical world that enables the lives we live. However, when traveling from one dimension of existence to another, the mind's disconnection with the world from whence one comes causes an individual to, well, forget."

"You mean like me?" I asked.

"Yes, and this was the phenomenon that your father expected to take place; this was what he meant by the risk," Josesh continued.

"But he came anyway?" I questioned.

"Yes, and there's more. Without the technology needed to receive him, there was uncertainty as to where he would end up, and he had suspicion that his body would be greatly affected."

"How so?"

"Temporarily disabled," Karesh answered.

"Another effect of moving something so complicated from one dimension to another," Sovia said. "Of course, we only know this because of your father."

"Before he left," Josesh added, "he made our people aware of these risks and told them what they must teach him in order to assist the return of what he once knew. You see, he had a great deal of confidence in the fact that, eventually, his memory and strength would return. Our people, of course, felt inadequate in teaching someone who knew more than us, but we promised to find him and do our best."

"Find him?"

"Yes, like I just said, he wasn't certain where exactly his final destination would be. Though he could expect, through his calculations, to arrive near us, there wasn't any way for him to be sure he would arrive in our city," Josesh returned, "not without the technology on our side."

"But they found him," I remarked with assumption.

"They did."

"Well, where was he?" I asked.

Josesh rose from his seat for the first time and paced about for an awkward moment before he stood behind his chair and looked at me. "We have always been an exacting people, John. We govern our own and anyone who lives within our reach by a strict order of conduct and self-governance. Any who are found to live beneath our expectations are cast out from among us and expected to answer to our rule from a distance, without the same privileges they may have once enjoyed. There have been times in our history when our own people have broken our law, and we've had to send them away because of it. Your father was found on the shores and taken in by a family we had driven out of our city.

"By the time we found him, he had already regained his strength and a good portion of his memory. He had taught the family, and all the other outcasts that would listen to him, many of the same things he had taught us, and he had gained many loyal followers and friends. My people learned from your father that he was just as exacting as we were, but he differed in the fact that he was willing to sympathize and overlook people's mistakes, even if it was at his own expense. He began to mediate for the outcasts and insisted that they be allowed to regain their place in our city.

"Naturally, my people were compelled to listen to him, and he and those who followed him came to our city for his sake. Afterwards, your father continued to have dreams, visions of his past that he shared with our people. They soon learned of things they hadn't in their first communications with him, and what they were taught incited their interest in the unity of our worlds all the more."

"Things like what?"

"They learned how much better a place your home is, and your father promised his friends that they could go back with him when he returned."

"So he found a way back?"

"Yes, he did," Karesh injected.

Josesh took his seat again and continued. "He was eventually able to regain all that he knew about the methods for sending life from one world to another, and along the way, he discovered how to do it without the relapse."

"You mean forgetting?"

"Precisely," Josesh returned. "However, being in our world had shown him that there were many who could not be trusted with such a power, and so, he hid it and told only those who he knew would never divulge its existence. Its secret has been kept with our people for a long time now, and we are under strict instructions to keep it safe."

"Where is it exactly, this secret?" I asked.

"I will tell you only because I have been told I can," Josesh said. "The secret, or the science, to send life to the world you came from is known only to your father for now, but he needed a special place for it to operate, and that place is on a certain island that you must tell no one about until instructed otherwise."

"Then why am I here?" I asked. "If he found a way back and means to keep one's memory, why am I here without any recollection of my life before? Have I been punished?"

"No, quite the contrary really," Josesh replied. "Before he came, your father was a highly respected man, the very best of anyone among his people. Because of his character, he was revered and respected, and there were many who considered him their ruler. When he returned home, he expanded this sovereignty by forming a royal council with those friends he took with him. Since those days, both he and your mother, along with those in his parliament, have sent their children here to experience the same thing that your father had. You and all the others had to come under the same circumstance that he came. The only difference is that our people from the island brought you to the shores."

"I don't understand. Why would he send me here like this? Didn't he care about me?"

"Care about you? I suppose he did," Josesh answered.

"Then why would he send me to such a place, and without even my memory to comfort me?"

"Well, I'm afraid I don't have the answer to that question, but your father told us that it was the very reason he sent you here, to figure it out for yourself," Josesh replied.

Chapter 16

I stayed in the city of the Justiton that night in accommodations even more comfortable than the glass room on the island. I thought a great deal about the strange building from Thomas's book and reasoned that it must be the place in which the science of all Josesh had told me operated. I tried to imagine what it looked like from inside and pictured in my mind what sort of action must befall it to send a person like me back home.

My mind was turned to thinking of my father as well, trying to envision what he looked like. I attempted to understand why he sent me here and what it was I was supposed to learn from it all. As I worked it over in my mind, I only became more frustrated with the lack of answers, and so, my thoughts turned, as if automatically, to the one matter that had calmed me in the past. But even my memory of Janaea was lacking in consolation after what Delvarus had told me.

I remember watering my pillow with tears that night as I tried to think on something that would allow me some peace. I thought of Thomas and Martha, but then I recalled the discontent in their faces when I left. Next, my thoughts were directed to Simon, but now he thought that I was up to no good. Finally, my mind rested on the little ones, most especially Susan and Timmy.

Susan had been a great strength for me from the beginning, and Timmy and I had grown all the closer in the past few months. I thought about the many moments the three of us had spent together playing games and catching toads in the pond. And when I pictured their smiles and laughter, I was finally able to rest.

The following morning started with a knocking on my door, followed by its slow opening. Josesh walked in, then Sovia, and then Karesh. "I hope you slept well, John, but now it's time to be going," Josesh remarked. "I'm learning that there are certain matters you are supposed to accomplish. I only hope you're up to it."

"Up to what?"

"You'll see," he replied.

As I walked out of my room, the three of them stood waiting for me. There were no words spoken, but they exchanged a glance, and Josesh nodded before turning to walk away. I followed, as expected, and made no attempt to speak to any of them at first. The Justiton were certainly a peculiar people, intent on showing next to no emotion or enthusiasm over anything. Delvarus was right when he said they were cold and calculating.

As we walked into the crisp morning air, the sun reminded me of the home I was missing. I began to long to be in the fields again, working the ground and toiling alongside Thomas and Martha. The city was an intriguing place, constantly alive with the movement of the contraptions they called cars or vehicles, but as I stood watching them pass in front of me, I wondered why it was that the colonists were left to employ far more simple methods of transportation.

"Why is it that such things as I see here aren't used in the colony?" I asked. "Like these cars for example."

Josesh stopped walking and turned to me as if he was surprised to hear me talk. "The colonists are not welcome to know of our secrets. They are a warring people, intent on destroying one another and themselves. If they were given our technology, they would only use it toward further destruction."

"You realize that is an unfair estimation," I said. "I know of many colonists who hate strife as much as anyone. The family that took me in, they are the kindest people I have ever met. Surely you don't think the same of them?"

"I know about Thomas and Martha, and they have done nothing to upset us, but that's not to say they wouldn't if we gave them the chance."

"You're dead wrong, Josesh," I answered with a small degree of force. "You don't know what it means to trust anyone do you?"

"Don't forget your place, John," he replied. "You are here merely because I trust your brother. You have yet to prove that trust to me." He turned from me with a look of stern reproach on his face and began walking toward a flight of stairs that wound its way to the roof of the building we just walked out of.

"Be patient with my father," Karesh whispered. "He's very fixed in the ways of our people. There hasn't been reason to trust the colony as a whole for a long time now."

I hadn't ventured to think that Karesh was the son of Josesh, but the idea seemed sensible. Although, there never seemed to be any sort of paternal bond from the side of Josesh in any observation I had. "He's your father?" I whispered back.

"Yes, and Sovia's my mother," he replied.

Sovia, who followed behind Josesh, looked back at us as if she had heard. "Come along, don't fall behind," she insisted.

When we reached the end of the stairway, a beautiful roof-top vista unfolded before us. Trees and flowers populated the stone-laden landscape, and a fountain sprung out of the center of it all. But what caught my attention even more was the strange contraption that stood on a large platform above the rest of the structure.

It was oval shaped with a long tail of sorts and a spindle-type blade at its end. Above its glass-covered center was another larger pair of blades that sat horizontally overhead. What this thing was meant to do was beyond me, but I was left to quickly assume that it was another vehicle of sorts, since we were walking toward it.

Sure enough, as we drew nearer, I saw six seats inside of it, and I was now certain that we would be taking this somewhere. "What exactly is this?" I inquired.

"Have you ever dreamed of flying with the birds?" Karesh asked. "Now you can."

"This thing is going to fly?" I questioned.

Karesh merely nodded in response and opened the door for me to get in. The interior was much like that in the cars, but it appeared to have more instrumentation on the panels that sat in front of the forward-most seats. Josesh and Sovia sat down and latched the doors behind them. Afterwards, Josesh turned a lever, and the blades that perched over us began to spin rapidly.

Before I had much time to react to the humming and pulsing sound that came from above me, we were already rising from the platform beneath us. I looked below me in astonishment and marveled at the distance that was growing between us and the ground. Josesh steered the craft away from the building, and we began moving forward, west of the city.

We soon passed the walls that Delvarus and I had entered a day ago, and I began to recognize the path that we had taken through the wilderness as it now ran beneath us. I sat in a vantage point I had never seen before, and I felt almost as if I could reach out and hold the world in my hand. The trees seemed so small, and the mountains looked like our footstool.

As we flew farther west, we came upon the beginnings of

what appeared to be ruins of a once-small city. Scattered and tumbled walls lay strewn beyond the same path, hidden within the forests that surrounded it. Josesh turned toward an open field and began descending slowly. The valley floor grew closer, and the trees appeared larger with every passing moment, until we rested on the grass and dirt beneath us.

Without a word, Josesh and Sovia, along with Karesh, exited the strange flying vehicle and motioned for me to follow. We soon found a road that took us out of the opening in the trees and back into the thicker growth that covered most of the mountains around us. This road, which once breached its line through the earth like a scar, was now laden with mud and rotted ash. Weeds uprooted the cobbled walkway, and grass sprouted between its cracks and crevasses, covering everything in a masking green. It seemed as if nature was torn between hiding the place from existence, or else consuming it altogether.

Farther in our course, we reached crumbled walls of rock and eroding pillars of wood and masonry. It was still and silent, as if the last words of the city's history had been uttered long ago but never heard. We walked through what appeared to have once been a doorway to some ornate building and into a large and dilapidated room. Beneath our feet sat a layer of charred blackness, as if a burning fire had permanently scorched the stone. Josesh walked carefully and quietly over the floor, and I followed after him. He continued toward the end of the room rather slowly, as if working something over in his mind, until he came to stop at the far corner.

"I brought you here under the instruction of Delvarus. He wanted you to see this place," Josesh said.

The scene that surrounded me captured my thoughts, and I began to wonder what tragedy had befallen it. "What happened here?"

"Hatred, lust, greed, and outright stupidity, it all happened here," Josesh replied. "This is the city of Jezria, or what's left of it. Here is where the colonists once lived in peace and prosperity." He paused for a moment and looked around him, returning to the same thoughtful demeanor he adorned earlier. "This is where the royal council of your father first began to send people. For many years, they lived here in complete harmony with our order, and we had no qualms with their presence. In fact, we welcomed it."

"Then what happened?" I pressed.

"Certain of the colonists began to rebel. They wanted to make their own order, contrary to ours. They wanted a government of kings and subjects rather than the constitution they had through us. Those who championed this cause wanted to rule over everyone else," Josesh explained. "Of course, we didn't have need to keep close watch on them then, and by the time we heard of it, we were too late. The rebels had gained too many followers."

"And then?"

"They marched against our city," Josesh returned. "Our people had no choice but to retaliate."

I looked around me at the heap of a once-civilized place and envisioned what it might have looked like in its peaceful days. "Were there any left alive?" I asked.

"None of those that rebelled," Sovia answered. "And when our people came against Jezria, those who were left fled into the forest."

"Were there none who were innocent of tyranny?"

"Our history tells us that most of those left behind were women and children, likely those who were uninvolved in the situation," she said. "This alone is why they were allowed to flee and weren't hunted down."

"But your people destroyed the city?" I clarified.

"It had to be done," Josesh answered. "The law has no tolerance for murderous intentions. The rebels intended to kill our own people in order to usurp the order that has been in place for eons before us. And we were intent on leaving them no leg to stand on, should anyone get the idea again."

I looked around me at the ashes in which the ground beneath us was shrouded and began to feel mixed emotions of anger and sorrow. "Why is oppression some people's fondest desire? What is it about peace that they find so unfavorable?" I asked these questions as much to myself as to those with me.

"The order we live is completely just and is intended to govern the actions of humanity for its own good. But there are some who think they know better. There are some who want to validate unjust desires, and they pretend to espouse freedom as their cause," Josesh returned. "Now, what is there to trust in such a people determined on destroying themselves and others?" he added.

"Not all are this way." I insisted, shaking my head as I stared into the grim scene of a fallen Jezria.

"Prove it to me," he replied. "In fact, that's what you're supposed to do, I'm told."

"What do you mean?"

"Delvarus tells us that you will be leading followers here to rebuild Jezria," Josesh answered.

"This is news," I replied. "He's said nothing of it to me."

"That's because we were instructed to tell you," Sovia said. "That's why we brought you here."

"But I have no followers," I returned.

Josesh reached in his coat pocket and pulled out a familiar-looking paper. "Of course you do. Why else would you have brought this to us?" He handed it to me, and I looked at the names on the petition, with my own as the very last. "We will be expecting these men and their families soon, but we will be watching Jezria very closely this time."

Chapter 17

I was taken back to the city of Litovia with the expectation that I would be schooled in all the details of the Justiton's order. It seemed to me that they were taking great precautions to ensure that rebellion wouldn't repeat itself. However, there was nothing spoken about Henry and his plans to storm the city. It was as if they weren't even concerned, but rather, considered him no threat at all.

"But what about Henry?" I asked as I sat in a large library of sorts the following day.

Josesh turned to me and seemed to give my question very little thought. "He's a fool. What about him?"

"He plans to march against your city with his army," I said, surprised at his lackadaisical response.

Josesh offered a smirk that seemed to suggest he found my concern over the matter humorous. "Don't worry. You should know by now that he is no match for us. Besides, we take orders from Delvarus, and right now, he is more concerned with getting the innocent out from amongst Henry and his lot."

"You mean the names on the list?"

"Yes, and any who haven't signed it that will. Remember, that's where you come in," he said. "But first, you must learn about everything to do with our government. Those who reside within these hills are expected to abide the highest law." He laid on the table in front of me a large parchment. "I take it you are familiar with this?"

I looked over the words and saw the same passages I had read before from the document in the home of Thomas and Martha. "Yes, it's all familiar."

"This is the very least we expect from the colonists," Josesh said, "but the government that we live here was adopted from your father's."

"You have the same government as my father?" I asked.

"Yes, and the same language too, as a matter of fact. Before communications were made with your father, my people's government was extremely similar to his own, but their language wasn't. His was superior, so my people learned it and have spoken it ever since." After saying this, Josesh moved to a nearby shelf of books and took several volumes from it, then he returned to the table at which I sat and dropped them in front of me. "Do you like to read?" he asked.

"I do, a little." I returned.

"Well, you're going to learn to love it in the next few days."

"Am I supposed to read all this?"

"Every page, and all in your father's language. How else are you going to teach all your followers about what's in there?"

"I've never been a leader before," I said, staring at the books and feeling altogether overwhelmed.

"I don't know about that," Josesh returned. "But you have four days in which to complete your study. After that, we'll be sending you back to the colony."

"Four days to read all of this?"

Josesh looked at the books and then at me. "There are seven volumes. That's only one and three quarters of a book per day. I'm sure you can handle it. At any rate, you'd best get started." He left my side after that and walked to the door. "I'll be sending you meals, and you'll have a chance to get some fresh air every now and then. However, you must be diligent. There are a lot of people counting on you."

When the door latched behind him, I opened the first

book and read the words that ran in bold lettering across the top of the page:

> "It is certain and evident to the conscience that for peace, truth, and justice to abide within any society that the beginnings of government must start with the individual..."

Following this preface were the words of a constitution of peace and self-discipline. Each article and passage I read served as refreshing evidence that my father was a man of great wisdom. Harmony and prosperity, both individually and as a whole, proved to be the underpinnings behind the words of the order. And each section was emphatically clear on the fact that no peace can be assured without first establishing peace within the hearts of all the people.

By the time I had gone many pages into the first volume, the premise behind what I read switched from general statements and axioms to specific rules of self-conduct. Each page that followed this transition outlined some basic and fundamental reflection of self-mastery and emphasized the constant need to check against complacency in such matters.

The reading went much faster than I had anticipated, and I found that it was all rather intriguing. Then, somewhere in the middle of the book, my attention was drawn to the sound of the door opening. "I brought you something to eat," Karesh announced as he walked toward the table. He set down a dish with a delicious and aromatic meal displayed on it, and I began to realize how hungry I was.

"Thank you, Karesh. Now that I think of it, I am really hungry."

"How's the reading coming?"

"I'm halfway through the first volume," I answered, somewhat pleased with my progress.

Karesh looked surprised at this statement. "Only half way? It's already past mid-day. You aren't going to finish in time at that rate. Are you reading every word?"

"How else would I read it?"

"Perhaps my father failed to mention that you're really only expected to get the general idea for now. You're going to have to breeze through some sections, you know."

I dropped my head in my hands and looked at the six other books in front of me. "Yes, your father failed to mention that," I replied.

"You'll be expected to have these volumes with you in Jezria eventually, and you'll have time to study it in more detail then. But for now just read as quickly as you can," Karesh added.

"I'm glad you told me. However, it is all very interesting. I don't know that I would mind reading every word."

Karesh offered a nod and then looked out the window. "You know, most of my people are leery about colonists returning to rebuild Jezria, because of what happened in the past. But between you and me, I'm not one of them."

I turned to look at him, and he offered a smile, (something not seen too often among the Justiton). "Why's that?" I asked.

"Because, your people intrigue me."

"How so?"

"Well, let me just say that something I witnessed once caused me to think very differently about your kind, differently than I had been taught at least."

"What was it?" I asked.

Karesh took a seat in the chair next to me and let out a sigh before speaking again. "Every three days, those who are assigned travel to the colony to collect the dead. Perhaps you've seen this before?"

"I've heard of it, but I've never seen it. Why is it the colonists aren't allowed to bury their own dead anyway?"

"It's your father's orders," Karesh answered. "The dead aren't permitted to remain within the colony but are entrusted to our care."

"Yeah, but why is that? It doesn't make any sense."

"I don't know if it's my place to tell you."

"Most would prefer to mourn over those lost to them and then bury their own dead," I added emphatically.

"I know, and I've seen it. You see, when it was my turn to travel to the colony on such an errand, I saw something I never could have expected."

"What do you mean?"

"When we were making our rounds through the outskirts of Caprecia, we came upon a home that had caught fire. We must have been the first of any on the scene, because we couldn't find a single person anywhere. We called to see if anyone was inside but no answers returned, and that was when she showed up," he said.

"Who?"

"A young woman who must have been returning from town. She was hysterical when she saw the flames and started shouting that her parents were in there. She ran for the door, but I stopped her. I couldn't let her go in with the fire as bad as it was. She kicked and screamed and elbowed me in the face until I let her go."

"So what happened next?"

"She went in the house to try and bring them out. I saw her coming to the door, pulling a body behind her shortly after, but then the beam over the entryway collapsed, and she was buried in the flames and smoke." Karesh reached forward and picked up one of the books. "No amount of loyalty to an idea is enough to risk one's life for another," he said. "That takes something more." He let the book fall to the table from his hand and then leaned back in his chair.

"Perhaps you would have done the same for your parents."

"What she did isn't in the nature of someone like me. I'm a Justiton." He rose from his seat and offered an expressionless face while he placed his hand on my shoulder. "You better get back to reading," he said before turning to head toward the door.

I thought about what Karesh had told me before I returned to my studies. The story of the woman caused me to think so highly of her that I began to imagine what I might say if only she had survived and I had the privilege of her acquaintance. It was a tragedy disconnected from my own life, but I felt as though I was part of it somehow. I felt as though the whole matter might as well have involved my closest friends. The look Karesh had in his eyes as he related the story seemed to suggest that he was as endeared to the woman for her noble act as much as I now was. And his apathetic reply appeared to be only a mask for what he was unwilling to feel.

For the first time since the news of Janaea, I found myself thinking of another woman, albeit briefly. My few sporadic memories of the woman of my dreams still caused a deep pain in my heart, but my adoration of the woman from Karesh's story was too real for these futile longings to quench its presence. If a reunion with Janaea were possible, as I once hoped it was, then the whole matter would have been different. I would never have allowed such emotions toward an unknown heroine to take place in my heart, but under the circumstances, my musings on the girl and her tragedy were a welcomed escape. Yet, the escape couldn't last long, for she too was gone.

I read quickly through the rest of the volume, and by the time I reached the second, the nature of the words changed and began to invoke a tone of caution. I slowed through this portion and read the consequences promised upon those who chose to disregard the order or all together fight against it. There was no tolerance for tyranny in an order of peace and freedom. Any opposition to such would mean oppression. Then I thought about Henry and his plans and began to wonder if he knew what awaited him.

Chapter 18

The days that followed were all very similar. Shortly after waking each morning, I would begin reading. I attempted to get as far as I could before Karesh would bring me my first meal for the day. Afterwards, I would commence reading again, eat later in the day, read some more, take a break for some fresh air, eat once more, and then read until I was tired enough to sleep.

It was a monotonous schedule, but my visits with Karesh helped to break things up throughout the day. I tried to continue our conversation about the woman and the fire, but he was reluctant to speak any more of it. Instead, I asked him what he knew about my father. "I've never met the man," he said as he sat at my table one afternoon. "But someday I would like to."

"What is his name? I've only ever heard him called 'father'."

"That's probably because whenever you've heard someone talking about him, they're talking to you, and that would be the most fitting reference under such circumstance. But you should have come across his name many times in your readings by now. He's the ruler referred to as Manaeus."

"I was wondering if that was him," I replied. "But tell me this, why would a self-governed people need a ruler? I thought that such a thing was against the order, to have a king that is."

"He isn't the kind of king you may think. He is a ruler merely because his people consider him one. Your father is so respected, because of what he's done, that everyone else is obliged to revere him as a leader. He makes no appointment of himself, but through his actions, his people have. You see the difference?"

I thought about the starkest example I could compare, and the Pridions were certainly a complete opposite to what I had been reading about my father. "I do now."

"Henry, for example, is a man bent on subjecting those beneath him. He coerces his followers into deeming him their ruler," Karesh said. "It's these kinds of people that use fear to incite a pretended loyalty. They don't have anyone's interest in mind but their own."

"What's going to happen to him, Henry that is?"

"Well," Karesh answered. "He's either going to come to his senses, or else, when he does march against Litovia, he'll be killed."

Surprisingly, I felt pity for the man rather than anger. I wondered if he knew how foolish he was being, or if he was merely lost and confused as to his real purpose. It seemed that the more I learned about my own situation, the more I saw everything in a new light.

By the end of the fifth day, I was excited to be heading home. Thomas and Martha, along with the rest of the family, had been in my thoughts frequently since I left. I longed to tell them everything I had learned about our place in the colony and the meaning it brought to our situation. I hadn't been told this time that I must keep such things secret, and I was ready to tell all. The island, however, was still to be known to no one else, and I could understand why now.

When we left Litovia, the weather was as blissful as I had ever seen, but as we approached the walls of the city, I could see rain clouds on the distant horizon. Karesh brought the car to a stop at the same opening Delvarus and I had entered several days ago. On the other side, two horses were there to meet us, one of which was Amos, who was as excited to see me as I was him.

"I'm afraid I'm on two matters of business," Karesh said as he mounted his horse. "Foremost, I'm making sure you get back to Caprecia, but I will be meeting others there to attend to the second."

"What is it?" I asked.

"I'm afraid the lot of searching for the dead has fallen to me again," he replied.

I'm sure none ever enjoyed attending to such a task, but I could see in his eyes that it was especially difficult for him. "I'm sorry," I said after a brief silence between us.

"For what?"

"I hope there is none to find," I added.

He paused for a moment before speaking again. "You and me both."

The rain persisted like a wall of water that was ever before us. The hours that passed were strange and quiet. Nothing had been said between Karesh and me, and there was no real communication apart from my following his motions through the winding mountain path. The only companion that spoke anything to me was the consistent whispering of the water as it fell through the trees around us, and it was one I could do without.

Amos and the horse ahead of us trudged through the weather as if the cold wetness was altogether absent while I, for one, was less than content with the abiding discomfort. My legs were soaked and my feet were damp, though my torso remained relatively dry. A steady stream of water dripped from the crest of the hood I wore onto my nose and chin. My hands clutched the cold reins with a lifeless grasp of knuckles, whitened by the cold water that pounded on them with every second.

After following behind Karesh for longer then I cared to account, I decided to attempt a conversation, if for no reason other than to pass the time. I slowly moved alongside his horse and offered a light observation. "Too bad we can't take the flying thing," I said. "It would be a lot faster and dryer for sure."

Karesh turned to me and offered a small grin. "That's true."

"It troubles you, this errand, doesn't it? Going to search for the dead?"

Karesh remained speechless at first. "Why should it?"

"Because of her. You've never been the same since, have you?"

"Of course I have," he returned in an unreal-sounding tone.

I was surprised to hear him respond in this way after what he had told me a few days ago. He appeared to have admired the colonists for what he had seen in the young woman, and now he sounded more like his father, which made me wonder whether he had spoken about it in some degree to Josesh, only to be reprimanded after. "Do you know what it means when your heart aches?" I asked. He turned to look at me, with surprise and question in his eyes. "It means you have one," I said. Karesh looked forward again, only this time it seemed as though my words had greatly affected him, and now he continued onward in silence.

I rode alongside him without speaking while the rain persisted in pouring sheets of water throughout the valley floor. I thought about home as we continued through the wet drudgery of our present surroundings. I looked forward to being in the presence of my dear friends again and wondered how they had been during my absence. After a long time of being left alone to my thoughts, I decided to attempt a conversation again.

"So," I chimed through the noise of the rain, "what's the next step?"

"What do you mean?"

"What am I supposed to do when I get back?"

"Delvarus will tell you that," Karesh replied. "In the meantime, you'll return to Thomas and Martha's."

Despite his present attitude, Karesh was someone that I was beginning to consider a friend, and I could tell that his mood was a depressed one. He was stiff and agitated as he sat in the saddle, and I knew it was in anticipation of his duties. "Do you want me to go with you?"

"With me where?" he said in a pretentious tone, as if he didn't know what I was alluding to.

"On your assignment, of course."

"No, it's a Justiton's business. We'll part at Caprecia."

"It sounds like this Justiton business needs a more human touch," I murmured.

"What is that supposed to mean?"

"It means you fight the greatest element of your nature instead of embracing it. You're so concerned about being like every other Justiton that you suppress the very thing that makes you human."

"Yes, well, my people have seen that thing perverted," he replied, "turned into hatred and vice. I've seen families torn apart by individuals who can't harbor restraint."

"Is that what you fear, that once embraced it can be turned?" He said nothing to follow my response. "Every light casts a shadow, Karesh, but it doesn't mean that darkness is its equal. It's merely what exists when it's absent." Karesh turned to me and offered a thoughtful stare, which seemed to reach beyond whatever earlier contemplations he may have had about the subject. Afterwards, he was silent again.

The rest of the time spent on our journey through the towering mountain peaks passed with some lighter conversation between us. By the time evening was upon us, it had stopped raining, and we were soon passing through the area where the landscape grew thinner in plants and trees. We came nearly to the end of it all, where the stretch of plateau extended to the horizon, but it was at this fringe of wilderness where Karesh brought his horse to a stop. "This is home for the night," he said as he dismounted.

We soon had a camp prepared, and Karesh's tent was something of a marvel when compared to my own crude shelter. I situated my bedding over the soft-but-still-damp grassy ground beneath my covering and laid on my back while staring into the cloth overhead. I turned on my side, and as I usually would just before falling asleep, took the necklace from my pocket.

With a new perspective on my situation, I was left to wonder about Janaea and what she must be doing back home. I thought about what Delvarus had said, but it caused a considerable amount of anguish in my heart. For the first time, I placed the necklace back in my pocket and hoped that I would not dream of her that night.

I woke the next morning to the sound of Karesh's orders. "Gather your things. It's time to be going."

I stammered awake, collapsed my tent, gathered my things, and inhaled what Karesh had left for me on the fire. "Alright, I'm ready," I said as I swung into the saddle.

"Very well then, let's go." Karesh kicked his horse and started into a bit of a gallop before slowing to the pace we would maintain for the rest of the day.

It was past nightfall by the time we made it over the plateau and through the hills of the country east of Caprecia. As we came upon the outskirts of town, I was feeling quite tired and could tell by Amos's slowing that he was as well. It was another hour or so before we would reach Thomas and Martha's, and I was hoping that perhaps the Fosters would put me up for the night.

"This is where you and I go our separate ways," Karesh announced as we came to the fork in the road where one side continued through town and the other turned toward the north.

"Well, best wishes," I said.

"You too. I will see you in Jezria soon enough."

"I guess so."

I continued toward Ernest and Sarah's home, and when I got there I hitched Amos to the post near the stable and made my way through the dark toward the door. The night seemed so still that I was reluctant to break the silence by knocking, but I could faintly make out a dim light radiating from behind the window, which encouraged me to follow through with it. I drummed three soft raps on the wooden panel and stood awaiting a reply. I heard the shuffle of feet and short slow steps drawing closer. The sound of a latch followed next, and the door cracked open just enough for me to see half of a face peeking through the breach.

"Good evening, Ernest. Do you have room to put a weary traveler up for the night?"

"John?" He questioned with surprise. He opened the door completely and stood with a demeanor of disbelief as he looked at me. "Come in, come in." I stepped into the house, and he quickly closed the door behind me, locking it with a firm motion of his arm. "Sarah!" he yelled.

She came around the corner of the adjoining room and paused with surprise upon seeing me. "It's good to see you're alright," she sighed.

"Yes, I'm quite fine. Why shouldn't I be?"

"We were so worried about you," Sarah continued.

"Worried, why would you have been worried?" She looked at Ernest and then back at me.

"Have a seat, John. There's something we need to tell you," Ernest said.

I slowly sat on the bench that stood near their door. I was growing slightly concerned as to how they were acting and why. I waited for them to address me again, but the wait was longer than I could stand.

"Well?" I insisted.

"Henry's been at work again," Ernest said. I rose from my seat and immediately felt agitated.

"What has he done?" They both looked at each other again and then back at me.

"It's Simon, he's not well," Sarah said.

"What do you mean?"

"You see, John," Ernest continued, "when you left, Simon came here to ask me if I knew what you were up to. When Sarah told him everything about your visit, he began to spread the news to everyone he knew that had signed the list."

"What happened?"

Ernest, a man of stoic determination and zeal, bowed his shaking head and covered his face in his hands. "Somehow Henry got word of it. Someone has betrayed us, John."

Chapter 19

"What of Simon then? What did Henry do?" I asked. "They really roughed him up I'm afraid, trying to keep him from spreading anything more about it," Ernest said.

"Thomas and Martha are pretty sure his leg is in pieces, and a few of his ribs are likely broken. He's bruised from head to toe and scraped up really bad," Sarah added. I took to my feet in a fit of rage. "Where are you going?"

"I'm going home. And Henry better watch his back from here on out!"

"John, wait. You need to stay here. Henry is looking to kill you. He has men all through these parts waiting for you to show up again," Ernest said.

"I can't wait around here."

"You can't go back alone," Sarah insisted. "Think what might happen."

"But what might happen if I don't?" I answered as I swung open the door and took a step into the chilled air of the night. Amos seemed to sense the urgency in my steps and began to grow restless at my approach. "Come on boy, we have to go." I grabbed the reins from the post and threw my foot into the stirrup, swinging over the saddle and jerking Amos in the direction of Thomas and Martha's.

Amos threw his feet forward and pushed from the ground with such force that we seemed to fly over the surface of the road with every stride. I hovered in the saddle with a nervous tension, and though the dark failed to effect Amos's vision, my limited reference to our surroundings made it appear to me that our speed was as great as a car.

All the while, I rehearsed the anger I was feeling and thought about the brutality that had been heaped upon my good friend. I clutched the reins with determination to avenge Simon, and as I did, I could sense the anger growing inside of me. Eventually, it reached a level where I stopped thinking about rushing home and began entertaining ideas of hunting down Henry.

I lingered in these thoughts for a time before I realized that it was deterring me from what ought to be my focus. I tried to calm myself and reassess my thinking. As we rode farther away from town and toward the open country, I recalled the words of Ernest, and though they might have concerned me under normal circumstances, my rage was such that I would have dared any man to try and stop me.

Later in our course, as we were nearing Thomas and Martha's in a steady maintainable gallop, there came a dark figure out of the shadows and onto the path in front of us. Amos made out the line of the opposing horse and rider just in time to come to a halting stop several paces from them. The man raised a small lantern from his side that illuminated half of his face and began moving toward us.

"Who goes there?" he yelled.

"Whose business is it to know?" I yelled back. He continued moving in our direction and stretched the light out in front of him. I remained still, as if I had no reason to be concerned with his approach. As he drew closer, I noticed two other riders following from behind him, and I moved my hand discretely to the hilt of my sword.

"What is your name traveler?" the man inquired.

"I might as well ask you the same thing, but what reason is there?" The riders made their final steps to come directly next to us, surrounding Amos and me on every side.

"The reason comes from Henry, leader of the Pridions. There's a traitor among us. Goes by the name of John. Chance you might know him?" he asked, raising the light to my face. I winced at his intrusion and leaned away from it, only to find a sword from another pointed toward my neck. "Or any chance you might be him?"

One man to our front and two to our sides made the chance for an escape a bit unlikely. Amos nervously jumped from one leg to the next, as if he knew the intentions of our intruders as well as I did. I could see only one way out, and Amos already seemed to have the same idea. I made a quick nudge to his side, and he bolted forward into the opposing horse.

The force was enough to send it into a whirl of imbalance and panic. It fell to the ground in a thud, and the shriek of the rider laying pinned under the animal pierced the night air as we flew out of the group and down the road. I looked behind me immediately after and could faintly detect the other two men riding in pursuit behind us.

Amos was a fast horse, faster than any I knew, so I had no real concern for outrunning my enemies. However, what I was to do when I reached home was an idea I needed to rapidly formulate. The rushing speed at which we cruised through the dark atmosphere around us nurtured assurance that I would have the time I needed to get the advantage on my two opponents.

Shortly, I was in the clearing that opened to Thomas and Martha's small settlement. Amos threw us off the crest of the final hill, into the air and down toward the house that sat in remote silence amid the rushing clamor that followed me. I leaped off at the barn and shooed Amos into the stable where I joined him in taking cover.

CHAPTER 19 | 153

Not long after ducking around the wooden wall, I could hear the approach of the two men as they came over the same hill. They rushed to the base and stopped in a pause of silence. I watched them exchange looks and gestures that sent one toward the house and the other in my direction. I witnessed in trembling aggravation as the one barged into the home and brought Thomas and Martha out into the cold night air.

"Where is he?" he yelled.

"We already told you. We haven't seen him," Thomas replied. The man threw him to the ground and took Martha in his grasp, pinning her arm behind her back. I grabbed my sword and drew it from its sheath. As I did, the other of the two stepped closer to the barn. Thomas and Simon had taught me how to fight with a sword for self defense. I remembered that they were impressed at how quickly I picked up on their instructions, and I hoped now that my knack for the skill was better than my opponents'. I waited as long as I could before I sprang from my hiding place and toward my approaching enemy, moving quickly enough to bring my blade to his neck before he had time to draw his own.

"Let her go!" I yelled to the other while his companion stood nervously at the end of my sword.

"Awe, so you want to barter do you? Tough!" he said as he tightened his grasp and I watched as Martha winced in pain. "Drop your sword or I'll break her arm." I lost confidence in my advantage and slowly loosened my grip on the hilt. The concerned look on the face of my captive began gradually to grow into a menacing smile.

"Let her go. Leave them alone and you can take me," I said to the man who held Martha.

"Drop your sword!" he returned.

"If I drop my sword, you will let her go!" I exclaimed. He threw her away from him, and I watched as she fell helpless to the cold ground. He drew his blade and let it rest on her neck. "If you don't drop your sword, I might not be generous for much longer." I looked at the man next to me and slowly withdrew my weapon from his gullet, letting it fall to my feet. He then took his own and brought it to my neck. The other left his place by Martha and walked over to me with an arrogant sway in his step.

"Well now," he said. "It looks like we got him." After saying this, he delivered a quick jab to my stomach that brought me to my knees, gasping for air. He then kneed me across the side of my head, and I fell to the ground with a racing pain that throbbed through my whole face. "Dead or alive is what the order said, but I think alive might be a little more fun, don't you?" he chuckled.

I tightly shut my eyes to regain as much strength as I could when next I heard a swift rushing of hooves coming from behind. Amos collided with the man whose blade had been drawn on me. He flew to the ground and kicked as much as he could to get away, but Amos pursued him and trampled his legs like snapping the limbs of a tree. His shrill cry echoed in the stillness of the night and was enough to distract the other sufficient for me to quickly take my sword into my hand again.

I rose to my feet and thrust it forward just in time to meet him with his own sword drawn and waiting. I wasted no time in moving on the offensive. One attempt to the next was countered by the metallic pinging of clashing blades. I saw a look of fear develop in the eyes of my opponent as he struggled to match my speed. I swung overhead and hit his blade into his own shoulder. I attacked to the right and knocked his sword back into his own leg—then to the left, quicker than he had time to react as I lopped off his arm at the elbow with a forceful blow.

His scream joined the moaning of his trampled co-part, and they both lay squirming on the ground in defeat. I rushed over to Martha and knelt at her side, trying to help her to her feet with assistance from Thomas, who had received a beating himself.

"Are you alright?" I asked.

"Yes, I'm fine," Martha said, "We were so worried about you." She wrapped her arms around my neck in a motherly hug, and Thomas placed his hand on my shoulder.

"I'm alright, but how is Simon?" I questioned.

"Simon isn't well," Thomas said. I looked back before entering the house and saw the two men struggling to get to their horses while Amos was making his way toward me.

I stroked his black mane and patted him on the head. "Thanks, Pal, I couldn't have done it without you."

As we entered the home we found Simon awakened from all the commotion, lying restless in bed. One eye was opened and looking our way as we came to his side while the other remained swollen shut. Timmy and Mary were waiting by him with looks of fear on their faces.

"John, you camed back!" Timmy exclaimed. Immediately following his excitement, his face turned somber. "What's goin' happen to Simon?" The others remained silent and still. I knelt at his side and looked at him with a great sense of concern. His face was marred with scrapes and bruises, and the rest of his body was covered under the sheets that had been tucked around him.

"Simon, what did they do to you?" I cried.

"John, you're back," he replied with a tone of relief.

"That's right."

"I'm in a lot of pain," he continued, "but Thomas and Martha are taking good care of me." He labored in his speech as if it hurt to talk. His eye flickered, and his brow formed beads of sweat. His jaw tightened after each utterance, and he shook with a slight spasm. "John, you have to leave. Henry will know you're here."

My thoughts turned to Karesh and those that would be

with him. If somehow I could get word to him, I would have all the help I needed. "Don't worry; I'll take care of Henry."

"Don't be a fool," Simon replied. "There are too many of them now."

"Well, it just so happens that there are some hill-dwellers in town tonight. I just need a way to get word to them of what's happened."

"It's no use," Martha said. "Henry has men all throughout the countryside looking for you. You'll never make it alive."

"I have to try," I returned. "Have you seen Delvarus? He said he would meet me in seven days," I stammered. "Has he been here?"

"We haven't seen him since you left,"Thomas answered. "Besides, you've only been gone six days."

"You must stay, John. We can keep you safe here. We can hide you where they won't think to look," Martha said desperately.

"She's right, John," Thomas added.

"I can't put you through the risk," I said. I rushed to the door and looked out. "The men are gone and they will be taking word to Henry. They'll know to come here. I've put you in too much danger as it is. I should have thought to keep them from leaving." Martha and Thomas exchanged a quick look and then turned to me again.

"Thing is, John, we're already in danger. Whether you leave or not, they'll come here looking for you," Thomas said.

"You're right," I replied in a moment of epiphany. "Whatever happens to me, you must listen to my brother when he comes. You'll have to do what I was meant to."

"What are you talking about?" Thomas exclaimed.

"I know what I have to do," I said. Amid the silent pause that followed, we began to hear the approaching procession of hooves that carried with it a foreboding sense of ill intent.

"There must have been others following me," I remarked.

"Martha, take the kids and hide," Thomas said. "I'll look after Simon. Now hurry!" Martha swung Mary and Timmy into her arms and guided them in the direction of the cellar. "What about Susan?" she cried.

It was then I noticed her for the first time, huddled in bed, looking very ill. "What's wrong with her?" I shouted through the confusion.

Thomas rushed to Susan's side and took her into his arms, wrapping her as tightly as he could with the blanket.

"What's hapning!" Susan screamed. "Where I going?" she said in a raspy voice.

Just then the door flung open. "There he is! Grab him!" a man yelled. Before I even had time to struggle, they seized me and forced my arms behind my back. They drug me out into the cold night air with Thomas yelling after them. I saw the face of little Susan smitten with fear as I was forced out of the house.

"Let him be, you fools! Let him go!" Thomas yelled. One of the intruders beat him over the head with the hilt of his sword and sent him falling to the ground. I kicked and moved as much as I could to extricate myself from their hold, but it was no use.

"Unhand me, or you'll be sorry you didn't!"

"Oh, and what are you going to do about it?" one of them hissed.

They threw me at the feet of a large group outside, and I soon heard the voice of one I recognized. "Knock some sense into him. Remind him who's in charge," Henry said.

They proceeded to tear my shirt from my torso, exposing my bare back. Next I knew, I was hearing the loud crack of leather and feeling the sharp sensation that came from my tearing flesh. It was enough to cause me to scream in pain with every return of the whip. They continued to administer the blows until I could feel the blood pool on my back. I was on fire with rage and the deep sting of mutilated skin and muscle. Several kicks to the abdomen from my assailants caused me to vomit so violently that my stomach felt as though it had turned on itself, as if it were about to dislodge from inside me and come up my throat. I felt as though I was slowly and painfully dying. They kicked me and spit on me afterward until I no longer moved but lay on the cold ground in a state that seemed to hover between life and death.

"Tie his hands and bring him with us. This isn't over yet," Henry said. They fastened a rough rope around my wrists and forced me to my feet. I could barely stand, but they beat me with clubs until I did. They brought me to a horse, whose back they draped me over, and tied me to it with course lashings that wore into my cut and bleeding body. "Now find the horse and kill it!" Henry shouted.

I lay helpless and unable to move as they forced Amos from the barn. He kicked and stomped but was soon met with the arrows of the archers that prowled around him like wolves. I watched as they pumped one after another into his neck and side. He screamed a piercing neigh into the darkest night I had ever experienced, and it was all I could manage to sob over the loss of my dear friend.

Amos lay lifeless on the ground as they took me away, and I thought that our eyes met one last time before his own closed forever. All at once, anger and sorrow raged through my veins, and I could hardly believe all that had just happened. The pain that I felt all over my body only added to making the whole experience nearly unbearable.

I had no way of telling where they were taking me. From my vantage point, I couldn't see anything but the ground that slowly passed beneath me. The blood began to rush to my head, and I feared that I would soon be passing out from the strain. My back throbbed with pain, and my stomach ached with soreness.

The next thing I knew, I was thrown into a cold dark cellar behind iron bars. My shirt was never returned to me, and it wasn't long before I began to shiver in the cold that seemed to permeate the walls surrounding me. I huddled in a ball in the corner and began to rehearse all the events of that night, a night that seemed as if it would never end.

Chapter 20

I don't recall sleeping at all. Moments of unconsciousness visited me with inconsistency, but with each occasion, it felt more like I was passing out again as opposed to actual slumber. By the time the morning sun broke through the small barred window, I had awoken from a spell of uncomfortable dozing. My body was severely chilled, as if my heart was no longer able to pump warmth through my veins, and I could hear footsteps approaching the wooden door which stood just outside my cell.

I stayed on my side, curled in the far corner of the room. When the door opened, I only saw the black boots that traipsed into the light. Then the person took a seat in the only chair that sat just outside the bars. When I looked up from the ground, I saw the most unwelcoming face, the very one I had no desire to ever see again. "I hope you like your accommodations," Henry said. "We built this place just for people like yourself, people who think they can change everything." He leaned forward in his chair and peered through the metal rods that separated us. "But the fact is—you can't."

After this, he rose to his feet and paced about the room. "Do you know why I have kept you alive?" he asked. "You've created quite a mess, trying to turn the hill-dwellers against me. But now you're going to fix it all. You're going to convince your crazy friends that the hill-dwellers did this to you," he said. "And do you know why you're going to do this, John?" He stopped moving and stood directly in front of me. "Because if you don't, I will kill Thomas, Martha, and all of their dear little family."

"Leave them out of this," I murmured through the pain in my chest.

"Oh, I hope you believe me. What we did to Simon should be a good sample of what's to come if you don't cooperate." Following this remark, he walked to the door and spoke to the men standing there. "Clean him up and get him ready to go."

When they opened the bars to the chamber, they threw cold water on me and drug me to my feet. They then proceeded to clothed me in a coarse and itchy coat, placing a black hood over my head, which they tied around my neck with a rope.

I was thrown into the cool morning air and, soon after, was loaded onto a horse. The long and silent journey that ensued was coupled with the pain of last night's assault. The coarse material of my covering rubbed against the open cuts on my back and made them feel as fresh and painful as they were when first administered. My head ached from dehydration and from being kicked and beaten several times, and the soreness in my stomach from the same assaulting blows and vomiting contractions was now accompanied by the pains of hunger and emptiness.

All this, and the fact that I couldn't see where I was going, made the trip a horrible one. It seemed to drag on for longer than any excursion I had ever taken. The persistence of the pain and the anxiety over my fate was enough to prolong the journey until it felt like a day had passed. Eventually, I began to hear the faint noise of what I guessed to be the beginnings of Caprecia. The horse's hooves began to clop on the cobbled walkway of the city's center, and the commotion of human movement and verbal interaction began to fill my ears.

"Off with the hood," I heard Henry whisper. The light

of the day made my head ache all the more as the brute to my left tore the sackcloth from my face. Gradually, as we moved farther in our course, I heard the voices of onlookers growing quiet as I passed, and I saw inquisition forming on their faces.

When the horse was finally brought to a stop, I was pushed off the saddle and caught on the other side just before hitting the ground. They took no care in how they dealt with me, and when their hands were pressed against my back the coat felt like sharp grains of salt being forced into an open wound.

Once they stopped me from falling completely, they dropped me on the hard stones and walked over my back before leaving me to rise alone. I screamed in pain and drew the attention of the townspeople my way. In the next second, they pulled me to a standing position and held me by the arms.

"Don't worry!" one of them yelled. "He's a criminal!" Unfortunately, this seemed to calm any concern, and the sounds that were earlier present in the city continued as before.

I walked forward in a pain-ridden stupor toward some unknown destination. I was dragged between two men, each on either side of me, holding both of my arms. Stairs soon followed, and then a door opened into a cool but stale-smelling room. I was guided to a chair where I was made to sit, and once there, I took notice of the faces that surrounded me.

"They're all here, your highness. Just like you requested," I heard a familiar voice whisper. When I looked up I saw the face of Charles Kilmen, one of the names from the list, speaking with Henry.

"Charles?" I asked through a swollen stare. He ignored me altogether and proceeded to take orders from the leader of this unlawful gathering. It was then it occurred to me—Simon, though zealous in spreading word about the plans to thwart Henry, would have been careful to share it with only those names on the petition. Henry had infiltrated our own people. We had been betrayed from within.

CHAPTER 20

As I took a closer assessment of my surroundings, I found myself in a room filled with the commoners of Caprecia. In front of me was a notable and rich man by the name of Samuel. He sat alone while everyone else occupied the rows of seats that formed a circle around the center of the room. "John, is it true?" Samuel asked. I turned my face to look directly at him. "Did the hill-dwellers really do this to you?"

"Good citizens of Caprecia," Henry began, interrupting Samuel's attempted conversation. "I know that we have not always seen eye to eye. You consider yourselves loyal to those that govern us from the East Mountains, and there are rumors that I plan to march against them. Well, let me tell you. I would never be so brash unless I had the support of the common people of Caprecia. While I have grown tired of their iron-fisted rule, I know that many of you don´t know what I know about them. They are tyrants! And they will stop at nothing to subjugate us."

After saying this, Henry pretended to wipe at his face as if he had formed a tear. "Look upon poor John here," he said. "He is an example of their ruthless cruelty and apathy toward our colony, and he has come to tell you for himself how they must be stopped once and for all!" Henry exclaimed. "They beat this poor man senselessly, without just cause, and all merely to send us a message."

After he said this, roars erupted from those around me. "Is it true?" I heard from the clamor. "Say it isn´t so," another voice rang. "Charles told us what happened," came another.

"Go on, John," Henry said loud enough for all to hear. "Tell them the truth."

I slowly rose to my feet, and silence settled on the entire crowd. Henry pretended to assist me by grabbing my arm but instead offered a tight squeeze to my bruised flesh, as if to remind me of his promise to harm my friends. I walked toward the middle of the crowd and looked back at the stern expression that formed on Henry's face. Then I did exactly what Henry had just asked me to do.

"As you should already know," I said with a voice as bold as I could muster, "Henry is a liar and a fool. But what you do not know is that we have been betrayed by a would-be friend, one of our very own." As I said this, I looked directly at Charles, and he quickly averted eye contact. Henry moved toward me as if to insist on taking me away, but Samuel stood in his place to stop him.

"The truth," I said, staring Henry down. "Is that Henry is planning a war. He and his army of Pridions are preparing to march against the East Mountains and turn the hill-dwellers against us all. He and his minions did this to me, and he did the same to Simon, whom many of you know, and all because we tried to raise a voice of warning."

Being perched in the middle of the crowd afforded me the safety net I needed. Henry was the greatest of fools to assume I would cooperate with him. The pity I once felt for Henry left the moment I heard news of Simon, and I was ready to seal his fate before all who stood with me. "Henry must be tried for his crimes!"

The crowd erupted again, and Henry and the few with him ran from the building and into the streets of Caprecia. A large group of townspeople pursued them, but by the time I had stepped outside, I could see Henry and his followers riding away fast enough to escape them. "I need a horse," I yelled. "He'll be heading toward Thomas and Martha's!"

"You're in no shape to be riding," Samuel said.

"I can manage."

"Then take my horse," he replied. "I'll find another and some men to follow after you." He stepped toward the posts that stood at the base of the steps outside the door and unleashed a black stallion. "Ride fast," he said as he cut the bands from my wrists with his knife and placed the reins in my hand.

CHAPTER 20 | 165

The ride was painful, and I soon realized Samuel was right. I was in no condition for the trip. After the initial adrenaline wore off, I was reminded of that fact with each second that followed. Every jarring gallop made my whole body ache, but the concern I felt for Thomas and Martha inevitably outweighed the pain. I slumped in the saddle and conjured enough strength to barely stay upright. The horse seemed to sense my posture and slowed to a manageable pace. Then I began to reproach myself and wonder what good I would be to Thomas and Martha even if I did beat Henry there. My only hope now was that Samuel and some others would be close behind.

By the time I reached the hill that stood before Thomas and Martha's house, I was relieved to see no trace of Henry, and the presence of a small caravan of hill-dwellers offered additional comfort, enough to help me raise my head as I approached the front of the home. As I made it to the door, I collapsed in exhaustion and pain, but before anyone was able to rush to my aid, I managed to stagger to my feet and step into the house.

I saw a sight that, at first, was most welcoming. Delvarus stood to greet me with open arms. "I'm so sorry, John," he said.

"I'll be alright," I managed. But then I saw Karesh kneeling at a bedside and my heart sank.

He turned to me and offered a face I had never seen him wear before. It was a face of sorrow. "I'm so sorry," he echoed.

"What's going on?" I demanded.

The next familiar face I saw was Ernest's, kneeling near Mary and Timmy. They were both crying while huddled at the side of Martha, who had perched on her knees at the head of one of the beds. "John, we followed after you as fast as we could, but we were too late." Ernest said in a somber tone while tears moistened his cheeks.

"Simon!" I cried.

Chapter 21

It was in the next moment that I took greater inventory of my surroundings for the first time. In the rush of excitement and fear, I had seen nothing beyond those individuals who first met me. "Simon's alright," Delvarus said. "I'm afraid it's little Susan."

As Karesh moved aside, I saw the small and fragile form of my tiny friend lying motionless and pale. Thomas was standing near Martha with his hands on her shoulders, trying to be the strength that she needed as she cuddled their children in her arms. And Simon, though incapable of moving, appeared to be suffering more than anyone. Mary and Timmy looked on with tearful eyes and expressions of disbelief.

I fell on my knees at Susan's side and began to weep with all the others. "What happened?" I wailed. "She can't be gone, not my little friend."

"She became really sick when you left," Thomas sobbed, "and last night was too much. Her little body couldn't fight any harder."

Karesh touched my arm to gain my attention. I turned to look where he stood gazing at me with a saddened countenance. "When Delvarus told me that I needed to come here, I was afraid it was for you. Then I saw Amos, and I thought that the horse was the reason." After saying this, I heard him choke on what he tried to say next. "I'm so sorry that it had to be her," he finally managed.

I threw my arms around Susan's cold and lifeless neck and sobbed into the pillow that cradled her small head. I felt Delvarus try to pull me to my feet. "Stand up, Brother," he said in a tone that bore the same remorse I was feeling. But I grabbed a hold of Susan. "No, you can't have her. You can't take her."

"It's going to be alright," Delvarus said, prying my arms from her neck and pulling me away. "Karesh will take good care of her; you'll see."

"Let us bury her," I insisted. "Don't take her away."

"I have to," Karesh replied in a quivering tone. "She deserves a better place than this."

"My baby!" Martha sobbed from behind streaming tears of anguish as Karesh lifted Susan's languid frame into his arms. "Please, not my baby!" she shouted.

Somehow, Thomas, though he groaned as much as any, was able to hold Martha tightly and offer the only comfort he could. Delvarus held me pinned from the side in his own grasp, and I witnessed a brief moment when his owns tears fell from his eyes to the floor beneath him.

Karesh offered one final look of sympathy before walking through the door and out of sight. Delvarus's restraint loosened, and I rushed out of the house along with Thomas and Martha. We saw the group of Justiton wrapping Susan's frame in a silken cloth of crimson red with the greatest reverence. Afterwards, they loaded her into a carriage of soft bedding.

I ran toward her, but Karesh stopped me. "Pull yourself together, John. She's going to be far better off with us."

"How can you say that when you're taking her away from those who love her?" I cried. "You, who refuse to know what love is, stand there and tell me to compose myself?"

I watched as tears formed in the eyes of Karesh for what was likely the first time. "I'm beginning to learn," he said.

We all watched as Karesh and the others mounted their horses and took Susan away from us. In a separate carriage that followed behind Susan's, I noticed, for the first time, the body of Amos sprawled in its bed. Delvarus came to my side and placed his hand on my shoulder. "Susan's death will be made right," he said. "But what about you? You look pretty roughed up. We need to get you some help."

Before I had a chance to ask him what he meant about Susan, and before I could provide any answer to his concern, a group of riders crested the hill beyond the field and made their way toward us. As they passed Karesh's small procession, they turned their heads to see the bodies in the carriage beds. Soon after, I noticed the familiar face of Samuel riding in the lead. "We came as fast as we could," he said as they dismounted in front of us all. "Where's Henry?"

"He's gone now. His wake of terror is all that remains," I answered.

"Are we too late?" Samuel asked.

"No, I was too late," I said as I wearily turned to walk back to the house. I rested on the post, almost falling to the ground, and cried over the loss of little Susan.

Ernest stepped out of the house and walked to my side. "Are you alright John? You should probably be seen to right away."

The pain that racked my frame was almost absent in the present anguish I felt over Susan, and as Ernest mentioned it, I was intent on letting it remain so. "I'm fine," I managed, though I really wasn't. I was capable, mobile, nothing was broken, but I was certainly in a great deal of discomfort and pain.

"I've sent the word, John. They will be coming now," Ernest returned.

I rose from looking toward the ground to meet his stare. "Who?"

"All of them, and then some. Every last name on the list that has not betrayed us."

Just then, Samuel stepped toward us. "What's this I hear of a petition against Henry? I'd like to add my name to it, and I know of many others who would also."

"I'm afraid I've lost it, along with other valuables," I replied, reaching to my chest where I would normally have felt the necklace perched in my pocket.

"Then we shall start another!" Samuel shouted. "Henry has to be stopped!"

"Leave Henry to me," I heard Delvarus say as he approached. "You and all that will follow must leave for Jezria at once, before Henry has time to come back with his armies."

"Who are you?" Samuel asked as he turned toward Delvarus.

"I'm your source of help."

"He's right," I added before Samuel had time to question any further. "We have to leave here. We'll only be safe in Jezria."

"I'm glad you realize that, John," Delvarus said. "Because you'll be the one leading everyone there."

I was fully prepared to follow Delvarus back to the Jezria, but I couldn't expect that I would be the one to take charge. "Me? Why would I be the one to follow? I'll follow you."

"Sure you will," Delvarus replied. "And then everyone else will follow you."

"My closest friends may be willing to, but what of everyone else?" I asked. "I'm hardly known to anyone in Caprecia."

"That much is true. But, you have Ernest on your side, and Samuel." He looked to both as he spoke and they offered affirming nods. "Ernest has plenty who are ready to follow him."

"But what of our homes?" Samuel asked. "Why not stay and fight for what is rightfully ours?"

"Yeah, what about all that we have back in Caprecia?" one of the men with him added.

"I'm trying to save lives, not risk them," Delvarus said.

"You're too outnumbered to stand a chance. You must travel with as much as you can manage. You'll be starting over in a more promising place. Take as many provisions as you can for you and your families, and all other resources that you are privy to. Take what you can for camp along the way and whatever comforts you can afford. Then you can meet in the country beyond Ernest's," Delvarus answered.

Samuel turned to Ernest as if to assess whether such a hasty endeavor was in his favor, but Ernest then turned to me. "He's right," I answered. "We have no time to waste."

Ernest's expression confirmed his resolve to follow through with the matter, but if this wasn't enough, his words should have been. "After knowing John for the short time I have, I've learned that he is a man that can be trusted," he said. "And we all know that Henry is a man that can't. I'll follow you John. You have my support."

Samuel paused for a moment. "Very well," he said. "If there's no other reasonable choice, then I'm in."

Once he was convinced, Samuel's small band seemed equally determined to espouse his same degree of consent. After confirming the details of the meeting place, they turned back toward Caprecia and left us to our own preparations. Delvarus turned and looked at me during the short spell of thought that I lingered in as I watch the horses ride away. "If it makes any difference, you are quite the born leader," he remarked.

"How do you know that?"

"It's obvious, isn't it?"

"Not to me," I said. "You're the one who's the leader. I'm just following you."

"Well, good leaders are born from good followers," Delvarus concluded.

Everyone went their separate ways, and while we all still anguished over Susan's passing, we had to work quickly to prepare for a very necessary departure. Ernest left to meet his allies at his home and to deliver the instructions to them, while Thomas and Martha gathered what things they could from the house and placed them in the only carriage they had, leaving what room was needed for Simon. The following hours were filled with a rushing movement of bodies and various supplies, and during it all, I tried to help with what I could. But I found that my strength was lacking.

Martha and Thomas attended to my wounds as quickly and as best they could, and they fed me what food they had available on hand. "How are we expected to bear all of this and still move on?" Martha cried as she sponged my back with a damp cloth.

I groaned in pain every time it touched my skin, but I tried to listen to all that Delvarus was saying. "You'll remember this one day and know that it wasn´t for naught."

"How can the last two days be remembered with anything but anguish?" Thomas cried.

"Where do you suppose Henry is?" I said through clenched teeth.

"Karesh has sent the other half of his convoy to search for him and his army. We´re guessing that they might be hiding in the northern forest," Delvarus answered. "Now is the best time to get the people out of here, while there´s still a chance."

When the painful process of washing my body was completed and everything that could be taken with us was loaded, I mounted the spare horse that Delvarus had brought with him and watched as Martha slowly closed the door to her home. She lingered for a brief moment in a sentimental daze, and I could see in her eyes the nostalgia that was clinging to the place she had grown to love.

Our travels carried on slowly and cautiously at first as we moved through the countryside, unsure if any of Henry´s brutes lay in wait for us along the way. Yet, with Delvarus leading us, the venture to the other side of town where Ernest and the others would be waiting seemed all the safer.

"Do you think we've seen the last of Henry?" I asked him as I rode alongside his horse.

"I hope so."

"What are we to do when we get to Jezria?" I asked in a quiet tone. "There is nothing left of it."

"You'll rebuild it. But until then, you'll have to live simply."

"I'm the only one who knows that we are heading into a wilderness without any providence for us. How can I ask all these people to follow me to such an end?"

"Don't worry," Delvarus returned. "The East Mountains are full of providence, and you will be taking with you a group of industrious people. Furthermore, this is the very thing father sent you here to accomplish."

I dismounted as we came to a massive group of people, horses, and carriages stationed in the fields beyond Ernest's home. Despite the grave nature of our circumstance, I was surprised to find that so many had gathered so quickly.

"We're all ready," Samuel said as I approached. "You give the word and we'll be on our way."

Suddenly, some inherent will to take on the role that had been issued to me surged in my heart. "Make sure all are accounted for. I don't want any left behind. We'll be traveling a good distance before we're done."

"Where exactly is this Jezria you speak of?" Ernest asked.

"It's in the East Mountains, outside the city of the hill-dwellers," I answered.

"And who is occupying it, hill-dwellers?" Sarah asked, who stood by her husband's side. "How do you know they will accept us?"

I was reluctant to mention the state of the place. I knew we needed to leave Caprecia, but I was afraid of what everyone might say if they knew we were heading away from civilization and into an unknown wilderness. I looked over at Delvarus and then again at Sarah. "We will be provided for in Jezria. Spread the word and tell everyone to be ready to leave within the hour."

As we left the outskirts of Caprecia, I could sense a spirit of trepidation among the host of people that followed me. Though they had brought with them every possession they could carry, as was instructed, they had still left so much behind them, and all because of the threat brought by one very delusional man and his followers.

The same path on which I had traveled only two days ago was accommodating for a rider on horseback, but not for carriages. Our expedition was slow for this reason, and by the time dusk had settled amidst the thinning landscape, we had only made it through the forest of the hills beyond Caprecia.

"It's going to take us a lot longer to get there this time," I said to Delvarus as we rode ahead of the others. "I'm worried about Simon. All this traveling can't be good for his condition."

"The sooner you get to Jezria the better," Delvarus returned. "Once we get there he can be treated as he needs."

I slumped in the saddle at the thought of arriving amid the ruin-laden landscape again. "How do you suppose the people will react when they see what Jezria actually is?"

"Hopefully, they will see it for what it can become," Delvarus said.

"I hope you're right."

Chapter 22

That night, I was restless. I slept very little from all the pain of my battered body, and a sense of dread lingered with me as I wondered whether Henry was pursuing us. Once within the East Mountains, we would have a greater assurance of safety. As I recalled what Josesh said about watching Jezria closely this time, I hoped that he had already placed eyes within it, as he assured me he would.

When morning came, our preparations moved quickly. Delvarus suggested that leaders be placed over every group of twenty five people in order to account for and assist everyone in the company. This helped our travels run more smoothly, and with reports coming from a handful of our comrades, I was able to rest my mind a little as to whether each person was being seen to as needed.

By the time it came to midday, our movement across the plateau seemed to be slowing. The time it took to close a reasonable distance was increasing, and it began to feel as though we were making little progress. All the women and children were allowed what seats were available, either in carriages or on horseback, and the men walked methodically alongside them.

Our slow travels carried on for several hours, but at long last, we came upon the mountainous ridge that enclosed the ruins in the small valley on the other side. Though we still had some distance to go, I was already beginning to feel relieved. Spirits seemed to lift with every encouragement I offered. Faces that once hung in bewilderment and fatigue seemed brightened with hope.

The coolness of the evening made travel more bearable, and dusk was a welcomed guest. As the sun began to touch down on the horizon behind us, it formed an orange blanket on the peaks ahead. The scene seemed so beautiful when coupled with the realization that beyond the wall in front of us was the chance for peace.

We came into a lush valley where the fresh smell of trees and the sound of flowing water greeted our group, a greeting that soon brought relief to many wearied travelers. After drinking our fill and relieving our animals of their burdens, we attended to quickly setting up camp for the night and eating what provisions we had for the evening. I knew that just over the rise in front of us were the ruins of Jezria, but I had no desire to chance bringing any disheartening news to an already tired lot. That would have to wait until morning.

After things had settled down and people were retiring for the night, Thomas came to my tent with Martha. They took a seat on the ground next to me, and then Martha began to cry. "What are we to do in Jezria?" Thomas asked.

"And where have they taken our little Susan?" Martha cried. "Surely you know. You've spent time among their kind."

I was silent for a moment, trying to hold back the tears. "I imagine they have taken her to their city, Litovia. I've been there. Maybe Delvarus can take us to see her grave." These words seemed to add hope to Martha's eyes, and Thomas appeared in a better mood about the matter as well. "As far as Jezria's concerned," I continued. "We'll live there in peace. That's what we will do."

Later that night, while everyone else was sleeping, I walked out of my tent and stood by the coursing stream that offered the only noise of the night. I looked at the water as it rippled under a moonlit sky, its consistent movement hypnotizing me as I lingered. I then peered into the sky overhead, and I pondered on the things that I had learned from the Justiton. I wondered what sort of stars might fill the sky over my true home.

When my sight came back to the ground, I was surprised by the outline of a rider on a horse. It was a woman, obviously Justiton by the nature of her apparel. However, the one difference was the veil which she wore over her face to conceal her identity. "Sovia?" I called. I stepped forward until both my feet landed in the water, forgetting for a brief moment about the stream that lay between us. My movement caused her horse to whirl about in a nervous tension, and Sovia seemed obliged to accommodate its mood. "Wait," I said, stretching out my hand as if I could hold her in her place. "Are you here to tell me something?" Suddenly, she nudged her horse in the side and spun around, disappearing into the night.

Her departure was sudden and peculiar, and left me wondering why she might have appeared in the first place. Josesh had said that they would be watching us very closely, but I had no idea that he would be sending his wife to do it. It was late and dark, and I didn't know the area that well. Prudence won over my mind, and as much as I longed to learn more of her mysterious appearance, I realized that it would be foolish to go after her.

As I walked back to the camp, I dwelt on the strangeness of our meeting. By the time I reached my tent, however, fatigue and soreness returned to the forefront of my mind, and I thought about Jezria and all that lay ahead of my friends and me. Tomorrow will be a day to tests the resolve of those who, for now, lay sleeping, peacefully unaware of the great work that awaited them.

"You alright, John?" Thomas asked the next morning as I sat staring at the camp fire. "You look as though you're mulling something over in your mind."

"I have a lot to think about," I said.

"How much farther to this Jezria?" he returned while raising a drink of water to his mouth.

I looked around us. No one else was very close. "Just over that rise," I said, pointing in the distance.

Thomas set his cup down, looked behind him where I had gestured, and returned a surprised look. "Why have we camped so close? We could have gone the remaining distance in less than an hour."

I rose to my feet and waved for Thomas to follow me. "Come with me," I beckoned. By the time we had walked outside of the camp, I stopped and stared in the direction of Jezria before turning back to speak to Thomas. "I know that Delvarus is right," I said. "We had to come here for safety's sake, but I'm about to tell you what no one else in this camp knows, besides me and my brother."

Thomas looked at me intently. "What is it, John?"

"Jezria was destroyed."

"Destroyed?" He answered in surprise. "By who?"

"By the hill-dwellers. It happened a long time ago. Those who used to live there attempted to wage war against the Justiton, just like Henry is planning to do."

"Then why are we here?" Thomas exclaimed.

"We're here to rebuild Jezria. But I'm worried about what everyone else will say when I have to tell them."

"It's not going to go over easy," Thomas concurred. He sighed deeply and wiped at his eyes. "We've lost so much, and to what end?"

"Well, Thomas, I can answer that in part now."

"How's that?" he asked.

"I mean, I know where we came from," I answered.

He turned his full attention my way. "How do you know?" he asked.

"Because, the hill-dwellers know all about us. They know why we're here."

"So what is it they told you?" he questioned with great interest.

"Thomas," I said. "We're not just strangers to this country; we're strangers to this world."

"John, what are you talking about? Let me check that cut on your head again."

"I'm serious, Thomas. If you had seen what I have seen, it might not seem so crazy."

"I never said it was crazy," he replied. "But talk of another world? You mean to tell me that we came from some place out among the stars?"

After he said this, I heard footsteps drawing close behind me. "Perhaps he needs answers step by step, just like you, John." When I turned around, Delvarus stood behind me. "Everything he's telling you is true, Thomas. But it might take a bit to sink in. When we get to Jezria, you will be able to hear about it all, just as John did."

"He will?" I asked.

"Not every building in Jezria was destroyed completely," Delvarus said.

I looked at Thomas to ensure he was paying attention as closely as I was, and then I turned back to Delvarus again. "Go on."

"Why don't I show you?" he answered.

"Are we leaving now?" Thomas asked with an inquisitive look written on his face.

"You are," Delvarus said, "and Ernest, and Simon. You need to bring back word to support what John will be telling everyone else when the whole camp is taken there."

"Simon?" Thomas questioned. "But is he up for the trip,

just to turn around and go back again? I think we need to make it as easy on him as possible."

"Our father insists that Simon be one of the first."

"And who is your father?" Thomas inquired.

"You'll know soon enough," Delvarus said. "Here, I've been saving this for the right time." He pulled from his coat an old weathered bottle. "Give this to Simon. It was the first he ever threw in. Tell him it's time that his questions are answered."

Chapter 23

"What do you mean your brother found my bottle?" Simon asked as I woke him from an uncomfortable sleep.

I held it up for him to see and watched as his eyes opened wide with surprise. "He told me it was your first attempt and that he's been waiting for the right time to give it back to you," I said.

He reached out his bruised and mangled hands and grabbed hold of the neck, carefully taking the cork from the top and emptying the small weathered parchment into his lap. Thomas and I watched while he read over it, as if to ensure that it was indeed his own. "Your brother has the answers?" he asked.

"He does," I replied. "And he's taking us to Jezria to show them to us."

A short time later, Thomas and Ernest helped load Simon into the carriage with as much care as they could manage. Though it was apparent that Simon was in a great deal of pain, he offered no word of complaint, as if the cost for knowing what he so longed to know was worth the discomfort.

The four of us followed Delvarus around the distant rise on the same road I had seen from the flying machine. I sat in the back of the carriage to assist Simon in any way I could.

Even though we had lined the bed with as much padding as we had, the jostling from the road made him cringe in pain time and again. I dabbed at his head with a wet cloth, hoping somehow it would help, and offered my hand for him to grasp for any amount of comfort it could render.

Eventually, we came to a stop within the dilapidated walls of Jezria, and it was not a moment too soon. Simon was sweating profusely from the pain, and all the while, I could do nothing but watch as he struggled to maintain composure. "I'm so sorry, Friend."

"Don't worry about me," he choked. "You've had more than your fair share to deal with."

"Things are going to get better from here, I promise."

Delvarus dismounted his horse a short distance from us, while Thomas and Ernest jumped from the carriage and helped Simon onto his only good leg. As they held both his arms around their necks, the three of them walked slowly toward Delvarus.

The road on which he stood extended beyond our view into a dense line of foliage. As we passed into the clearing on the other side, our sight was directed to a round building at which the road ended. "What is this place," I asked.

"A good place to instruct," Delvarus said.

Just then a loud commotion came through the trees and brush behind us. As we all turned around, we saw the emergence of a large four wheeled contraption much like the cars and other vehicles I had seen in Litovia. This one, however, sat much higher from the ground, and the black encasement that surrounded its wheels looked as though it could crush anything in its path. "What in the world?" I heard Simon mutter under his breath as Thomas and Ernest stood speechless. All three remained motionless with astonishment written on their faces.

The thing came to stop within several feet of us, and once

it did, I immediately recognized the man operating it. "We got your message Delvarus, sorry we weren't here any sooner," Karesh said. Two others came out of the vehicle, and all three of them approached us. "I wish I'd had the right equipment with me when I first saw him," Karesh added. He stepped up to Simon's side and appeared to be examining his physical condition. "We have the essentials, but we may need to take him back to Litovia."

"That will be fine, but I will need to talk to him before you go," Delvarus responded.

"Take me where?" Simon said.

"To a place where you can be treated for your injuries." Delvarus said.

"I thought we were going to some place called Jezria," Simon questioned.

"I'm afraid you just saw what's left of it," I chimed in.

"Litovia is the city of the hill-dwellers," Delvarus concluded.

"Right, I will need to take an initial look at the damage before we go there anyway," Karesh added. "And it looks as though you will need some attention as well, John." Soon after saying this, his assistants assembled a long table of sorts on which they laid Simon. Karesh spent a great deal of attention on his leg, inspecting the swelling that engulfed the whole right side. He pushed at a few places and bent his leg at the knee as if to assess the movement. Both occasions made Simon scream in pain. Nonetheless, he seemed to understand that Karesh was attempting to help and was very patient through the whole ordeal.

After injecting some liquid into Simon's arm through a small needle and administering a strange smelling substance to his cuts and bruises, Karesh looked at his leg with a peculiar apparatus that displayed a black and white outline on a screen. Following this, he wrapped his leg in a strange material that rendered it totally immobile. "I don´t know that we will need to take him to Litovia, actually," Karesh concluded. "His leg is broken, and he will need to stay off of it for a while, but it should all heal on its own from here."

"That´s good news," Delvarus said.

"Now let´s have a look at you," Karesh added as he approached me. He gave me the same attention as Simon, with the use of his portable table, but since I had no broken bones, the worst of it was when he dressed my back in some liquid that caused it to burn. "Don´t worry," he said. "The pain means that it´s cleaning the cuts." I gripped the table and endured the remainder of it in silent anguish.

When it was finally over, I rolled slowly off the table and onto my feet. "Thank you," I said.

Karesh nodded but said nothing. He then went to the vehicle and came back with a pair of crutches for Simon. "These will help you get around until you can walk again. As for you, John, I wish I could give you something more to help with your back. They tore you up quite badly, I´m afraid." After this, he turned to Delvarus. "In which case, what are we going to do about Henry?"

"I will need some equipment first. But I´m leaving tonight to look for him," Delvarus said. "I have my suspicions that he and his army are hiding out in the hills north of Caprecia, just like we thought. "Once I find him, I will be assessing his intentions."

"Very well," Karesh said. "We will wait to hear back from you." He and the others walked back to their vehicle, and before getting in, Karesh offered a wave. I waved back and wondered if I was going to see him again anytime soon.

"I don´t understand," I said as I turned to Delvarus. "I thought Henry made his intentions pretty loud and clear. Why not stop him before he has a chance to do any more damage?"

"We're working to get him to change his ways before it's

forever too late."

"Do you really think he's going to change?" I asked.

"We have to try."

"I'm done trying. The man is a vile wretch!" I exclaimed.

"Yes, but that wretch is our brother," Delvarus returned. "He doesn't know that, but now you do."

His response left me speechless for a moment, and I tried to come to grips with the fact that the man I loathed the most was a brother. "How can...? Our brother you say?"

"That's right. Henry used to be quite good. He was very supportive of our father's plans to send us here, but then he turned once he came here. You see, John, that's part of the reason we were sent, to allow our true selves to take form."

Thomas, Ernest, and Simon had been intently listening up to this point. "How can Henry be John's brother?" Simon asked Delvarus. "He's old enough to be a father to both of you."

"Yes, at least he is here," Delvarus said.

"What? I don't understand what you mean," Simon replied.

"Let me show you."

We followed him into the circular building, and I immediately saw some very familiar illustrations on the decaying ceiling overhead. Paintings of the same solar system I had seen in the chart room at Litovia remained faded but still intact above us. But there was no imaging table in the middle of this place. Instead, there sat a large sculpture of the three concentric circles that Josesh had shown to me on the imaging screen in Litovia.

Around these circles lay an old stone floor. And the walls looked, at one point, to have been painted with a deep rich blue. In every way, it looked very much like the room in which Josesh, Sovia, and Karesh had instructed me, the primitive nature of the place being its only real difference.

The one which was designated to represent the realm of origin looked to be made of silver, another appeared to be made of gold, and the third took on the lesser luster of bronze.

"What is this place?" Thomas asked.

"This is a place that was used to instruct the colonists who lived here long before you," Delvarus answered. "All that I am about to tell you used to be known to those who lived here. And this room was built as a reminder to the colonists, a reminder of their origin and purpose."

"Origin?" Ernest asked.

"That's right. This was the very thing that John was sent to learn from the hill-dwellers."

"John, you know what he's talking about?" Thomas asked.

"Yes, I do."

"Perhaps you should explain it to them," Delvarus offered. "Tell them what you remember, and tell them about everything you don't."

I walked to the center of the room and touched the cold metal rings. I turned to look back and saw Thomas, Ernest, and Simon staring at me with faces of intrigue. "We're not from here," I told them.

"Well, I think we know that," Ernest chuckled.

"No. We're not from this world."

The three of them were quiet for a moment. "This world?" Ernest inquired.

"Yes, the hill-dwellers, or the Justiton is what they're actually called, they told me that this image represents the system of stars and planets in which we live." I pointed to the ceiling overhead and watched as the others looked above them. "The Justition know a lot about many things, but the greatest discovery they made was what these circles represent," I said, resting my hand on the bronze portion of the structure.

"What is it?" Simon asked.

"It is an example of the idea that there are worlds beyond

this one, worlds that exist in an entirely different system of stars and planets."

"I don't know that I follow you," Simon said as he grew weary from standing on his crutches.

Delvarus picked up an old chair that sat toppled in the far corner and dusted it off. He walked over to Simon and set it behind him. "What he means is that there are entire systems of stars and planets that exist outside of this universe."

"Well, I don't know much about stars and planets," Simon said while taking a seat. "But are you proposing that we came from some distant planet far away from here? Seems an awfully strange idea."

"Distant isn't the word for it, really." Delvarus went on. "Tell them what the circles are showing, John. Do you remember?"

"Yes," I said. "The circles mean to show that the other realms, as they called them, are all within the same space."

"Same space?" Thomas questioned.

"They're around us, but we can't see them or interact with them, because...well, it's something to do with—"

"Their nature," Delvarus interrupted. He walked over to my side and pointed at the large golden ring. "This is the place we call home. We, all of us, come from a realm beyond this one. One whose laws are higher than here, and one composed of a substance different from this world. That's why its presence isn't visible to us. However, our father found a way to move between them."

"Wait, you mean we come from the same place as you?" Ernest asked.

"That's right," Delvarus confirmed. "In fact, we are all brothers. That's why I brought you here with me, to explain all this to you. Our father had you in mind when he told me his plans. He said that you would be teachers."

We all looked at each other and pondered on what he said.

The idea was as new as me as to any of them. "How old is father if Thomas and Ernest are his sons?" I asked. "I don't mean to say that you're ancient or anything," I hastened to add, "but how?"

"Remember what the Justiton told you, John, and what I've just reiterated. The world we come from and everything that surrounds it, well, they aren't the same as things are here."

"How are they different?" I asked.

"Here, things have a way of falling apart. Matter decays and returns to a disorganized state. Chaos is the nature of this place. However, the laws that govern our home are quite the opposite. Order is nature, and life moves forward unobstructed by the forces that end it here."

"You mean there's no death?" Thomas asked.

"Correct," Delvarus returned.

"So how old is father then?" I asked again.

"Older than you can probably guess right now."

"So, what of the others?" Thomas asked. "Where do they come from?"

"Every single colonist, and that accounts for anyone who is not living in Litovia, all that aren't Justiton in other words, come from the same place, or else they are the son or daughter of someone who came from our world. All the colonists here are the children of the council."

"But that's thousands of people," I said. "How could a small council of mothers and fathers have so many children?"

"You're still thinking in terms of this realm, John. Besides, there's nothing small about the council."

"What is this council?" Ernest asked.

"Those individuals our father took back with him from this world. And all others like yourselves."

"Wait, our father has been here?" Simon inquired.

"Yes, a very, very long time ago."

"Wait a minute, what do you mean—others like us?" I asked.

"The answer to that question is the thing you should always remember. The reason Father and his friends have sent their children here is to prove them worthy of the council. You are working now to become council members yourselves."

"But why is it that we remember none of this?" Simon asked.

"Your lack of memory is due to the effect of coming here, moving from one realm to another. And father and his friends have used this to your advantage. It's all part of their plan. You're here as part of a test, one which father and the council began a long time ago. You see, there is an element in everyone that they wish to bring to light, one that must be isolated from other matters of influence in order to be truly assessed."

"What element?" Ernest asked.

"The element of self."

"I don't understand," Ernest returned, and he wasn't the only one. I could tell from the looks on Simon and Thomas's faces that they, too, were uncertain as to what it meant. As was I.

"Though you cannot recall who you are and what you have learned, for now," Delvarus continued, "the wisdom you acquired before coming here remains deeply rooted within your personality. Your memory is only half of what determines your identity. Thus far, you have been able to discern between what you can think and what you can feel, between what lies present in front of you and what lies beyond it. This is what you have been sent here to learn."

"It must be nice to have a memory of home," I said.

"What do you mean?" Delvarus asked.

"I mean you. I'm glad you are able to teach us all this, but will we ever be able to go back home and see everything that we left?"

"Yes, the whole idea is that you go back home better and stronger than when you left."

"And when does that happen?" I asked.

"Do you remember how the Justiton told you that Father found a way back without losing memory? Or did they tell you?"

"Yes, they told me," I replied. "But they didn't tell me what it was."

"Well, the way to get home is not an easy one," Delvarus continued. "But it is worth it."

"What is it?" Thomas interjected.

"Death," Delvarus returned. "And by the way, John, I don't remember our home either."

Chapter 24

I wasn't sure what question to ask first. I had been presented with two facts I could never have expected. I had assumed up to this point that Delvarus had been going between our worlds, due to all that he knew and his close association with the Justiton. It hadn't once crossed my mind that he was like us. "I don't get it. You mean to tell me you're a colonist too?"

"Yes, I am."

"Then how do you know so much?" I questioned.

"I've spoken with our father. But in many ways I know what I do through the same means you know about Janaea."

"From dreams?" I asked.

"Tell me this," Delvarus said. "Did you notice that the more attention you gave to the dreams, the more often she appeared in your thoughts?"

I thought back on my recollections of her and began to grasp what he meant. "I see." The others looked on with confused expressions, but Thomas appeared deep in thought.

"The more attention given to matters before coming here, the more likely they are to come back to you eventually," Delvarus continued.

"So the dreams I put in the book, they're real?" Thomas asked, turning to look at me.

"Yes, they are." I said.

"This isn't the strange building I saw, is it?" He asked.

"No, that building is somewhere else," I answered. "The island is no rumor. It actually exists, and that..." I almost forgot that I could say nothing about what I had seen there. I turned to Delvarus to beg his pardon, but he finished what I was about to say.

"The building you saw, Thomas, was likely the building through which we all got here," Delvarus said. "And the same through which we will return."

"But, what is this matter of death?" Simon asked. "How can dying be anything good, and how would some building play into it? It doesn't make any sense."

"It will shortly," Delvarus replied. "It's time you know all about it." He walked to the circles and turned to look at us, placing his hand on the silver one as he did. "The mind of all living things—you could say the essence of what makes you what you are, is something with no beginning or end. It exists within its own realm, a universe of light and energy. We call this the realm of origin, because it is from here that connections with worlds such as this one are made. However, when death occurs, the mind's connection with this place is broken, and your consciousness remains alone in the place it has always been. Without the limitations this world imposes, you will remember everything, all that you have always been and all that you ever knew."

"Everything?" I asked. "You mean all about our home?"

"That's right. But there's more. Father theorized that these connections could be remade, if the dormant frame was returned to a place where nature was order and organization law. And he found out that he was right."

"I'm afraid I don't follow you," Thomas said.

"What it means," Delvarus continued, "is that life can be reformed. That's the reason for the law that our father gave to the Justiton regarding the dead. That's why Susan was taken from you."

"What are you getting at?" Simon questioned.

"Rest assured," Delvarus said. "Susan is alive and well. She's in a place where death doesn't even exist."

"You mean she's in our home?" Thomas asked.

"That's right, and you'll see her when you go back." I looked at Thomas and saw tears welling in his eyes. A slight smile came to his face, and his expression was enough to carry the same joy to all our countenances. "That is why the Justiton gather the dead," Delvarus went on. "They take the bodies back to the island to send them home, where the connection with their minds is renewed."

What once seemed so mysterious about our place in the colony now appeared so systematic and grand. However, the reason behind sending us here still remained somewhat vague. "Then why is it that we came here in the first place?" I asked.

"I've told you already," Delvarus answered, "remember? We were sent here to learn."

"Learn what, exactly?" Ernest chimed in.

"All that you have, and then some." Delvarus answered. "Now, remember everything I have told you, because you will be delivering the news to the others."

"Why not you?" I asked. "You know so much more."

"I have to be going now. There are other matters I need to attend to."

"With Henry?" Thomas asked.

"Yes, I'm afraid so."

When we stepped out of the building, the sun was brighter and warmer than it was when we first entered. The clouds that once obstructed the morning light had dispersed and created a day as perfect as any. As we walked toward the road that would take us back to camp, I pondered on the one matter that didn't seem to add up.

"If you remember what you know from dreams, then how do you know so much about what happened between me and Janaea?" I asked Delvarus.

"I don't, I only know what Father told me to tell you."

"You mean he was the one that said I needed to move on?"

"Indeed."

"But when did you speak to him?"

"When I was in the city of the Justiton," he answered.

Delvarus gave each of us a brotherly hug before departing. "Show all the others the hope you have in better things," he said. "I will see you again, but I have my suspicions that it won't be for a while." As he spoke, his voice was somber, in a way that I hadn't heard it before.

"What do you mean your suspicions?" I asked.

"Don't worry about it," he answered with his voice back to its stoic tone. "Karesh has been placed to watch over Jezria in my absence, so you will answer to him until we see one another again." After this, he mounted his horse and gave one final look toward us all. "Rebuild this city to its former glory. You have all that you need around you." With these final words, he turned to leave and soon disappeared into the forest beyond us.

"What do you think he means?" Simon asked as he limped to my side on his crutches. "About not seeing him for a while?"

"I don't know."

Our trip back to camp was one of heightened spirits. We spoke about what Delvarus had taught us, and I said more of what I had been told by Josesh about our father. Simon inquired with great interest about Litovia and the island. I recounted my stay in both places to him, Thomas, and Ernest and spoke about the peculiar things I had seen.

By the time we arrived back among the others, there was a buzz and excitement in the air. The first sight we came to was that of families attending to tasks of clean up and packing, as if they were in a hurry to be going. Martha approached us quickly when she saw us riding toward her tent. "Everyone's been asking where you've been," she said, "so I told them. Now the whole camp is in a bit of a frenzy to be getting to Jezria."

"That's good," I replied. "But we have news to share with everyone before we leave."

"News? What news?" she asked.

"The best kind there is," Thomas said. "Susan's alive, Martha!"

She offered a confused look as he jumped from the carriage to embrace her. "What are you talking about?"

"Here, come sit down and we'll explain it all to you," I offered. As we took a seat outside the tent, many others who had seen us arrive began to gather around. Eventually, the group consisted of the whole camp and was too large for all to hear us.

We decided then to divide the host of people into four smaller groups, so that Simon could speak to some while Ernest spoke to others. Thomas explained all that we had learned to Martha and those that surrounded her, and I proceeded to inform those remaining beyond the sound of his voice.

Without the same visualization that my brothers and I had, I found it somewhat of a challenge to relate the more intricate details to my audience. But I promised that the building we had visited would be shown to everyone and the story of our place in the colony would be made clear. "But what do you mean Jezria is in ruins?" I heard someone murmur when I told the crowd the nature of our situation.

"We have to rebuild?" others asked.

"Yes, we will," I said. "But it is a small thing to ask in order to be free from tyranny."

"I'm not so sure you're right," a certain man said. "Perhaps we would have been better off taking our chances with Henry.

We've left behind livelihoods that took years to build, and just to come out here to camp in a strange wilderness? Besides, who are you to tell us what's best? Ernest is a man I can trust, but I don't even know you." After he said this, the same small number that had raised concern gave ear to his words and support to his viewpoint.

"Please, remember the reason we're here," I implored.
"My brother said—"
"You mean the man with dreams?" a voice echoed from the bunch as another man voiced his discontent. "We're staking everything on such a story as you've told us? You may be willing to risk your all for some good idea, but how can we be so sure that it's even true?"

I was surprised, to say the least. I hadn't accounted for any opposition to the idea that I had so fully embraced. There were many others who remained firm in their hopes that I was right, but now there was a small number that didn't think I had an ounce of sound reasoning.

"Really?" a woman spoke. "Haven't you questioned how we all got here, where it was we came from? John has answered that question for us, and it makes sense to me."

"I know it's true," I added. "If you had seen what I have seen, perhaps—"

"Have you seen this other side?" the first man interrupted. "Have you? I'm against Henry as much as anyone; that's why I signed with Ernest's petition. But all this talk of things that can't be proven! There needs to be some evidence."

"Perhaps you'd like to ask Ernest about it," I answered. "He's over there saying all the same things I've been saying to you."

The man was silent for the moments that followed. "Even still," he finally said. "I say we march against Henry and reclaim our lands." A bit of an uproar came from his group of followers after he said this.

"His armies are too big for us," I said. "And besides, this is meant to be our land. That's why we were shown here."

"It all sounds grand and good," the leading man said. "But I just can't believe it." Others expressed the same sentiment after this, and all the groups were eventually joined into one due to the commotion of my own. Though Thomas, Ernest, Simon, and I all tried to convince them to stay and go with us to Jezria, we lost a small number of our friends to skepticism that day.

When the remainder of us arrived amid the ruins, we made camp again and gathered the necessary provisions. Despite the somber mood that the opposition had caused, we all soon returned to the high hopes we had for the place. That evening, everyone came to the building my brothers and I had been instructed in and saw the faded paintings on the ceiling and the sculpture of the three metal rings in the center of the room. Many received a greater understanding of the matters we had related to them after seeing the place where those before us had learned.

Later that night, after everyone else had grown subdued and quiet, I ventured on a walk through the surrounding area. As I moved away from the sleeping camp, the only sound that I heard was the soft trickle of the river and the beginnings of the cricket's evening chorus.

The beauty that surrounded us in our journey to this place continued throughout the entire valley. Trees and shrubbery dotted the open canyons in a quaint but arbitrary fashion, leaving spots of open glen exposed to the full gleam of the moonlight. With a fresh perspective on matters, I was all the more grateful for the gift of the moment. I couldn't recall ever seeing a scene so serene, and I was left to relish in the perfect peace that the moment had conjured.

I walked toward the sound of running water, allowing the river's melody to draw me nearer. As I came through the

CHAPTER 24 | 197

trees and into the small clearing that the banks of the river had formed, I looked upon its crystal current moving westward toward the wilderness we had traversed. While I stood thinking over the events of the day, my eyes caught sight of something I didn't expect to see so soon again. There she was, Sovia and her horse, only a stone's cast from me on the opposite bank.

Chapter 25

She looked to be stooping by the water to get a drink, and with her veil wrapped behind her neck, I got a brief glimpse of the left side of her face. Though the distance was too great for me to make out any considerable detail, there was one thing of which I became certain. It wasn't Sovia after all.

Her face looked different than any I had seen, and at my distance, it appeared as though all her features were blended into a mass of flesh. I stepped closer, wondering if the moon's light was playing tricks on my eyes. When she heard my feet crunch on the rocks of the banks, however, she turned from my approach so quickly that I could scarcely see the same blur of flesh before it was immediately covered by her veil.

She mounted her horse before I could even make out what I should say, and the deep interest I had in finding out who she was moved me to action. I ran back the short distance to camp and quickly unloosed Claudia from the tree I had tied her to earlier. I swung myself over her bare back and spurred her toward the river. When we arrived, the woman had vanished, but I took Claudia across the shallow water in pursuit.

We cautiously made our way through the large and dark forest of trees, and I began to wonder whether a chase was a wise thing to start at such an hour. Riding without a saddle was something I wasn't accustomed to, and there were moments

I almost fell off completely. Claudia maintained a steady trot at my insistence, and by the time we made it to an opening in the foliage, we had gone a good distance into the woods past the river.

Then I saw something that caused me to pull the reins and stop us in our tracks. In the distant line of trees, barely visible amid the deeper darkness that the forest provided, was a small cabin. Adjacent to it, and equally hidden by the shadows, was a fenced area large enough to contain the horse that stood as still as the night within its enclosure. Discovering that this mysterious woman was our neighbor made me all the more interested to learn more about her.

I carefully drew closer and noticed a faint light coming from within the home, but reason stopped me from going any farther. The woman had run from me in fear or trepidation, and knocking on her door in the dead of night to assure her that I only had intentions to introduce myself and our people would seem odd.

Aside from this more obvious reason, I didn't know whether she lived alone in the home or if she had a husband, which in turn would make an approach seem all the more strange. Instead, I decided to take note of the location. I would return tomorrow with others to offer our friendship and learn more of her then.

The journey back to Jezria was accomplished by attempts to glean some understanding of my surroundings in the dark, ultimately hoping that I hadn't gotten myself lost in a frenzy of intrigue. The time it took to get back to camp was also coupled with a great deal of thought as to who this woman was and why she lived in seclusion. Up to this point, I had operated under the assumption that there were none in these hills but the Justiton, and though she looked just like one, the fact that she lived outside the walls of Litovia seemed peculiar.

Then it occurred to me. Perhaps she was once a Justiton,

but no longer. I remembered what Josesh had said about my father appearing among their outcasts and reasoned that this woman could be one of those the Justiton had shunned. She must be a vagabond, now living a lone and secluded life away from everyone else. My heart went out to her. If my father had taken to calling such his closest friends, I would do nothing less. I would invite her to our new home and make her welcome to live among us.

When considering my sudden and speedy departure from the ruins, I half expected to find a small group of concerned friends awaiting my return. However, I was pleasantly surprised to find that my flight had left the camp as undisturbed and peaceful as before. I was tired by the time I laid my head down on the ground beneath my tent, and it didn't take more than a moment to fall into a peaceful sleep.

I was awoken the next morning by Thomas shaking my shoulder. "John. John. Wake up. There's someone here to see you," he said.

"Who is it?" I asked as I slowly sat up, still half dazed.

"He said his name is Karesh. It's the same man that helped you and Simon."

I rolled off my covers and stood on my feet as quickly as I could. "Where is he?"

"Just outside."

When I walked out of my tent, I saw Karesh standing with Martha conversing about something. "Good morning," I said as I approached. "Delvarus told me that I would see you now and again, but I'm sorry—I didn't expect you so soon."

"No matter," Karesh replied. "I came to make sure you knew where to go for what you needed."

"What we need?"

"Yes, you will need certain resources to rebuild this place. Now gather your things. We have a few places to go."

I attended to his instructions with a sense of urgency. The sooner we could begin rebuilding the city, the better. A short time past before I was swinging my foot over Claudia and looking down at Thomas as he stood near us. "It only makes sense to put you in charge while I´m gone," I said. "In fact, I wish it could remain that way."

"Nonsense, we need your ambition to guide us," Thomas returned. I offered a smile and turned Claudia in the direction that Karesh had already begun to go. As we passed through the waking crowds, I received looks of question, as if all who saw me wondered where I could be going.

Shortly after we left the ruins of Jezria behind us, Karesh offered the first words between us since his earlier instructions. "Jezria was a built in a very ideal location, an ideal location to build a city, that is."

"How so?" I asked.

"Well, that is what I aim to show you, and the reason Delvarus asked me to come here."

I was silent for a moment, contemplating what I was about to say. "I recently learned something of my brother that I don´t understand."

"What do you mean?"

"The fact that he is a colonist like me."

"Why should that seem so confusing?" Karesh returned.

"Well, it seems as though your people view my people as a bit of a menace, and yet you take orders from him. But then he´s one of us."

"We don´t view the colonists as a menace; we merely have seen that trusting them is a liability. But your brother, Delvarus—he´s different."

I knew Delvarus was different, but I didn´t know what Karesh meant by it. "How is he different, aside from the fact that he knows so much?"

"He was the one sent here to fulfill a promise that your

father made to my people," Karesh said.

"What promise?"

"When my people complained to your father about Jezria and the rebellion, he promised that he would send someone here who would do exactly what he once did."

"What my father once did?"

"Yes. He told my people that he had been training someone who had a heart as strong as his own."

"Delvarus?" I questioned.

"Correct."

"But what was it that my father did exactly?"

"He united my people with their outcast. You don't remember us telling you?"

"Yes, I do. But how did he go about it, uniting your people that is?"

"I'm not sure," Karesh answered.

I found this most surprising. "What do you mean, you're not sure?"

"Everything I have told you is what has been passed down to me, either by word of mouth or the written record of my people, but the history was never clear about it. My ancestors didn't bother to mention it. They only said that he accomplished the union by a power greater than all others."

I wondered about what he said and what it could mean, but before I could continue our conversation on the matter, our short travels brought us to the base of the nearby mountain peak under which Jezria once sat. Karesh pointed in front of him, deftly changing the subject. "Here is where you might begin; there is an abundance of ore in these mountains. You can make whatever tools you need with it. I hear there is a talented blacksmith among your group."

"There is."

"Follow me," he returned.

I followed him toward the ravine that breached its way

through the summit above us and the peak to the east. Water flowed at a rapid pace through its opening and formed the river we had seen on our journey into the mountains. "See up there, on the shoulder of the peak?" Karesh asked.

"What?"

"That's granite. Those who built Jezria established a quarry amid these cliffs, and this road will take you there. You'll need pack horses and stone masons. Do you have any among your group?"

"I'm not sure."

"I hope so," he said, turning to follow the river down the hill.

As we traveled farther in our course, entering the lush green valley on the other side of Jezria, the denseness of trees covered the floor like an emerald garment of life. A breeze blew out of the ravine and made the forest seem alive with movement as the scents of grass and all manner of growth swirled in the air. "This valley provides more than enough to build your homes. You will have no shortage of lumber. You have plenty who know how to work timbers; that I know."

After viewing the scene, I followed Karesh back to Jezria along the weaving river bed that flowed toward the western side of the rise on which the ruins sat. The rippling current reminded me of the woman in red. I thought back to the events of last night and the questions that arose in my mind, which had been postponed by the tour Karesh had taken me on. However, Karesh also happened to be the best person to field my pressing questions about the woman. "Are there any others that live in these hills?" I spoke out of the silence that had settled between us.

"Why?" Karesh replied in great interest.

"Because I saw one of your kind. At least, I think she was one of yours."

Karesh pulled his horse to an immediate stop and turned

my direction. "So you've seen her already?"

"I suppose. That is if we're talking about the same person. Who is she?"

Karesh took a deep sigh. "It's fitting you should ask, because that's the other reason I came here."

"What reason?"

"To tell you about her."

"Go on."

"Do you remember the story I told you of the woman and the fire?" Karesh continued.

"Yes, of course."

"Well, they're one in the same."

Chapter 26

"But I thought she was dead."

"I did too, at least at first," Karesh continued. "But I haven't told you the rest of the story."

I brought Claudia to a stop and swung out of the saddle to show Karesh that I had intentions of going no farther until he had related the whole matter to me. "Well, please do. I'm all ears."

He followed with the same action and walked toward a fallen tree he spotted several paces away. He took a seat and stared at the ground for a moment. "You have to understand that what I've done is against the order of my people."

"How's that?"

"I brought her here," he replied. "If my father were to find out, I would be banished."

"Well, I have no intention of telling your father, if it makes any difference."

Karesh folded his arms over his chest and looked at me with a serious face. "I'm glad we're in agreement. I knew we would be."

"So, tell me the rest of the story," I returned eagerly.

His face grew somber again and turned from looking at me to the space in front of him. "When the beams collapsed on her I thought she would have died instantly. That was my initial thought, at least. The others with me that day were paralyzed from the sight. We were mere observers after she ran from me, but when we saw her coming to the door I'm sure we all had hopes that she was going to make it out just fine." Karesh paused for a moment after this and appeared as if he were in a trance. "She didn't though. She wasn't fine."

"How did she get out then?"

Karesh answered my question without even breaking his stare with the near horizon of trees. "It was only a short moment before something came over me," he continued. "It all happened so fast that I was unable to analyze what it was. It was an influence that made me frantic and desperate toward a woman I didn't even know.

"I ran about to find something to quench the flames, but it was several moments before I spotted the well that sat near the house. I pulled on the rope as fast as I could until the bucket came to the surface. Everyone else watched me as if I was a stranger to them, but I didn't care. I rushed to the doorway and threw the water over the beam that was holding her down.

"It was enough for me to push it off of her and pull her body from the fire. When I looked at her charred and bleeding face, I realized I was too late. She was badly burned and not moving the slightest. She was a very pretty girl, but the fire had taken it away from her in an instant. Her face below her right eye was gone, she no longer looked like the same person. Her left side was laying against the ground when I got to her, so it had taken less heat from the flames, but it was still pretty burned as far up as her neck and chin."

"But she wasn't dead?" I questioned.

"The body has within it an inherent way of fighting to live," Karesh answered, "even when the stakes are against it. I suppose she was no exception. But it happened so much later that it surprised me when it did."

"When what happened?"

Karesh looked at me and then back in front of him. "After I pulled her from the fire, we waited for the home to be safe to enter. It took a long time for the flames to die, but once they did, we pulled out the bodies of the others. We quickly covered them, so no onlookers would see how disfigured they had become. I took care to cover the younger woman's body myself. We loaded them on the carriage to take them away.

"When we were taking the bodies toward the shore, the younger girl moved beneath her cover, but only very slightly. If I hadn't been watching at the moment, she wouldn't have warranted any attention. But I saw the black blanket moving over her face. I had the drivers stop the horses immediately to tell them that she was yet alive, but after that we weren't sure what to do."

"What do you mean?"

Karesh sighed deeply again. "We couldn't take her to the island if she was alive, and she couldn't go to Litovia. Ever since the events of the former Jezria, it has been firmly held in our law that no colonist was to know of our technologies or benefit from them. Of course, Delvarus is changing all that. But this is why we operate by the same primitive methods when we are among you. I had the ability to treat her burns but, according to our order, I couldn't. And should I take her back to the colony, who was left to care for her?"

"So the others were dead too then?"

"Yes," he replied. "I imagine they were gone long before we had even arrived."

I watched Karesh stare forward as he related the events of that fateful day. He seemed affected on a human level I hadn't seen in him but once before. He paused in silence for a moment as if he was reliving the worst part of it, and my observation beckoned me to move the conversation along for his sake.

"What did you do," I asked.

"I went against our order," he said. "I brought her into

these hills and hid her in the forest. I nursed her back to health the best I could. I built a small cabin for her to live in and provided a horse for her to get around. I had told the others that I was taking her back to the colony, but I realized that I couldn't leave her there."

"So she's been here ever since," I concluded.

"That's right, and if any of my people find out, she will be banished along with me. You understand, John, our order accommodates no sympathy, only exactness."

"Don't worry," I said. "Her story's safe with me." I felt a great excitement over the news that the woman was still alive, and that I had already met her in some small degree. Where once this same excitement had been extinguished in the very moment it had risen in my heart, it could now be fully realized. I was anxious to speak to her, to tell her how honorable a character she was, to offer any words of reassurance I could.

"Good," he remarked. "I was rather hoping you could help her. You see, I built the home close to the ruins for a reason."

"What reason would that be?" I asked.

"She belongs with you and your people. Tell me you can make her feel welcome."

All this affection toward a stranger was something unbecoming a Justiton, but it made me realize that the Justiton could be persuaded to consider our plight if they were willing to see as this man was seeing. Perhaps if the whole lot of them had witnessed what this woman had done, they would be thinking the same as Karesh. "Karesh, you have a great heart. You're closer to a colonist than you are a Justiton."

"You'll take her in then?"

"Consider it done, and an honor." I answered.

We both mounted our horses and began again toward Jezria. Along the way, our conversation about the woman continued and Karesh offered more valuable information. "You should know that if you try to approach her she's likely to turn away. She's very self-conscious about her scarred face."

"I'm afraid I know from experience," I said.

"You've already encountered her?"

"Yes, I told you I saw her."

"Well, that could have been from a distance," he replied. "At any rate, don't take it too hard. Like I said, she has reason to be quite shy. She merely lacks the courage to approach people again."

"Yes, I suppose you're right."

"Let me talk to her, tell her about you and your group. Then I'll show you where she's been living."

"That sounds like a good idea. But I must confess that I already know where she lives."

Karesh looked at me with a surprised face. "What did you do, follow after her?"

My silence answered his question well enough, but I felt obligated to explain myself. "It was the second time I had seen her. I merely wanted to talk to her."

"So you ran after her?"

"Actually, Claudia did all the running."

"Well, perhaps I will start by telling her of your ambitious nature," Karesh chuckled.

"It would be the perfect place to start," I said with a smile.

We rode on in silence afterward. All the while, I thought about the poor woman with whom fate had dealt so harshly. I wondered how she was coping with so much loss and longed to tell her all about the news that made my place in this strange world so much more sensible and worthwhile. Even though there was great hardship in the unanswered question as to why my father would send me to a place so ravaged by corruption and uncertainty, I nonetheless felt purpose-driven with the knowledge I now had.

The afternoon sun was growing rather warm, and I was beginning to wish I had a fresh drink of water to carry with me the remaining distance back to Jezria. "Are you thirsty?" I asked Karesh as we traveled along the sound of the nearby river.

"I'm alright, but we can stop if you need."

As I walked to the water's edge, the woman was still on my mind. When I stooped to drink from the current, I imagined seeing her again on the opposite bank reaching for a drink as she had the night before. I imagined what I might say to her when I finally met her. I wondered if she knew I had chased after her, or if that fact was a matter known only to myself and Karesh now.

When I approached my horse, I paused before getting on and turned toward Karesh. "You know so much about my father. What do you know of this woman's parents? Did I hear your father say something about a directory when I first came to Litovia? Is there any information in there about such things?"

"Now I know why you haven't been talking this whole time. You've had a lot to think about. I'm glad to see that you have taken such an interest. What motivates your concern?"

"What do you mean?"

"I think you know what I mean," he chuckled. "But to answer your last question, yes, we have such information in our directories."

"Where do you get it all?"

"Where else?" he replied. "Before anyone comes here from your world, your father provides us with all the information we may need about them, including a picture of the individual, so that they can be identifiable to us. Then we file the information in our directories to keep track of all of the colonists."

"So you know who her parents are?"

"Yes, I know who her parents are," he replied.

I swung into my saddle and readied to go. I looked at Karesh, waiting to hear his answer, but he said nothing. Instead, he just looked back at me as if to assess whether I was ready to go again. "So who are her parents?" I asked.

"I was a little surprised when I found out," he returned. "After bringing her to this place, I figured I should know all I could about her, so I looked up her information. I didn't know her name, so I had to search for what I remembered her face to look like, before it was disfigured of course. It took awhile to find her, but eventually, I was able to locate her file in our database." He paused after saying this, long enough for me to wonder if he was going to tell me what had surprised him.

"What did you find that was so astonishing?" I begged.

"I found out who her parents were."

"And?"

"Well, John, her parents are Justiton," he said.

Chapter 27

"Justiton? I thought she was a colonist."

"Oh, she is," Karesh replied.

"I don't get it."

"I didn't at first either, but it makes perfect sense to me now. In fact, it makes me wonder why I didn't consider it before."

"Do tell. I'm afraid I must be lacking in perfect sense right now."

"It's simple," he said. "When your father came here, he did so to unite our two worlds. His hope was to show my people a greater existence. He wanted to continue life, taking it from a world where it ended, to his own, where it didn't. It mentions in our records that he took with him those he called friends, but I never understood who that included."

"I thought you said that his friends came from the outcasts," I offered.

"They did, but I always assumed that was the only place they came from, mostly because they're mentioned so much."

"Are you saying there were those who followed him from Litovia?" I asked.

"Yes, and I never even realized something so simple. Your father's design was to take with him all those who were ready to live the law of his world, or the high law, as he called it. Some of my people must have been ready, so why wouldn't they have gone with him?"

"Well, that makes perfect sense," I said in a jesting tone.

"It does, very much so," Karesh responded, as if he didn't get my joke. "But there's still something I don't quite understand."

"What's that?"

"There is a riddle in our history concerning your father. It says that when he came, he brought with him this high law, one which acted as both a capstone and foundation for all the others."

"What is the high law?" I questioned.

"I don't know. That's the riddle, you see. It only says that those who returned with him were those who had learned to live it. It's been a bit of a mystery to my people ever since."

"Well, if anyone's to figure it out, Karesh, I'll bet it's you."

"I don't know. I've looked through the books time and again, but it still eludes me to this day. At any rate," he continued, "the woman's parents must have been some of those Justiton that figured out what I haven't yet."

"Perhaps we can ask Delvarus," I said. "When will we see him again anyway?"

"I'm not sure. He didn't say."

"Well, when he gets back we'll find out all about it, I'm sure."

The idea behind this riddle was something interesting enough to keep my mind busy for days on end, but my thoughts were very much elsewhere at the moment. The selfless sacrifice of the woman I had seen by the river pulled on my heart in a way I didn't quite expect, and I thought back to the time when Karesh first told of her and how much I now wished I could have been there at the fire that day when she came to consciousness again. I wished I could tell her that she was brave and great and still beautiful. It seemed a little unusual at first to think of a woman whose face had been marred as beautiful, but then I knew I was interested in an essence beyond what eyes could see.

Karesh left shortly after we returned to the ruins. The remainder of the day accounted for more work at the same tasks that occupied our energies previously. The most pressing matter at hand was hunting and gathering the needed resources that would see us through to harvest and the days of labor that would follow. Along with this, we worked at preparing the ground for crops, and with Thomas and others' experience in the area, we made considerable progress in little time.

That night, my body lay still and tired on the ground of my tent, but my mind raced between two trains of thought. The first was the conversation that Karesh and I had earlier in the day about the Justiton and my father, and the second was the woman. I wondered what was to be understood about this high law mentioned in the history of Karesh's people. Why would something of such paramount importance, as it was, be so unclear to an entire people? I thought on this for a time before I concluded that I would wait to ask Delvarus.

Once my mind rested from this, however, I began to imagine what my meeting with the woman would be like. I recalled what Karesh had said of her shyness and hoped to be able to gain her trust early on. I had been advised to wait until morning before venturing to her home, and so I determined that I would make it the first matter of business tomorrow.

I rose with the sun the next morning and saddled Claudia, taking care to remain as quiet as possible. A mist of fog covered the valley floors, but I was afforded an unobstructed view of everything above it as I left the rise on which the ruins stood. Descending into the mist reminded me of the uncertainty that awaited my meeting with the woman in the forest. Would she be eager to receive company, or would she be there at all?

CHAPTER 27

The song of birds and the eventual rays of sun that pierced through the morning clouds helped to keep me in an optimistic mood. Claudia's rhythmic movement was enough to relax my body, and the encouragement I had received from Karesh regarding our meeting served as a sufficient reminder to incite a good deal of confidence in me.

When I finally reached the cabin, I lingered several steps away, running scenarios through my head in hopes to aptly prepare myself for any response. I approached the door with timidity and quietly rapped a few knocks on the wooden panels. I heard a movement of feet and then nothing. A long pause followed before the door creaked open, creating a small crack that the woman peeked through.

For a brief moment, I saw a portion of her face that the shawl failed to cover. It was scarred by a reddened and irritated mask of skin, raised above the remnant flesh of her youth that remained in a small area closer to her nose. "Are you John?" she asked in a raspy whisper.

"Yes, I am. Karesh told me where I could find you."

"So he said."

"Right, and I understand that he's probably told you a little about me," I continued.

She stepped back and opened the door the remainder of the way where she stood in her tall and slender form. Her face was veiled completely now, and her head was covered in the same red shawl. The only part of her exposed to view was her deep piercing eyes and the smooth delicate-looking hands that were marred in spots from the burns.

"Please come in," she whispered. I stepped into the small and humble abode and took a seat in the wooden chair that she offered me. Another sat a short distance across from it where she slowly came to rest, all the while maintaining unbroken eye contact.

"Is it true then?" she asked. "Are you from Caprecia?"

"Yes, well, just beyond it really."

"Forgive me. I didn't know who you were before."

"And you do now?"

"Karesh, he stopped by and told me about you, said I should listen to what you have to say. I didn't mean to seem rude before."

"It's quite alright. I'm glad I finally caught up with you." She sat silently, poised for my next words. She turned in her place as if to look out the window, and I could see the contemplation in her stare. Her eyes were a marvel to behold and stood out amid the cloth that veiled her. "Karesh told me your story," I continued. "I'm so sorry for your loss."

"It was very good of him to do what he has for me, and at such risk, but I'm afraid even Karesh doesn't know all of what's happened to me," she replied, wincing a little afterward.

"Well, I would like to know. If you care to tell me."

She grabbed at her throat and cringed again. "I'm sorry. It pains me to speak most of the time. I'm afraid my voice will never be the same."

Her raspy whisper sounded so sad when considering how she got it, and I felt a sincere pity for her that only added to my increasing respect for her character. "What is your name?"

"Katherine," she answered.

"My name is John. But of course, you already know that."

An awkward silence followed where I forgot entirely what to say. "I wanted to ask you if you would like to come live among my people. We're all colonists, just like you." I finally said.

"Most people aren't so welcoming to a woman behind a mask," she said.

"If the eyes are the window to the soul, then you aren't wearing a mask at all." I remarked. "I can see that you are a beautiful and courageous woman." I found myself a bit astonished after saying this, fearing I had been too bold too early.

"Thank you, but you don't see the rest of my face."

"But if I could it wouldn't change my opinion of you."
"And who's to say the others will be such idealists?"
"They'll consider you just as I have. Trust me."
"How can you be so sure?" She asked.
"I know these people. They're my friends; they're like I am. You're a brave and amazing woman to have done what you did. They will be able to sense that in you just as I have." She sat very still for a moment, working the offer over in her head, hopefully considering it with some real seriousness. "It's what Karesh wants for you," I added.

"I've lived alone for so long now," she said.

"All the more reason to come be with us."

She sat in complete silence again, and as I looked into her eyes, I could see that she was crying.

"Have I said something to upset you?" She shook her head and brought her hand to her face to wipe away the tears.

"I'll need some time to think about it," she concluded.

To be frank, I felt a bit dejected, but I wanted to respect her wishes. "I understand." But really, I couldn't fully understand. I had never been in such a sad situation as hers. "Perhaps I could come back in a few days and we could talk again."

"Yes, that would be fine," she replied through clouded eyes.

I left feeling very unsatisfied with the outcome of my visit. I thought that after being alone for so long that she would be eager to return to the company of others, but then again, I've never known the anguish she must feel at the thought of showing her scarred face, albeit mostly veiled from sight.

When I returned to camp, Thomas, Martha, and Simon were waiting for news about my trip. I had told them of my hopes to visit with the mysterious woman, and when I shared the news regarding her hesitancy to join with us, they seemed as forlorn as I was. Yet Martha appeared to understand something the rest of us couldn't. "Well, I know very well why such a decision would be a difficult one to make," she said.

"Why's that?" I asked.

"It doesn't take vanity or pride for a woman to be concerned about her looks. A modest woman still finds great importance in her appearance. And if she once had beautiful features, as Karesh told you, then she's likely to feel as though she's lost a bit of identity from the whole ordeal."

Martha's words left us in a state of acceptance, and I began to take what she said to heart. "I think you're right."

"Yes, and the only difference is that I know I'm right," Martha returned.

Though there was plenty of work to occupy my time, the next few days passed agonizingly slowly. I kept thinking about Katherine and wondered whether she would be more receptive to my invitation when I returned. I also tried to center my thoughts on her plight. I wanted to understand her reticence in joining with people again, and as I spoke with Martha about the matter, I received valuable insight and advice. Eventually, my wait came to an end. After three days, I swung back into the saddle and took off toward Katherine's small cottage in the woods.

Upon arriving at her door, I drummed three soft raps against it. I waited, but nothing happened. I knocked again and waited, but still there was nothing. I looked over at the corral where her horse stood watching. Surely she was home, but why was she not answering? Then, as I raised my hand to knock a third time, the curtain in the window to my right parted. Following this action, I heard light steps and then the door slowly creaking on its hinges.

"I didn't know when to expect you," she said. "Please come in."

I took the same seat I had a few days ago, and she sat across from me again. For a moment, I wasn't sure what to say, and I sat awkwardly searching for the right words to start a conversation. Then Katherine saved me from my fumbling. "I´ve been thinking a lot about your invitation."

"Listen, I want to apologize for making you cry last time. I don´t know what I said that—"

"It wasn´t anything you said," she replied. "And there is no need to apologize."

"Then what did I do?"

"I lost what friends I had in the fire," she said. "I´ve never felt so lonely as I have here, and then you come along and offer what I´ve longed for, but..."

"But what?"

"How can anything ever be as it was before? No one can look at me and see past the scars on my face."

I wasn´t sure what to say, but I thought about Martha´s advice and spoke the first thing that came to mind. "I can."

"I don´t think you have any idea what it´s like," she returned. She pulled at her veil as if to insure it was in place and then slowly rested her hands back in her lap.

"I would like to. Besides, I know what it´s like to feel alone."

"How could a man with a host of followers know what it´s like to be alone?"

"It wasn´t always that way. There was a time I had no idea where I came from. Have you any idea about that?" I continued with interest.

"I´m an orphan," she said. "An older couple took me in. I´ve never known who my parents were."

"How long ago were you taken in?"

"I don´t remember," she said.

A smile came to my face when I heard this. "What if I told you that I know where you came from?" I said.

Chapter 28

"How can you know that when you have only just met me?"

"I know that you come from the same place I do," I answered.

"And where is that?"

"Well, that's the very thing I wish to show you. Come with me to Jezria, and you will learn everything I know."

She sat for a long time just looking at me and saying nothing. "Why are you being so kind to me?" she finally asked.

"Why wouldn't I?"

"Well, many people are only inclined to offer kindness when they expect something in return."

"I would expect kindness for kindness, nothing more."

"Somehow I believe you," she whispered in her restricted tone.

"So you will come with me then?"

"Karesh did say it would be best for me," she returned while looking out the window again. "And after taking time to think about it, I believe he's right."

"I believe he's right too."

I was happy that she consented to follow me back to Jezria. I assured her that I wouldn't pressure her to stay with us, but that I would be most happy if she did decide to. I was very thankful that she had come. Despite the fact that she said nothing unless I addressed her with a question, I was beginning to enjoy her company and wished all the more that she would decide upon joining our small community.

"What were your parent's names, those who took you in, I mean?"

She looked at me with somber eyes and turned back to peering forward through the trees. "Elizabeth was the woman's name; Matthew was her husband."

"Did they have any children?" I asked, hoping to keep a conversation going.

"No, they told me they were unable to have them, but they treated me like I was their own."

I paused for a moment before asking the next question. "How long ago was it that they died?"

"The fire was a little less than a year ago. But some days make it seem like it was yesterday."

"I can only imagine," I said. "I'm sorry to ask so many questions; you say it hurts to talk?"

"It's alright," she replied. "I've grown a bit used to it, I suppose."

"You know, when I heard your story from Karesh, I never thought I would get to meet the brave woman he spoke so highly of. It's a privilege to be talking to you." She had nothing to say following my comment, but I looked at her as we rode through the forest, and I could see that she appreciated what I said. "You are very brave, you know."

"I'm not so sure about that," she finally replied. "Even still, I didn't end up helping anyone in the end. Now I only bear the scars of my failure."

"Is that how you see them?"

"What else is there to see?"

"I think they're tokens of love and courage," I said. "I see it in no other way." She turned to me with another look of validation, then remained silent for a long time after that.

The woods offered a quiet serenity that eventually helped to conjure another conversation and move it slowly forward. "You say you didn't help anyone. I happen to know you did." Her eyes met mine, but she said nothing at first. "Who?" she asked.

"Karesh."

She almost chuckled at my answer before she managed to speak again. "I think you have the story switched around. Karesh was the one that helped me, remember?"

"Oh, he did alright, but you helped him in a way you don't even know."

She looked confused after this. "How could I have helped Karesh?"

"You helped him see what makes us different from his people," I replied. "What he saw in you, he tried to return by bringing you here and caring for you." She had no reply for this, but seemed to ponder on the idea for a time. "And there's another you've helped as well."

"Another?" she asked. "And who might that be?"

"Me."

It was clear that she wasn't prepared for this answer, and she was speechless for a moment before finally expressing her astonishment in words. "How could I have helped you? Aren't you the one trying to help me?"

"Yes, but meeting you has helped me through a very difficult time," I replied.

"How's that?"

"Perhaps I can tell you all about it someday."

After wading through the forest of trees that sat between Katherine's home and Jezria, I began to recognize our surroundings more readily. The fertile glen that sat just beneath the rise of the city's ruins burst before my eyes with a new light. In the midst of the field was a small multitude of people tilling the ground in preparations for the seed that we had brought with us. Foremost among them, and the one who seemed to be in charge of the matter, was Thomas himself.

"We don't have much now, but we are soon to rebuild a city," I told Katherine as we drew closer.

"You intend to restore the ruins?"

"More or less. Karesh told me that he built your home near this place so that you would meet up with us eventually."

"How did he know you would be coming here?"

"That's part of everything I want to tell you," I replied. As we approached the field I could sense the apprehension building inside of Katherine. "Don't worry, you'll be greeted like an old friend," I promised. She slowly rose from looking at the ground and her gaze turned toward me.

"Are you really that confident in something so uncertain?"

"I am."

"Well, I hope you're right," she said.

I was happy to see that she wasn't opposed to putting a degree of trust in me, and I was beginning to wonder what all Karesh must have told her. The more time I spent in Katherine's presence, the more interested I became in her. As we drew closer to everyone in the field, she carefully followed behind me as if she was hoping to shield herself from any approaching stranger.

Thomas was the first to take notice of our approach, and he stood waiting to greet us. "I don't suppose we expected you back so soon," he said as I jumped to the ground a few steps from him. "And you must be Katherine," he continued, offering her a warm welcome. Thomas, Simon, and Martha all knew where I had gone and had planned to help prepare everyone for a new arrival.

"Yes," she answered softly.

"We've been eager to meet you. It's an honor." (I realized then that if we were going to err on any side of things, it would most likely be on the side of smothering Katherine with hospitality.)

I was delighted with the result of her meeting so many after that. She was treated like she had always belonged with us and was welcomed with open arms. Not a single person was brash enough to ask her about the veil or draw any attention to it, and after my introduction and explanation that she came from Caprecia, there was no reason for any to question her rightful place among us. If she came from Caprecia and had no association with Henry, they knew that she must be a friend, and they took her in accordingly. Katherine appeared, as expected, reserved and reluctant to return much by way of conversation. Still, I felt as if I could sense she was happy to have come.

As we walked down the road that disappeared into the overgrowth of trees and shrubbery, Katherine moved nearer to my side. I looked at her and tried to imagine what was going through her mind, but she offered only small cues of contentment. Over the course of the day, we had begun to grow comfortable around one another, and her closeness was a welcomed guest.

"Where does this road lead?" she asked.

"To answers," I said as I pulled aside two branches in the path before us. We weaved carefully through the overhanging trees that shaded the road with their leaves. I was careful to keep them all as far from Katherine as possible, knowing that if her fragile skin came in contact with any one of them, it would prove far more painful than for someone without the scarring left by fire. When we walked through the final thick of it and stepped into the open glen, she looked at the building with surprise in her eyes. "Who would have known that this was here?" she spoke.

"It is a bit hidden."

"Yes, in all my wanderings through this place I never knew that anything lay beyond this tree line."

"You mean you've been here before?"

"Many times," she replied. "Since being in these hills, I've often wondered what these ruins were all about."

"Well, I'll tell you," I said. "But first, I want to show you what's inside." I stepped forward and opened the door, ushering her through with a wave. The room was lit as dimly as before with only the sunlight that came through the atrium overhead to illuminate it.

After we both stepped into the room, I noticed something that I had failed to on my first visit. The glass dome that allowed the rays of sun to penetrate the room served, not only as a light with which to see, but also as a representation of the light around which the world we stood on orbited. It served as a live and moving center to the amazing tapestry above us.

As I brought my gaze down from this view, what I saw surprised me. Katherine was standing still and quiet with her hand raised to her veiled mouth as if to silence a gasp. She stared at the three metal circles in the center of the room. "Is something the matter?" I asked.

She turned to me and slowly lowered her hand. In her eyes wasn't fear but astonishment and marvel. "I've seen these circles before," she said.

Chapter 29

"Where was it that you saw them?"

"It's going to sound so strange," she answered. "I don't know what to make of it."

"Try me," I offered.

"I've seen them before in my dreams," she replied. "It's all very vague and only every now and then, but it's these same circles, all three of them, just like this."

I smiled at her and began to speak. "I know why you've seen them."

She turned toward me with a surprised look. "You do?"

"Yes, that's why I wanted to bring you here. It all seems so mysterious right now, I know, but it's about to make a lot more sense."

She stepped closer to me and turned all her attention to my face. "Go on. Tell me the mystery."

As I explained to her everything I had learned, both from the Justiton and Delvarus, I was mesmerized by her keen interest. She drank it in as if it were the most delicious nectar she had ever consumed. Her eyes were deeply fixed on me as I spoke, and her attention to my words was such that she followed my comments with questions that prompted further thought and discussion.

"So you and I come from an entirely different world?" she

asked, "a place we can't even see?"

"Yes, you, and I, and everyone else considered a colonist."

She pondered on this clarification for a moment before looking back at me. "It seems so real to hear it from you. And somehow I believe it, but has no one ever questioned the existence of this world?"

"Quite a few have, I'm afraid, but they returned to Caprecia already."

She was quiet again, then moved to the chair Simon had sat in days ago. As she took a seat, she appeared to be deep in thought. "What do you suppose will happen to Caprecia? Now that you've told me what the Pridions did to you and your brother, well, it makes me worry for those who stayed behind."

"I know," I said. "We tried to convince everyone we could to come with us, but we had to be shrewd about it at the same time. We couldn't let word get to Henry about where we were going." I turned to look at her directly. "Ernest, the man you met today, laid a good foundation beforehand though."

"What foundation?"

"Before I even showed up here, Ernest had started a petition of sorts, a list of followers equally united against Henry. They all were entrusted to keep matters between themselves, so that Henry couldn't have the upper hand. Ernest's system was what allowed us to mobilize so quickly."

"I see," she replied, turning her head to the ground only to raise it again a moment later. "Do you think Henry will ever find us?"

"I hope not. I hope he isn't even looking."

Katherine was quiet again. "Do you think Karesh's people will fight for us if it comes to it?"

"I don't know," I said in a somber tone, wondering why she was concerning herself with the idea so much. "If anyone can convince them to do so, it's my brother."

"You mean the one you told me about, Delvar—?"

"Yes, Delvarus," I finished.

"You said he'd left, but where is it he's gone?"

"Back to Caprecia. He's gone back to find out Henry's intentions, try to plot his next move."

"Isn't there danger in returning? Henry and his Pridions, they're ruthless. Of course, you know that better than I do."

"I don't know if Henry even knows who Delvarus is. If that's the case, my brother will have the advantage."

"I hope so," she said.

We talked for a while longer, and when we finally left the round and secluded building to venture back toward the camp, our friendship had passed its stage of infancy. I was already beginning to feel more in tune with Katherine's personality and the story that enable us to meet. Her understanding of everything I told her was both surprising and endearing. She seemed to catch on rather quickly and wonder the same things I had once wondered.

Katherine was happy to stay among us the remainder of the day, but she stayed aloof from most everyone except me. Mary and the rest of the young girls took a keen interest in her presence, and seemed to gravitate around her in some undefined admiration. Between these moments of distraction, I answered questions from Katherine about my earlier days in this place. I told her of all that had brought me here, and I found that with every occasion I was willing to share something about myself, she was willing to do the same.

Time passed quickly with her around, and as the day reached evening, and as the sun began to set over the western hills, Katherine stood staring into my eyes as I told her of Litovia and all that had happened there. She didn't seem as though she wanted to leave or stop talking, nor did I want her to ever have to go back to her lonely home in the woods. I offered my tent to her in hopes that she would stay, but I was uncertain whether she would prefer to sacrifice the greater monetary comforts that she had in the cabin merely for the company of a developing friendship.

"Your tent?" she asked when I proposed the idea. "But where would you stay?"

"Tonight is going to be perfectly clear and not too cool, I think. I can manage a night under the stars."

"No, I wouldn't have you inconvenienced like that."

"It's no inconvenience if it means you'll stay. Unless of course, you'll find it more comfortable in your house."

This comment placed her in an introspective mood that she lingered in for a while without speaking. "I've had a certain comfort here that I've lacked for a long time now," she finally replied. "There's much to be said for having friendly company. I think I might choose it over a bed any day."

"Then you'll stay?"

"Perhaps I can sleep under the stars."

"Of course you won't. No honored guest should have anything but the best that can be offered. I insist." I had grown tired from working with all the other men in clearing the roads and moving some of the larger debris from the fallen structures throughout the day, so I wasn't worried about being able to fall asleep just about anywhere. Katherine offered an expression that was certain to mean she accepted my invitation but was reluctant to voice it. "Then it's settled," I said.

Thomas and Martha offered for me to stay with them in their tent, but I had no intention of crowding them, although I was happy to accept some extra blankets to sleep with. After I settled my things under the thatched roof I constructed with tree branches placed over some of the pillared ruins we had removed from the road, I walked back to my tent to wish Katherine a peaceful night's rest and to ask her if she would like to make a trip back to the cabin to retrieve her things in the morning.

"May I come in?" I asked as I approached the slit in the

overhanging cloth which served as a door. I heard a soft sniffle followed by a choking and almost suppressed 'yes'. As I parted the covering, I saw her sitting on the ground with her legs folded to her side. While drawing closer, I noticed that her eyes welled with tears. "What's the matter?" She turned her head a little and wiped at her face with her sleeve. "Are you unhappy about something?" I begged to know. She sniffled again and turned back to look at me.

"No, it's quite the opposite really."

"So everything's alright?" She nodded her head ever so slightly and took a moment to better compose herself.

"I've never had so many people offer so much kindness to me. It means a lot to someone who has spent nearly a year almost entirely alone."

"Now you don't have to worry about that ever again," I said. I felt compelled to kneel next to her and place my hand on her shoulder. She turned to me and offered a smile that I could see in her eyes. "Good night, Katherine."

As I rose to my feet and turned to leave, I heard her voice calling to me. "John," she spoke in her low and restricted tone, "thank you."

"You're welcome."

"No, I mean thank you for not telling anyone about my face or what happened to it."

"Yes, well, it's not my place to tell."

Her eyes smiled back at me again, and I returned a smile of my own. "Promise me something?" she asked.

"What's that?"

"That you won't ask to see my face."

"You've no reason to worry about it. I only see beauty when I look at you," I dared to say, recoiling with a degree of timidity and thinking that perhaps I was growing a bit sappy in my answers.

"It's worse than you might think." I considered her request

for a moment, and I felt sad for how self-conscious she was of her condition. I had never been in such a situation and could only imagine how difficult it would be if the idea of showing my face caused such concern as she had.

"If that's what you want, then I promise," I said.

Though I might have expected the night to be one of restless hours dispersed amid moments of light sleep, I found that I was far too tired to even stir. Once my head lay back on the padded ground I had created, my eyes slowly shut, and I didn't wake again until the following morning.

The coolness of the air and the beams of sunlight that streaked across the landscape of the mountainous region were what roused my mind from slumber. As I sat up in my bedding, I noticed that a few others had woken already and were tending the fire pits that dotted the grounds of the camp. I looked toward my tent and wondered if Katherine had slept well.

The sun was low in the sky, but it was enough into the day that I felt it would be alright to call from outside and see if she was awake. I rose to my feet and walked toward the door. When I got close enough, I spoke her name softly through the covering and waited for a reply. After a brief moment of no response, I called her name again, this time a little louder, but still there was no answer. Proceeding my third attempt, I was compelled to enter, but when I pulled the covering of the door back, I saw that Katherine was gone.

Chapter 30

When I turned around, I spotted Simon walking with his crutches in my direction. "Have you seen Katherine?" I asked as I approached him.

"You mean this morning? I haven't seen her since last night."

"She's not in the tent," I said.

"Is her horse gone too?"

"I don't know. I'll go check." I ran to the field where we were keeping the horses and looked around to see if I could spot hers. It was the only one of its uniquely-amber color, so it took no more than a few seconds to see that it wasn't there. I then returned to the tent to find Simon waiting to hear the news. "It's gone too."

"Maybe she went back to the house you said she has," Simon suggested.

"Perhaps you're right, but what would have caused her to leave without saying a word to anyone?" Simon simply shrugged his shoulders and said nothing more. "I'm going to go look for her. Let the others know where I've gone, if you would."

"I will."

All the while, as I readied Claudia with her blanket and saddle, I thought about Katherine, hoping that she was alright. I couldn't reason why she would have left, but I was willing to

CHAPTER 30 | 233

assume that she had returned to her home. As I journeyed on the road that wound down the hill on which the ruins stood, I looked around me carefully in case Katherine was anywhere to be seen. It wasn't long before I came within the sound of the river, which now reminded me of the first time I had seen her. When I approached the turn in the road that directed its course toward the western mountains, I left the path to venture through the dense cover that lined the banks.

The presence of two trees, relatively close to one another, made for a larger-than-usual breach in the growth that surrounded the river. I recognized it as the same path Katherine and I had taken back from her home, and I knew that it would be the same course she would have taken to return. So I followed, through the trees and onto the pebble-laden ground on the near side. To my surprise, I immediately saw Katherine's horse.

I brought Claudia to an abrupt halt and jumped from the saddle. She had to be close. As I looked around me, my eyes fell upon a scene that sent an instant surge of panic coursing through my veins. In a thick bed of grassy earth lay her motionless body. I rushed to her side, and as I came closer my heart settled. It was then I saw that she was lying on a blanket with another draped over the lower half of her, as if she had picked this spot to sleep.

"Katherine," I spoke. "Katherine." I placed my hand on her shoulder and gave it a gentle nudge and then a shake.

Her beautiful eyes slowly fluttered open and she stared at me with surprise. "John?"

"What are you doing down here?" I asked.

She slowly sat up and adjusted her veil to make sure it remained in place. "I'm sorry," she returned. "I didn't mean to cause you any concern."

"Don't worry, it's alright now. But why are you here sleeping on the ground?"

"I'm afraid I had a very restless night."

"So you came here?" I asked, a bit surprised.

"Yes, the river and its sounds, they soothe me."

I took a seat next to her. "I see. Were the accommodations that uncomfortable?" I asked after a brief pause.

"No, not at all," she replied, turning to me with a look of worry. "Thank you again very much for offering it to me. "I can't sleep some nights; that's all."

"What is it that keeps you from sleeping?"

She turned from facing me and stared at the river's current. "The fire. I relive it in my dreams so vividly some nights that I'm afraid to even fall asleep."

I didn't know what to say to this, so instead, I did something audacious, but something that seemed so natural at the same time. I reached around her back and pulled her in toward my side, hoping that she would welcome an embrace offered for consolation. I was delighted when she returned the affection by resting her head on my shoulder and curling up closer to my side. "I'm sorry you have such troubles," I whispered.

"Have you ever had dreams that cause you unrest?"

"I used to," I said.

"What about?"

"A lost love."

It seemed as though this answer sparked empathy in her heart and caused her to feel as though I was the one who needed the comfort. She reached her arm around my back and the other around my chest in a full embrace. "A woman from back home?" she inquired.

"Yes. We remained speechless for a while, and for a second time since the anguish I had felt for Janae, my heart seemed as though it was repairable. With Katherine's head perched on my shoulder, I rested my cheek on the shawl that covered it. It seemed as though our actions were communicating the words we didn't speak, and in that moment we grew closer than any conversation could have brought us. It all seemed so fast, to have met as we had and to already be drawing so close. This sort of thing happens to the infant romantic, but surely more mature minds would prevail over such impulses—and yet, it felt so right.

At length we came to stand hand in hand by the riverside. Her cool soft touch was a welcomed guest, and I began to feel the beginnings of a grand affection for a woman I had, up to this point, merely admired. "I've spent many nights near this river," she said as we listened to the melody of its undulating movement. "It's been the one thing that has helped me rest since being here."

"It is a soothing sound," I concurred. "Perhaps a certain kind of friendship will replace your river someday."

She held my hand tightly after I said this, and I sensed assurance that she knew what I meant. "I hope so," she replied.

The following days accounted for vast amounts of work among our group. The preparation for crops, the gathering of fruits, and the dressing of game we had acquired were all attended to by a group of most capable and wonderful people. The men labored on the reconstruction of the roads and the building of homes, along with continual errands to hunt for deer, of which the forest was so abundant. Even with the crops several months out, our people never wanted for food. The excess of timber and granite, when coupled with the skills of our craftsmen, allowed all to eventually possess beautiful houses to call their own. Life quickly became a great joy to all that lived in the new Jezria.

Days turned into weeks and weeks into months, but I had heard no word from Delvarus in all that time. Karesh hadn't visited us since showing the area's surroundings to me, and I began to fear that no news from either could mean that some ill fate had come to my brother. I wished I could return to Caprecia to find where he had gone, but I knew that I would be risking, not only my own life, but many others if Henry were to learn of our whereabouts. For the sake of my friends, it was best to remain in Jezria and let Henry conclude, if he would, that we had disappeared beyond his reach.

"I'm sure he's alright," Katherine said as I sat musing over the matter one day in her home, the one which had been built for her in Jezria." From all that you've told me of him, it sounds as though nothing can stop Delvarus from what he sets his mind to do."

"Maybe you're right. But why has he sent no news of his whereabouts to us?"

"I'm sure there is a good reason," she replied.

I let this suffice and tried to turn my mind to other matters. I rose to my feet and held Katherine's hands in my own. "I find myself in a very difficult situation," I told her.

"What do you mean?"

"I have a deep desire which can't be satisfied without compromising a promise."

"What promise?"

"My promise to you," I answered.

She held her hand up to her veil and stepped back slightly. "My face? But you promised you would never ask to see it."

I held her by the shoulders and pulled her in close again. "And I will keep that promise forever. Don't worry."

"I just want you to see me as you envision my face to look," she continued. "It's hard enough for me to see it, and I don't want you to have any such memory of me."

"I love you, Katherine, and I merely long to kiss you. I've wanted to for a long time now."

She turned her face and rested her head on my chest while hugging me around my waist. "I would love for you to just as much, but there's no need for you to see my face. It's strange to kiss with eyes open anyway, isn't it?"

"Yes, it certainly would be," I chuckled.

"Let me guide you then, and you´ll have no need to look at me until my veil´s in place again."

"I promise."

She turned and stared at me with a smile in her eyes as she had so many times before. "Keep to the left side of my lips," she begged.

"I will." With that, she raised her soft hands over my eyes and closed them. I waited and listened as she removed her veil and placed her hands back on my cheeks. As she pulled me in, I felt my mouth touch her scorched skin. Slowly, I lingered on her cheek as she moved me toward the center of her face. When our lips touched, she pulled me closer, and I was more than obliged to do the same.

After a moment that could have lasted forever and still felt too brief, we parted, and while my eyes remained closed she returned the veil to her face. We looked at each other, and I brought her to me again with a full embrace. "Sometimes I feel like I can't hold you close enough," I said.

"I know the feeling."

Just then, our moment was disrupted by a small commotion, the thundering sound of horses. Katherine and I exchanged a look before leaving the house to see what was going on. When we stepped into the beaming sun of a cloudless day, we immediately saw a group of horses carrying a host of red-cloaked riders. At the lead was a man we knew well, and as we approached him, he swung from his saddle to greet us.

"Karesh, we haven´t seen you for so long," I said.

"Yes, it has been some time hasn´t it?" He turned toward Katherine and offered a smile. "How are you Katherine?"

"I´m very happy here."

"I knew you would be," Karesh said. "Jezria appears to be coming right along. It´s looking very promising, John. I feel proud of you, you know."

"Thank you," I said. "Are you here to stay for a time then?"

"No, I'm afraid I can't. I'm simply here on a matter of certain business."

"What business is that?"

"I bring news of your brother, Delvarus."

Chapter 31

"You've heard word from Delvarus?"

"No, I haven't actually."

"Then how do you have news?" I inquired with a great deal of confusion.

"I said I bring news," Karesh replied, "and the news comes with her." After saying this, he pointed behind him to a woman in a red dress who sat on a horse amid all the other riders. Even from a sitting position, I could tell that she was tall and rather thin. Her face seemed welcoming beyond the general expectation I had of most Justiton, and she had the same pretty complexion as Sovia, only far younger. "This is my sister, Coleena," Karesh added as she dismounted her horse and came to his side. "She came to me yesterday and said she had news to deliver to you, something that Delvarus wanted you to know."

"You know Delvarus?" I asked her.

"Yes," she said. "He's my husband."

"Your husband? I didn't know...well, there's not a whole lot I do know, I suppose."

"Yes, well, we've only been married a short time, less than a year," she said. "But, there is something very important that I was told to tell you."

"What is it?"

She looked around her and hesitated for a moment. "Perhaps such matters are best discussed in private."

"Of course." I turned toward Katherine. She returned a nod and then began walking toward the door.

As we entered Katherine's home, Karesh took a moment to assess the appearance of the furniture we had brought from her old house. He did so as a casual recollection of his own handiwork and seemed delighted to see that she was still using it. Eventually, he took a seat at the table he had built for her. His sister sat next to him and said nothing for a moment, so I took the opportunity to ask the question that seemed most pressing. "Is everything alright?"

She quickly fought back her emotions and began to speak again. "Delvarus wanted me to tell you that his absence would be considerable, but not to worry."

"Where is he?" I questioned.

"Surely he told you before he left," she said. "He's gone to Caprecia."

"He only said that he was leaving to see what Henry planned to do next. But I didn't think it would take so long."

"I'm afraid it will," she answered. "You must know that he hasn't gone merely to assess Henry's plans. He's gone to overthrow them. He's among the people of Caprecia as we speak."

"But how does he plan to do that? He's only one man, and all those against Henry are here in Jezria now."

"I'm not sure," she replied, "but I have to trust that he knows what he's doing. He said that he possessed a power that was far greater than anything that could oppose it, something that could unite your people and mine."

I dwelt upon what she said for a moment. "What is this power he's mentioned to you?"

"I don't know, but he wanted me to tell you that he doesn't want you going back to Caprecia for any reason."

"I can't say that it hasn't crossed my mind," I returned,

"not with hearing nothing from him for so long. I was afraid something had happened."

"Yes, I was afraid you might have thought that," Coleena continued. "I'm sorry it has taken me so long to tell you. It's just that I was hoping things might change, that he might come back sooner than expected."

"When do you think he'll be coming back?" I asked.

Once I said this, Coleena quietly began to cry. Karesh put his arm around her and tried to console her. "Don't worry. He'll be back. He promised." Coleena turned from us and buried her face in her brother's sleeve. Then Katherine said something that turned her attention away from her sorrow. "I imagine it's a hard thing to have a husband away for so long," she said. "How did you and Delvarus first meet?"

Coleena wiped her eyes and regained her composure. She looked surprised at the sudden change in conversation, but she answered the question still the same. "When he came to live among us."

"Live among you? When did he live among you?" I asked.

She looked at me with a degree of bewilderment. "Has he not told you his story?"

"Only a small part," I replied.

Coleena looked over to Karesh and then back at me. "Delvarus told us to tell him his father's story," Karesh said in answer to her critical glare, "not his own."

"Then I will tell it to you," she replied.

Katherine sat as poised and ready to listen as I was while Coleena continued speaking. "When your brother came to our world, my people were waiting for him. Your father told us that Delvarus would be the one to reunite the Justiton and the colonists. We weren't quite sure how he was going to do it, but we trusted that he could, and your parents made plans with mine to accommodate his appearance. My father, Josesh, was instructed to tell a certain couple among the colonists, one that your father had decided upon, to go to the shores on the day of your brother's arrival, just like someone came and found you, no doubt. The couple did as they were instructed, and everything followed according to plan afterward."

"How's that?" I asked.

"Well, your father said that Delvarus would come to realize his origins faster than anyone else, and that, eventually, he would travel to our city to gain further instructions."

"You mean like I did from your parents?"

"Sort of," she replied, "only he didn't learn anything from my parents. They learned from him."

"Then who was he receiving instructions from?"

"Why, your father, of course. He communicated with him in the same way that we have, and he was reminded of all that he was to do here."

"So is that how he knows so much?"

"Partially, yes. And all that he has told you is what your father wanted you to know."

"How long was he in Litovia?" I asked.

"Delvarus was with us for seven months, and during that time I never thought a man such as him would ever take interest in me," she said. "Observing him was as if we were reliving our history books and all the stories of your father. I've never met your father, John, but based on everything I have learned about him, Delvarus is the same. That's why I wasn't sure what to think when he sought after me with considerable interest. He told me that he saw something special in me, something that wasn't common among my people. He told me that I was ready to live the law of his world. I don't know what he meant by it, but we soon fell in love and were married," she concluded.

When she finished, the sadness that had come over her returned, but she tried to hide it as best she could. "Let's get you home," Karesh said. He helped her to her feet and started for the door. "Continue as planned, John. If we hear anything more we'll let you know."

We followed them outside and watched as they mounted and prepared to ride away, but there was some clarification I needed before I was content to let them leave. "Karesh," I called. "What am I to do if I continue as planned?"

"What do you mean?"

"I mean what is the plan from here?"

"Live the law and live in peace," he replied. After this, he said nothing more but took the reins and followed after all the others as they rode down the hill and out of sight.

Time passed and seasons changed until we came to commemorate our first year in the beautiful valley. By now we had developed the beginnings of a quaint township. The roads had been renewed, and homes had been finished for all the families. The crops came in with great surplus, and we held a wonderful feast at the end of harvest.

"For the first time in a long time, I feel rather fortunate," Katherine said.

"You mean, to be here?" I asked.

"And to have met you."

Such words were like a cool drink to a thirsty soul such as mine. "I know what you mean," I returned.

I took her into my arms and held her close. Her essence was something unmatched in its serenity. Everything about the way she managed herself from one day to the next was a treasure to me. From the nature of her walk to the manner in which she interacted with the children, all seemed to convey some greatness untainted by the misfortunes that had come to her. She was a splendor to behold, and an even greater splendor to hold close to my heart as I did now. Every moment I took in drawing nearer to the intricacies of her character was time that couldn't be better spent.

"I love you, John," she whispered in my ear as we stood at the place where I had first seen her. We gazed at the stars overhead and watched as the moonlight rippled over the river.

"And I love you just as much," I answered.

"You know, my scars don't pain me so much when I'm around you."

"What do you mean?"

"I mean, if these scars are what brought me to you then, well, I'll take them." I looked at her with the deepest, most special love I have ever felt. I raised my hand to gently touch her veil. She held it there with her own while I placed a soft kiss on her forehead.

"I'm sorry you have to live with the effects you do," I said. Her eyes smiled back at me.

"But what if I hadn't been caught in the fire and then never met you? That would have been a much greater tragedy, don't you think?"

"Far greater." I pulled her closer and hugged her as tightly as I dare. The right side of her body was very sensitive to touch, having received the greatest effects of the fire. I tried as much as I could from holding her there, but on some occasions I was too reckless and would send a brief spasm of pain coursing through her. I was most careful not to disturb the moment with any negligence on my part this time, and we stood in calm and perfect peace as we held each other as closely as we could.

"I'm so glad you found me," she said.

"I am too," I replied.

The following days brought similar moments, moments overwhelmed with the blissful experience of being in love. Each time I was around Katherine, I felt that fate had somehow played a small role in bringing us together. I looked to her with increased affection the more time we spent together, and eventually, it came to the point that it was too much to keep outside of us. I wanted her to have and to hold as my dearest companion.

The wedding approached as if a dream and passed in a similar manner. Amid the small festivities that our friends provided, I can remember only one thing with any degree of detail—the gleam in the eyes of Katherine as I gazed at her across the altar. Her veil became a tapestry for my imaginations of how beautiful her face had once been. And as I stared into her loving eyes, I started to feel as though I was always meant to be with her.

When we walked that night along the river, she turned to me and kissed my cheek. "The river isn't the same to me anymore," she said.

"Why?"

"It's been replaced."

A smile grew on my face. "I'm glad to be your new river," I said.

"You're more than that. The river used to soothe me, but you give me strength."

"It's no wonder I adore you so much. You, too, gave me strength, and a reason to hope again." I felt greater peace when I was around Katherine. With her, my life was fuller and brighter than I could have expected, but in that night, when everything seemed almost too good to be true, I dared to wonder if such peace could last forever.

Chapter 32

"I think it's finally happened," Katherine said as we woke one morning.

I turned on my side to face her and looked into her bright eyes that were staring at the ceiling over the bed. "What's happened?" I asked.

"The thing we've been trying for now for over a year," she said, moving closer to me.

"You mean...?"

"Yes, I'm sure I must be pregnant. I just know it."

I took her into my arms with a great sense of closeness, and we held each other for as long as reason would allow. "Really?" I continued, pulling away from her long enough to look back into her happy countenance, "but are you sure?"

She nodded her head slowly and quietly. "We're finally going to have a child."

I gently placed my hand on her stomach. "How far along do you think?"

"About six weeks, I would guess."

At that moment, I remembered the nights that Katherine had cried on my shoulder, wondering why she couldn't conceive a child, hoping that her fortune would change. She told me once how she felt that I must have regretted marrying her, now that I knew she wasn't going to be able to bring any children to us. I assured her, vehemently, that I would never regret marrying her, children or not, and that she was the greatest happiness of my life. "She's going to be as beautiful as her mother," I remarked while moving my hand over her stomach again.

"You think we're having a little girl?"

"It's just a hunch. But if I'm right, perhaps we can name her—"

"Susan?" Katherine finished.

"Yeah, what do you think?"

"I love the name," she said.

Seeing Katherine pregnant was a joy when considering how long we had waited. Although, for her, I'm sure it wasn't so blissful and that the discomfort only increased with time. Eventually, she was unable to work in the fields harvesting the crops with the other women, and instead was confined to the more manageable tasks of sewing and cooking, which she happened to enjoy.

We had determined that by the end of the pregnancy we would have been in Jezria for three years, and if the days continued to pass as quickly as they had, they would all be behind us far too soon. At the same time, we heard nothing regarding Delvarus from Karesh, or Coleena, or anyone else during the months that transpired. Karesh would visit every now and again on matters of business, matters surrounding the nature of the Justiton keeping tabs on Jezria, but aside from this, he never had any news for my questions about my brother.

With this being the case, Katherine and I were often worried about Delvarus's safety, and on more than one occasion, I was intent on leaving for Caprecia with a rescue party. I had become convinced in my own mind that he had fallen into the hands of the Pridions and had been dealt with just as I had. However, the only thing that stopped me from ever going was the fact that Karesh eventually brought news back with him one day after a visit to Caprecia.

I was working in the stable re-shoeing Claudia for Thomas on a certain afternoon, when I heard his approach. I stopped what I was doing and waited for him to bring his horse within a reasonable talking distance. "Where are all the others?" I inquired, knowing that he most often came to Jezria accompanied by a small group of fellow Justiton.

"They're waiting just outside the city," he said.

"Won't you come in and stay for a while?" I asked, motioning toward my and Katherine's home.

"I'm afraid I have to report back in Litovia shortly. I have to be moving on very soon, but I wanted to bring you word."

"Word?" I questioned. "Word about Delvarus?"

"I've just come from Caprecia."

"Did you hear from my brother?" I asked with considerable eagerness.

"Actually, I did."

"And?"

"All is well, John. Delvarus is actually living among the people that are left in Caprecia. He's amassed a bit of a following too."

"So he's safe then?"

"Definitely."

"What of Henry?" I asked. "Where has he gone?"

"I don't know. I imagine he's still in hiding."

"Why don't the Justiton hunt him down before he has time to wreak havoc again?"

"Because Delvarus told us not to."

"He still thinks he can help him?"

"Yes, he told us that it wasn't time yet, that he still had sympathy to exhaust toward Henry. Delvarus is intent on giving him every opportunity to come to his senses," Karesh said. "Now I really must be on my way, but I'll see you again soon enough." With a wave of his hand, he bid his final goodbye then rode quickly out of sight.

As I stood lingering in the relief I felt from knowing that my brother was alright, I heard a voice of urgency coming from behind me. "John, come quick!" When I turned around, I saw Thomas running in my direction. "It's Katherine. She's having the baby."

By the time I reached the house, Martha was kneeling at her side, dabbing her forehead with a damp cloth while Mary knelt at her other side to offer any support she could. I fell at her shoulder, next to Mary, and grasped her hand in mine.

"It's too early," I said while looking to Martha. "This shouldn't happen for at least two more months."

"I know," she replied.

"What can I do?" I asked Katherine.

"Don't let go," she said between panting breaths, "and stay close; don't leave me."

"Never, I will be here the whole time."

As the hours dragged on, I could do nothing but watch as my sweet wife shook in exhaustion and pain. By the time night fell, however, the child's head was visible. Martha placed herself at the receiving end, coaching Katherine with each push. After every shriek of pain, she grasped my hand all the tighter. Tears streamed down her face, and I could see that she was worried.

"The head's out!" Martha exclaimed some time later. "Come on, one more push." Katherine's eyes shut in a wincing grimace, and she shouted as much as her wavering voice could manage; one last push and a new cry broke through the night. "It's a girl," Martha announced. Mary quickly brought me a cloth and Martha set the child in my arms. As I wrapped her tightly against the cool night, I feared for her small and fragile body. It was clear that she was underdeveloped. Her tiny frame was thin and shivered in the night air.

Even still, her whimpering cry and crinkled face was a miraculous sight to behold. As I held her in my arms, I felt as if I had been given a possession and responsibility more important and more cherished than anything I had yet to imagine, outside of my companionship with Katherine. In that moment I felt a supreme closeness to my wife, one which caused me to deeply contemplate the great promise of life that our sacred union had created.

I looked at Katherine with moistened eyes while the dearest most innocent-looking creation snuggled closely to my chest. I saw in Katherine the same joy I felt in my own heart, and our silence exchanged what words could not. "Meet your mommy," I said as I brought her to rest on Katherine's chest. Her eyes were filled with tears that seemed to replace the look of exhaustion that had been her sole expression for so long. We wiped the blood from the child's face and brought her little head to Katherine's mouth for her to kiss the baby with motherly adoration.

"Thomas, fetch me another towel for the blood will you?" I heard Martha say.

"Is there that much?" I asked.

"I'm afraid so. It's more than usual."

"What's that mean?" I inquired in a tone that tried to conceal the despair that was suddenly creeping into my mind.

Martha looked at me with worried eyes. "She may be hemorrhaging, I don't know."

"Someone has to go get Karesh. He has means we don't," I cried. "Someone has to go."

"No one knows the way to the city, but you," Thomas said.

"Don't leave me, John," I heard Katherine whimper.

I returned to her side with our child still wrapped in my arms and stared into her eyes. "I won't," I promised.

She gripped at my forearm, but already her strength seemed to be departing. I felt Thomas rest his hand on my shoulder in the next moment but couldn't bring myself to break eye contact with Katherine. "Tell me where to go, John. I'll go get Karesh," he said.

I turned to him and looked at a face that seemed as urgent as I felt. "You know the path through the mountains that we took here? That same path, as it goes toward the east forest, if you stay straight on it, you'll come to the walls of Litovia. Don't veer in any other direction at any fork, just stay eastward," I said.

"How do I find Karesh when I get there?" Thomas asked.

"Just tell the guards that you need to speak with him. Tell them that it's an emergency. Tell them it regards an old friend." With no further questions, Thomas offered a nod and disappeared out the door.

Moments later, Katherine complained of feeling cold. The bleeding continued, and Martha did the best she could. I handed our little Susan to Mary and wrapped my dear wife in a blanket, holding her as close as I could. "You'll be warm soon enough," I managed while hugging her tightly. "Thomas has left to get Karesh. He'll know what to do."

"I feel so weak," she whispered.

"It's alright, just rest."

I looked to Martha again, and her face failed to offer any expression of comfort. Her hands were stained in blood, and she motioned with her head for me to follow her. "John, come and help me fetch some more water."

"I'll be right back," I told Katherine, caressing her forehead and leaving a kiss. I followed Martha out of the house and into the early night. We walked only a few steps before she pulled me aside and choked on her first words.

"John, I don't know what to do. The bleeding isn't stopping."

"What are you saying?" I asked desperately.

She remained silent and looked at me with sympathy. "I'll

keep doing what I can. Stay close to her while I go get the water."

I returned to Katherine's side and held her cold hand in mine. Neither of us could keep the tears back now. When Martha returned, the bleeding still hadn't stopped and Katherine was growing weaker. I felt powerless to do anything for her, so I held her as close as I could, whispering in her ear all my love and admiration for her.

"I love you too," she said, "so much. You were there when I needed you most. You showed me love I'd never known." After she said this, her grasp grew looser with every passing second, until her hand fell lifeless in my own. I lingered in a spell of disbelief. The reality of the situation coursed through my veins like a cold wind. I placed my arm around her neck and touched her scarred but precious face against my own. My wife was gone, and I lay at her side sobbing like a child.

I tried all I could to help our baby after that, nestling her against the warmth of my chest, but by the time the night was old, her fragile and unprepared body had fought all it could, and I lost our little Susan as well. I cried so much in the following hours that sleep eluded me entirely. I passed through intense fits of anguish, realizing on each occasion that the woman who was my world was no longer with me, and that the little child who was born from our love was gone with her.

Chapter 33

Eventually, my grief exhausted me to the point that I fell into a subconscious stupor. I woke hours later to the sound of my door swinging open and a cool morning breeze following it. The light of the rising sun came into the room from around the figure of a tall and wearied man, who I was sure was Thomas. As he approached, I noticed his bloodshot eyes, his haggard stare, and the sorrow that was traced on the ridges of his face. "I tried, John. I did all that I could, but they wouldn't let me past the walls," he said. "They wouldn't let me talk to Karesh or even send a message to him."

"All the same," I said. "It's too late."

"I'm so sorry, John." He knelt down and gently placed his hand on Katherine's head in a way of offering his final goodbye. "What of the child?"

My lips began to quiver as I removed the blanket from over the tiny body I was holding close to my heart. "It looks like we've both lost our own Susan, Brother."

Tears streamed down Thomas's face with a deep and sincere empathy. "We have no friends in these hills but our own people," he remarked. "The Justiton will do nothing for us."

"Then we must stick together for all that it's worth," I said, trying my best to sound strong, even though my heart felt dead along with my cherished wife and daughter.

Thomas raised his head from the opposite side of Katherine and looked at me with indecision in his eyes. "What are we to do?"

In some pretended stoicism, I dried my eyes and stood up. "I'll take them to Karesh. There's no use waiting for him to show up here."

I wrapped our small Susan in the arms of Katherine and bundled them both in the finest blanket we owned. It was difficult for me to see much through the tears that were ever present in my eyes. My world was underwater, and I was barely keeping my head above the surface.

I managed to secure them in a peaceful cocoon of cloth with the assistance of Martha and Mary. I laid the blanket carefully over Katherine's face and recalled how glad I was the day she had grown comfortable enough to remove her veil in our presence. She had continued to cover her face in public, however, and I knew that's how she would want to be remembered in the eyes of everyone else.

Timmy and Simon both looked on in despair, and their disheartened expressions carried a weight that was apparent in their postures. Thomas helped me manage the bodies with as much reverence and care as possible, and when we stepped out of our home and into the morning's sun, a large crowd of people stood to greet us. "Word's traveled fast." Ernest said. "Everyone's come to pay their respects." It was then I noticed that the crowd carried on down the main road of our little town as far as its end.

As we moved past the closest group of fellow mourners, the crowd parted to revealed the finest carriage in town. And standing next to it was Mr. Samuel. "Only the best we have to offer," he said. "Take her in this. It's the very least I can do." He ultimately maintained his composure but looked as if he wanted to cry along with me.

"Thank you," I managed.

"Katherine was loved by us all," he said. "She will be greatly missed." He placed his hand on my shoulder and looked at me with compassion in his eyes. "You have the support of everyone around you, Friend."

I nodded my head. "Thank you," I said again.

Samuel had lined the carriage with fine linen and a spread of wild flowers that had been gathered for the occasion. My tears flowed freely when I saw those surrounding us shedding their own remorseful cries. The great care Samuel had taken to prepare for her departure touched my heart and made me love my friends all the more.

As the procession slowly moved down the road, Thomas, Ernest, Simon, and Samuel were obliged to walk alongside the carriage. While passing through the crowded lines, young children and women stepped up to the side of the carriage to place flowers over the bodies of Katherine and Susan, and every man stood with their heads bowed in reverence. The morning brought with it the deepest sorrow I have ever known, but it wasn't until now that I realized how closely knit our people had become.

When we came to the end of town, I looked back, and I saw that the crowd had formed behind me like the ripples of a wake behind a slow-moving ship. It was a moment both bitter and sweet in its nature. Katherine had touched many lives in the short time we had been together. Her amiable personality was a treasure, and I now realized how much everyone else had cherished her.

Suddenly, while all was still and quiet in the atmosphere of mourning, a commotion began to rise up the hill toward Jezria. It was a sound that I had heard once before, and in a short time, the perpetrator of the noise was made known to all. It rolled up the hill onto the road in front of us and came to stop just before the carriage. When the door was opened, Karesh came from inside and slowly walked toward us in observance of the somber scene.

He approached the carriage and looked at me with sorrow on his face. As he peered into the bed, I saw his eyes fill with tears, something I had only seen from him twice before. "I'm so sorry, John. I came as soon as I heard."

"I was just leaving to bring them to you," I said.

"The guards at the gate told me that someone had come asking for me, some colonist."

"It was me," Thomas spoke.

Karesh turned to look his way. "They didn't let you pass, I assume." Thomas merely shook his head in a defeated stare.

"Perhaps it wouldn't have changed anything," I offered. "She passed so quickly."

Karesh returned a look my way. "John, let me take her back. You need to rest. I can get her home faster."

I turned in my seat and stared back at the house that Katherine and I had made. She belonged with me and I with her, and the thought of parting was extremely difficult for me. Katherine was the owner of my heart's dearest sentiments. They were hers ever since she first told me she loved me, and I realized that in her absence those fine sentiments would be absent too. Yet, with her body still in my possession, they seemed to linger in the essence that surrounded her stillness.

I stared past our home and into the memories I had of Katherine. There I remained for a good amount of time before Karesh carefully called my attention back to the present. "John," he said. "The sooner I can get her back the better."

I turned and looked at him with my thoughts still lingering in a nostalgic episode. "Right," I answered. "Whatever's best for her and Susan."

"So the child hasn't survived?" Karesh asked in a tone that was sympathetic but lacking in surprise. I shook my head but said nothing. As I crawled down from behind the reins, my body felt weak and drained of life. I forced my steps to bring me to the carriage bed that held my world in its walls. "I have a stretcher we can use, John," Karesh offered. "It will make the transfer much easier."

He walked toward the strange vehicle and brought back two long rods that were connected by a hammock of thick cloth. With the help of Thomas and Karesh, I was able to move the bodies into the stretcher with little effort, but what was lacking in physical exertion was made up for in emotional strain. As we carried them to the doors of Karesh's transport, I felt as though I was parting with them a second and final time.

"I'll take the best care of them," Karesh informed me. "I'll have them sent to the island immediately."

"Thank you for your help," I said.

As the doors were shut, my heart was again open to the memory of last night. I watched in my mind as Katherine uttered her final words while she slowly slipped away from me. Now she left in a vehicle as strange to me as death, toward a distant eastern horizon.

Everyone in the crowd watched as Karesh drove out of sight, and though I was saying my final goodbyes from a distance now, I was glad that he had come, glad that he was able to send my dear ones home within the day. He had taken some risk bringing an advanced thing such as that vehicle to Jezria. He was likely to have taken it undetected by anyone else in Litovia, because such an act wouldn't have been permitted by their law, even under dire circumstances. Karesh had risked his standing with the Justiton twice now for the sake of a colonist, and I was indebted to him for both occasions.

Everyone else eventually returned to their homes while I was left standing alone, peering down the road toward the east. I couldn't bring myself to leave the spot where I last saw her, where I turned her care over to a friend. She was gone to me now, but a part of her still remained and caused my heart to ache for her presence.

Chapter 34

The following weeks were more difficult than any I had endured. I couldn't help but count the days that we figured would have brought Katherine to full term. I remember crying myself to sleep the night the counting was through, and though it marked the time of our third year since meeting, it was the emptiest commemoration I could imagine without her present.

I had learned to carry on in the affairs of daily living, but life had ceased to start again for me. Surviving was all I was doing. My heart yearned for the cherished moments of the past, the moments when I held Katherine in my arms and was left wanting nothing more. I found myself revisiting the spot where Karesh had left with her body entombed in the vehicle from Litovia.

One particular morning, as I stood at the end of the road where I had bid my last farewell to Katherine, I thought upon our small Susan who had passed that night with her. It seemed a great injustice that a woman should suffer so much to bring a child into this world, only to have that child die without the chance to see morning. I found myself lost in this thought as I stared down the road that wound into the trees and disappeared from view.

Suddenly, a voice woke me from my mournful contemplations. "John," it said in a familiar tone. I turned around to find

Thomas standing behind me with a look of trepidation on his face. "There's a man that's come to town asking about you, says it's urgent."

"Who is he?" I asked.

"He says his name is Peter. He says he comes from Caprecia."

"From Caprecia?"

"Yes, and there's a very worried mood about him."

We wasted no time in returning to the center of town where we saw a small group of our people huddled in a mass. As we approached, those present made room to reveal the personage of an exhausted and defeated-looking man, who sat on the ground next to a horse that had collapsed to its knees. He looked at me as I neared, and while still breathing a bit heavily, as if he had sustained the same strain as his four legged companion, he rose to his feet. "Are you John?" he asked.

"I am, and you must be Peter."

"Yes."

"I don't recall ever meeting you before. How do you know my name, and how did you know to find me here?"

"I'm a friend of your brother, Delvarus. He told me where to find you."

"You know my brother?"

"Is there somewhere we could speak?" he asked. "I'm afraid the matter is quite urgent."

I looked at Thomas and then back at Peter. "Follow me."

As Thomas and I walked toward my home, Ernest left the crowd and joined me at my side. "What is this all about?" he questioned. I had no answer for him; neither did Thomas. The one man who did, however, opted to say nothing. When we reached the door, the group that had followed us stopped and waited to hear an explanation for the man's arrival. I turned to look at them and then back at Peter. "Let us speak first," he said. "There's no reason to incite pandemonium."

Now I was really worried. We walked into the house and took a seat at the table while Thomas and Ernest stood at the wall by the entrance. A moment later, a loud knock came to the door. As I rose to answer, Thomas opened it to reveal Simon standing at the threshold. "I came as soon as I heard," he said. "Rumor's spreading in the street that someone's here from Caprecia."

"Yes, this is Peter, I said. "He brings news of Delvarus."

"Indeed, but I'm afraid I bring grave news, John." His eyes grew very tired looking, and he appeared to be holding back grief as he said this. "Your brother is dead," he spoke with a painful tone. "I´ve been fortunate enough to escape to tell you and to warn you."

I was speechless for a time before I managed to express my astonishment. "Delvarus is dead?"

"I´m afraid so."

I fell back in my chair in silence as I turned it over in my mind. "How can that be?"

"I´m afraid he was killed by the very man he was trying to save," Peter replied.

"What do you mean?" Thomas asked. "Who´s done this?"

I sat up in my place. My hand grew tight into a fist, my teeth clenched until I felt they might shatter, and my blood boiled in rage. "It was Henry, wasn´t it?"

"Yes, it was. Henry and the Pridions murdered Delvarus."

"How did this happen?" Ernest cried.

"I hadn´t been in Caprecia long when I first met Delvarus," Peter said. "But shortly after I had, his story began to spread. He soon gained a number of followers and that's when Henry began to feel threatened. He and the Pridions tried to convince everyone that your brother was a lunatic, and that his stories about other worlds and high science were all lies. But it didn´t work. So they took him away." He paused and let his head drop into his hands. He pulled at his hair and tightly shut his eyes as if he couldn´t bear to say what happened next.

"What did he do to our brother?" Simon insisted.

Peter looked up at him with reddened eyes and an expression of pity in his face, as if the task that was asked of him was most difficult. "I was able to get away and follow after them undetected," he finally continued. "I saw it all."

"All of what?" I asked.

"Henry and his followers tried to drag it out of him, but he wouldn´t budge," Peter answered in mild hysteria.

"Drag what out of him?" I begged.

He regained his composure and began to speak again. "Your location. Henry has been looking for you and everyone that followed since the day you left. When he realized the connection between Delvarus and your people, it was just a matter of time before he tried something crazy. But your brother wouldn´t tell him anything." He fell silent again and wrestled with the anguish inside of him. "John, I´ve never seen a man as strong as your brother reduced so low. They tortured him within a thread of his life, as if they intended to witness his worst sufferings before finally letting him die." Peter buried his head in his hands again in an agitated manner.

"All is lost now," Ernest said. "Who can stop Henry if Delvarus can´t?"

Peter continued speaking while staring forward into space, as if in some trance imposed by the horror of the tale. "When they brought him to the town square the next morning, he was barely alive. It was difficult to even recognize him after they had beaten him so severely. They made all those present watch. They made an example out of his opposition to the rightful order, as they called it. Then they hung him from the large tree in the center garden till he was dead."

"What has become of my brother´s body?" I asked with great concern.

Peter looked us all in the eye before speaking again. "But it´s as if he knew it would happen," he said.

"What are you talking about?" Thomas asked. "Where is the body?"

"Don't worry," Peter replied. "I've hidden the body. It's safe. He had told me where to put it. He also told me that if ever his enemies were able to take his life, they would be sealing their own fate," he said, turning to face me directly. "It was about a year ago that he said it, but I've never forgotten, because he gave me such detailed instructions along with it. He informed me of your journey to a place called Jezria and exactly how to find it. Then he told me that I was to waste no time in coming here if ever he were killed. He said that once I told you about his fate, you would know who to give the news to."

"Karesh?" I questioned. "But..." I fell silent and marveled at the epiphany that struck my mind in the next moment. It was then that the mystery became clear to me, as if Delvarus himself had explained the matter in his great simplicity. When I realized what he had done, my heart swelled with loving admiration for my dear brother and friend. Then Peter, in his urgency, insisted that I speak. "John," he said. "Whatever it is we are to do, we must be quick. Word of your location has leaked from men of lesser constitutions. I'm afraid Henry knows where you are."

"How could he?" Simon insisted. "Delvarus is the only one that knew, except for—" he stopped himself, for he must have realized what came to me next.

"Except for those few who left us," I said.

"Word was traveling fast when I left, and I heard of Henry's plans to march his army into these hills," Peter continued. "Whoever it is you're supposed to inform, I hope he can help."

"They can, and they will," I said. "Thanks to Delvarus." I rose to my feet and stood at the side of Thomas. "You must charge the people with everything we've just heard. Prepare them as best you can for Henry's approach, but I will soon be back with help."

"From where?" Thomas inquired.
"From Litovia," I said.
"The Justiton? But, John, they won't fight for us."
"You're right, but they will fight for Delvarus."

Chapter 35

Claudia ran with an ability beyond her age as we made dust our wake on the road to Litovia. As I listened to her panting rhythm, I knew that she wouldn't be able to keep the pace for long. Yet, she continued on her own even after I had ceased to kick at her side with my heels. It was as if she could sense the urgency which hung in the air like a dense and formidable fog.

The trees flew past us and rushed with the wind of our speed as we careened through the narrow passageway that took us toward the walls of the city. Eventually, Claudia's pace slowed, but I could tell by the movement of her muscles that she was keeping the quickest speed she could manage. "Come on girl," I insisted. "You can do it; keep it up."

With each encouraging statement, I could sense her resolve thicken. Her breath billowed through her nostrils loud and strong, and I began to wonder if this loyal horse was willing to give her life at my command. Reason brought me to my senses, and I knew that if I didn't force her to slow, we might not make it at all. "Whoa girl, keep it steady; keep it steady."

By the time we finally reached the bordering walls of Litovia, Claudia began to stagger in exhaustion. "Come on girl; we're almost there," I urged. "It's within our sight. See, there's the city. Steady now." As we approached the entrance, the guards looked at me as if my presence was a great surprise to them. I jumped from the saddle and approached them with haste. "You have to let me through to speak with Karesh," I said. "It´s urgent. Henry has killed Delvarus, and now he plans to march against Jezria."

"Wait a minute," one of the men said, "Delvarus can´t be dead, why he´s—"

"I tell you he is!" I cried. "A man from Caprecia has escaped to tell us. My brother has been murdered. Karesh must know." The two men stared at me with bewildered looks on their faces, as if they couldn´t believe what was being said. "We have to act quickly," I insisted. "Henry could be approaching Jezria as we speak, and he does so with the belief that you will do nothing. Don´t let my brother´s death be in vain," I said. "He died to protect us."

"Right," the man replied. He turned away from me and spoke some strange wording into the radio in his shirt and then motioned to another man standing near the tall tower that overlooked the valley in every direction. A moment later, a car sped away down the large road protracting into the heart of Litovia.

The man began again to speak into his radio box, and after saying what sounded like, "code red, I repeat, code red," he turned to me and offered a serious stare. "Go back to Jezria now; we´ll take care of it from here."

"But what are you going to do?" I demanded. By the time I finished uttering these words, the man had already turned to run and never looked back. I felt defeated and alone in dire circumstances. Surely they planned to do something, but I couldn´t wait around to see what. I hopped back into the saddle and steered Claudia toward home.

The trip back was fraught with sorrow, uncertainty, and frustration. Claudia was unable to maintain the pace she had before, but her zeal pushed us toward our home with a brave determination. "That a girl," I said. "Keep it up; you can do it," I encouraged.

As we rode time seemed to pass very slowly. I worried all the while that the Justiton wouldn't do anything in time to stop Henry and that my friends and brothers would have to face his murderous tyranny. I clutched at the reins in wholehearted anger and determined that I was going to have to take matters into my own hands. If Henry was going to come against us, he was going to pay a heavy price for it.

When we returned from the forest and made our way up the rise on which Jezria stood, I heard a sharp whistle and then a painful neighing sound coming from Claudia. A fraction of time whirled before my view as I saw an arrow lodged within the side of my companion. She fell to her knees mid gallop and crashed to the ground, just outside Jezria's bounds, throwing me through the air. I fell to my stomach on the hard and rock-laden floor of the valley, finally coming to a stop with my face buried in the dirt. Scraped and bleeding, the next thing I heard was the slow but steady crunch of feet walking toward me.

"I was beginning to wonder where you had gone," a familiar but heinous voice spoke. "We've been looking for you for a very long time. Though I must say, I never thought you would come here," Henry laughed maniacally. I tried to rise to my feet with my arms, but my right shoulder was immovable and throbbing with pain. "You know, I never thought that you would have been foolish enough to challenge me either," Henry said as he stooped near the ground by my face. "But I told you what would happen if you didn't cooperate, and I am a man of my word, after all."

Suddenly, a rope was flung over my neck and cinched tightly around my throat as the horse to which it was attached moved forward. In reaction, I lodged my hands between the rope and my flesh just before the horse took off galloping, dragging me all the way to the center of town.

When the rider finally brought the horse to a stop, I felt barely alive under the strain of suffocation. I rolled on my back and saw Henry approaching from behind. He pulled on his horse's reins and swung out of the saddle. "Put him next to Thomas," Henry hissed.

The rope remained around my neck, though it loosened enough for me to breathe easier once they cut it from the saddle. I soon found my arms bound behind me, and though the pain in my shoulder was multiplied in intensity, the pain of the scene that came to view was far greater. I anguished as I looked upon Martha and Thomas kneeling beneath the blade of two Pridions. Their arms were bound behind their backs just like mine, and their heads were bowed to the ground. An army of archers stood in line around them and held all the others in Jezria at a distance.

"Let them go!" I yelled.

I was punched in the stomach and thrown to my knees by Thomas's side. I heard the crowd of our on-looking friends screaming for mercy on our behalf, but their screams fell on ears that considered it laughter. I felt the heavy cold steel of a sword placed on my neck, and the sharp edge cut into my flesh as I turned to try and see Thomas and Martha again. Thomas seemed surprisingly calm and still, and Martha appeared the same, but I could see tears coursing down her cheek as I looked closer.

"I suppose this is the end, Brother," Thomas choked.

"I'm so sorry," I said.

"And you should be," Henry exclaimed. "It's because of your defiance that your friends are in this situation. Had you listened to me, I might have made you my servant. You all could have been in the service of a great leader, but this is the miserable end you chose instead."

"We're brothers you fool. Don't you realize what you are doing?" I yelled.

"Brothers?" he laughed. "You sound like that lunatic, Delvarus, with his elaborate stories. Are you really so stupid? Do you actually think that there is some special reason you wound up here? Wake up! This place is what you make of it, and you and all your idiotic friends don't have the spine to be great."

"You're a coward and a fool, Henry. You're delusional to think you are some leader. You're merely a pathetic malicious slave driver."

Henry pushed aside the man that held the sword to me and took the weapon in his own hand, sending it running across the back of my neck where it formed a searing laceration that spilled blood down the top of my back. "We'll see about that," he said.

As he finished saying this, a rumbling sound turned everyone's attention to the forest beyond the city. In an instant, some twenty or more vehicles similar to the one Karesh had brought to the city breached the tree line and rolled toward us. In the following moment, they came to a stop, and a small army of men proceeded from inside the vehicles and stood with large metal-like rods pointed at Henry and his men.

It was this distraction that afforded me enough time to push to my side and knock Thomas and Martha to the ground. I quickly rose to my feet, stepping past Thomas, who lay huddled over Martha to protect her from any harm. In the next second, I ran into their would-be assassins, pushing them into the crowd of archers that stood in line behind them. As I did, I felt an excruciating pinch and a nauseating pain that gripped at my bowels as the sword of one impaled my stomach.

I fell to the ground in a daze and felt my midsection convulsing in pain. My heart raced, and with each thump, it sent blood spilling into my throat. As I lay on the ground in the grips of fleeting life, I saw shock and horror in the eyes of Henry when, in the next moment, the Justiton's weapons issued forth a loud and breaking noise as fire spit from their ends and caused Pridions to drop like flies.

Henry was one of the first to fall, and I watched as his lifeless face fell to the ground in front of me. Before any archer could draw back an arrow, they were pummeled to the ground with the shots taken by the men in crimson red. In the following moment, Henry's people were retreating back toward Caprecia, but the Justiton remained in their stance against them, mowing them down like grass against a wild fire.

Thomas crawled to my side and lifted my head in his arms. "Brother!" he cried. "Stay with us. Don't go!" The next thing I saw was Karesh hovering over me.

"Karesh, take care of my friends," I said as the blood choked my words. It was soon after this that my sight grew dim. I labored more and more to breathe, and eventually everything fell dark.

Chapter 36

I remembered. When my eyes grew dark, I saw Karesh and Thomas and the events of my death play out again. I saw Henry and his people destroyed by the weapons of the Justiton. I saw Thomas and Martha bowed to the earth at the feet of a Pridion army. An arrow had pierced the side of Claudia. We were running to Jezria as fast as her tired body could manage. Then I saw the guard speaking the code into his radio as he ran past the walls of Litovia.

I watched trees fly past my view and the sight of Claudia's head bouncing with her quickened stride. Peter cried over Delvarus at the table in my home, and Thomas, Simon, and Ernest all listened with me as he told us of Henry's plans. I watched as Peter rose from the ground and made it to his feet, while his horse still lay panting on its knees. Next, I was peering off into the distance and thinking of Katherine.

Then I saw her in Samuel's carriage, the beautiful form of my wife, shrouded in crimson silk, and all around her were the people who came to see her one last time. I saw the child, Susan, lying close to my chest trying to fight against the cold. I saw Katherine lying on the bed in our home, weak and pale. I looked at her and the light in her face was fading.

I then saw her pushing in pain as she labored to bring our daughter into the world. After this, I saw her eyes, and she was staring at me again in some heavenly way. I viewed her first meeting with Thomas and everyone in Jezria and then the trip from her home to the ruins. I saw her running away from the river on the back of her horse as I stood watching.

I witnessed a procession of people following me into the hills beyond Caprecia, and afterward, saw the gathering of the same large group in the countryside near Ernest's home. I saw the old house of Thomas and Martha, and standing around it was Samuel and his people, listening to me speak. I witnessed the death of my little friend, Susan, and watched everyone present lamenting the loss of the cherished little girl.

Next, I saw the commotion caused by my speech about Henry's intentions, witnessing him run at the approach of those against him. I watched a group of angry individuals who beat me incessantly, and then I was fighting with one. I saw Amos breezing through the trees of the night, and then I saw Karesh on horseback, Litovia, the library, the chart room, and my journey with Delvarus across the plain.

I remembered my trip back from the cottage in the south forest. I recalled Janaea and how my heart ached for her. I saw Delvarus piloting the boat across the waters with considerable speed, and then I remembered the underwater ship and my visit to the island with the strange building. Then I saw that strange building in the book that Thomas kept.

I saw the fields of my first home and the children at play. I saw a bottle thrown in the ocean and Simon walking toward the shore. I saw a night that found me riding to the shores in a carriage under a bundle of cloth, and then I saw Martha bringing a spoonful of soup to my mouth and the eyes of little Susan peering down at me as I lay on the sands of the shore.

Afterward, I saw the face of a most gorgeous woman with tears welling in her eyes as her hand reached out to mine and our grasp slowly parted. Next, I found her in my arms staring at me. Her beautiful face beamed between the silk-like strands of hair that met her shoulders in a graceful touch, and her lips spoke words that tugged at my heart.

"I love you, Markeus," Janae said. Then I remembered who I was and all that I had been.

The scenes which had flashed before my eyes ceased, and I mused on all that had returned to my memory. My real name was Markeus, and Janaea was my espoused wife who I had missed so much back in Caprecia. But as I finished this thought, another replaced it, one that caused even greater sentiment. It was the memory of Katherine.

For the first time since I left for Caprecia, my mind recalled all that I had experienced with Janaea, but my love was turned to the woman whose face had been scarred by her bravery. I reached out to Katherine in my thoughts and lingered in the moments with her that were more precious to me than anything else. Yet, upon doing so, for what seemed to be a mere second, everything went dark, and I suddenly felt a surge of energy, as if it coursed through once-lifeless veins.

Chapter 37

When I opened my eyes, I found myself lying on my back looking up into a blue sky through a large dome-shaped pane of glass directly above me. The clouds that hung overhead slowly coursed across my view, revealing the rays of the sun as they pierced through the covering and onto my face.

The floor beneath me seemed to be made of glass, underneath which was a vibrant blue substance similar too the sky overhead. All around me circled a silver-looking wall with golden trim at the base, and throughout the entire building there wasn't a single window, apart from the atrium overhead. It was then I realized that I had been in this place before.

I heard a latching noise and the release of air as if a large seal was being broken. I looked to the right of me and noticed a massive opening in the wall swinging outward to reveal the bright sunlight coursing through the entrance. There appeared the outline of a man whose features I couldn't see until my eyes adjusted to the increase of light. I squinted and opened them again to a better focused world. "Delvarus?" I questioned.

"I'm very pleased with you, Markaeus," he replied. "You've learned the law of our world and lived by its influence. Welcome home, Little Brother."

I patted at my face and chest to assure that I wasn't dreaming but was actually alive. "You mean I'm back?"

"Yes."

"But how did the Justiton get me back so quickly? I was only dead for seconds."

"Well, it may have seemed that way," Delvarus replied, "but that's because you were confined alone to the dimension of your mind, or the realm of origin, as we call it. Surely you remember the discussion we had about it back in Jezria?"

"Yes, I do."

"Then you will recall that the realm of origin is a world of light, because the mind is light, and in such a place time has no reference," he said. "I've spoken with Karesh since your death. It was actually three days before they got you back to the island."

"I see," I answered, looking at the man I now remembered admiring from the very beginning. Then my thoughts turned to the news I received of his death. "The Justiton found your body."

"Yes, I got back not too long ago myself," he answered. "Peter was able to show them exactly where he had taken it."

"What is to become of Henry?"

Sorrow came to the eyes of Delvarus, and a brief moment elapsed before he spoke again. "I tried so hard to get him to change his ways, but he wouldn't listen. I warned him what would happen if he didn't repair his wrongs and turn from a life of harm and hatred."

"But you let him kill you," I remarked.

"Yes, and if I hadn't, countless others would have died at his hand. I knew it would take a power above all others to convince the Justiton to fight for our people. I knew it would take the high law."

Silence followed while I thought about his decision. "And we all are indebted to you for it," I finally said. I paused for a moment to think about all those Pridions who had died because of their lust for power. I thought back to the moment I

watched fear come into Henry's eyes, right before he fell lifeless to the ground. "He's dead now. Henry I mean."
"Yes, I know."
"What is to be done with him?"
"He'll be brought to justice. He'll have to stand before you, me, and the entire council. He will have to cower in the presence of all those he betrayed. The very thought is likely causing him unrelenting fear at this moment."
"You mean he knows?"
"Yes, I warned him. And now that he remembers everything once more, he will have time enough to think about what he has done. Then he will be banished forever."
"Where will you send him?"
"We've found a place for Henry and all his followers, but don't worry about it. "You're home now, and that's what matters," Delvarus concluded.
All frustration and sorrow departed from me when I heard these words, and I stared forward in a daze of elation and amazement. "How is it that death can be overturned?"
"You remember what I told you of the difference between our world and Caprecia?"
"Yes, you said their natures were opposite."
"That's right," he returned. "In Caprecia, the nature of chaos is bound to destroy the connections that form life, and when this happens, the link between your mind and body is lost. However, there is no chaos here at home. Order and life are the nature of existence."
"So, how was the link to my mind reconnected?" I questioned.
"You're body was sent here," he returned, "or rather, the composition of your body was changed to something more pure, changed so that it existed in this dimension."
"You mean, like a change in frequency, as Josesh explained?"

"Yes, I've heard him use that comparison before, and it's a good one. The building you are standing in now is exactly same as the structure you saw on the island, and it's in these buildings that the science of this change occurs. Once the material that composes your physical existence is caused to pulse at the frequency of this world, your body ceases to exist in Caprecia and disappears to this realm. Here the connection with your mind is renewed, because this world and the realm of your mind are so close that matter and light are infused together to form an immortal harmony."

I stood still in astonishment as I worked the idea over in my mind. "It's amazing to think about and difficult at the same time," I said.

"Don't worry," Delvarus returned. "You'll learn at an increased rate of speed here. It will be elementary to you soon enough." Now come along. There are many old friends waiting to greet you."

As I stepped out of the strange building, I noticed that its appearance was identical to the one I had seen on the island of the Justiton. But a my attention was immediately drawn to the person I saw in front of me. There he stood, a leader among leaders, the man I had always wanted to emulate just as Delvarus had done so perfectly. His appearance was as amazing and inspiring as was his personality, one that epitomized all that a man should be. His eyes seemed as deep as eternity, and his countenance expressed the form of a man old in years and wise beyond their number. Yet, his smile and stature seemed to convey a never-ending youth. He appeared as though he was the father of time itself, and yet, portrayed in word and deed, a man forever in his prime. "Welcome home, Son." He said as he embraced me the way a father does a child that has been gone for a long time. "I'm so pleased with what you've done."

Next to him stood a woman of unsurpassed majesty, whose face told of innumerable levels of maturity and goodness. My loving mother offered a sweet hug around my neck and looked into my eyes with deep appreciation. "I'm so glad to have you back home now," she whispered. "It's a hard thing on a mother to have her children away, and in such a place as you were. I missed you, my dear Markaeus."

Tears of joy streamed from my eyes as I stood in the presence of my parents. "I missed you too, Mother—Father."

They stepped to my side, and my father placed his arm around my shoulder. As I peered forward, I saw a multitude of familiar faces. I found myself standing in the center of a majestic city that seemed to shine as brightly as the sun that beamed from the rich blue sky overhead. Vibrant fields of green and roads of smooth marble extended into the distance beyond the crowd, and all around us was a constant warmth and energy that seemed to make us all as one in mind and heart.

As I approached the group, they all raised their arms and lauded me with shouts of joy and excitement. A reunion of friends was never sweeter. I couldn't hide the joy that swelled in my heart, and I continued to offer tears of gratitude as I encountered long-lost loved ones.

When I waded farther into the crowd, those present before me began to part and leave an opening in the road beneath us. There, in the middle of all the excitement, was the same little face that I first saw on the shores of Caprecia. "John, yer not dead no more," Susan exclaimed as she ran to wrap her arms around my legs.

I pulled her away and knelt down to give her a hug in return. I was so happy to see her alive and well that I hardly knew what to say at first. "Susan, you cute little thing!"

"Dat's whut day say," she shrugged. "Know sometin? I missed you John."

"I missed you too," I chuckled, "very much."

"Are my mommy and daddy otay?" she asked, "cause I bet dey miss me rill bad."

"Oh they do, little Susie, but they'll be back here with you before you know it."

Just then, I noticed beyond the face of little Susan, a complexion very dear and familiar to me. As I looked up, she approached and dropped to her knees in front of us. "I'm so glad to see you again," she said, throwing her arms around my neck.

"Janaea," I replied. "It's been a long time."

"Yes, it's seemed so long."

My heart was overjoyed to see her again, and I recalled the memories that graced my dreams while in Caprecia. But as soon as this joy came, a degree of turmoil followed. For, though I recalled at that moment all that I had loved about Janaea over the years of my life, I couldn't help but ache to see the woman whose love had borne our child. Katherine owned my heart, even in the presence of Janaea, and I couldn't be fully comforted until I saw her again.

As I turned to my side, I noticed that my crowd of friends had departed a small distance to give us space to ourselves. Susan had left and had begun playing with some other children in the nearby field of grass, and all that remained around us was uncertainty. "Have you been waiting for me all this time?" I asked.

"Of course, waiting with an eager heart," she said.

She leaned forward and kissed me, and I couldn't help but return the affection in the moment, though immediately after, I felt guilt for the fact that it hadn't been Katherine. As our lips parted, Janaea could see it in my eyes.

"What's the matter?" she asked, as if she was about to cry.

"Delvarus told me that you weren't waiting at home for me?"

"Why wouldn't I wait for you?" she stammered

"I figured that he meant you had moved on."

A welling of tears began in her eyes. "Did you hope I had?"

"No. I dreamed of you in Caprecia, and my hopes to see you again tormented me in your absence. Then Delvarus told me I had to move on, and, well, I did eventually. Oh, Janaea, I once loved you with all my heart, but my heart belongs to another now."

As I said this, she wiped at her eyes and began to smile. "You don´t recognize me, do you?"

"Of course I do. You were my dearest love before I left, Janaea. We were engaged to be married."

"We are married, John," she smiled.

"What?"

"I was sent to Caprecia too. It´s me," she said. "It´s Katherine. And look, there´s someone else waiting to meet you." She smiled from ear to ear before turning around. A man, who I recognized to be her father, came toward us with an infant in his arms while her mother approached at his side. He handed the child to Katherine, and he and his wife smiled at me without saying a word. "Say hello to your daddy," Katherine said as I stood to look at the face of my dear little Susan. Her eyes beamed back at me, and a tiny smile grew between her plump and rosy cheeks.

I looked at my wife and lost myself in her deep and glorious eyes. It was too much to take in all at once. Never had I felt a joy so full. Tears came without restraint. I reached my arm around her back and kissed her beautiful lips where her own tears mingled with mine. When I looked down at Susan again, I saw her mother's face in her tiny features. "She looks just like you."

Katherine returned a smile and passed her over into my arms. I held her close to my heart as I did on that fateful night in Jezria and kissed her small forehead. "You were born of the most amazing woman," I told her.

"And of a courageous father," Katherine added.

When I looked back at her, I caressed the side of her face where once the scars had destroyed her smooth flesh. She held my hand against her cheek then brought it away to kiss it with affection. I had missed her when she visited my dreams and lost her a second time after she had become my dream. Now she stood before me, never again to leave my side or create a hole in my heart. She was with me forever.

"You know the necklace you gave me before I left? It conjured memories of you. It did exactly what you hoped it would," I said. Katherine smiled back at me but remained silent. "Did you never recognize me in Caprecia, never have any dreams of me?"

"I did," she said.

"And you never said anything?"

"I was rather hoping you would learn to love Katherine more than Janaea," she answered.

As I stood with my dearest love in my arms and the child whose life was born from our union, I gazed around me at a world of beauty. My parents and Katherine's came to stand at our sides, and Delvarus placed his hand on my shoulder. "I knew that things would turn out very well in the end."

"You always knew," I said.

"Or, perhaps, I had hope."

"Well, it was your hope that got us here."

I held Katherine closer than ever before and peered off in the distance, into a world of wonder that now held new meaning for me. Where once travail and sorrow were my companions in Caprecia, I now stood with new perspective in a place where life continued forever forward, where joy had no bounds, and where love was law.

About the Author
Jordan Arey

From his earliest years, Jordan wanted to understand who he was, why he was, how things worked, and for what purpose. He passed through a childhood stage of eager questioning, riddling his parents with countless inquiries". He can remember the repetition of a certain phrase from his father as a child: "Why all the questions? Are you writing a book?" he would ask. Well, he wasn't then, but he can see now that all his questioning was preparing his mind to do so later.

After high school, Jordan turned to further studies in his faith and attended an institute of religion from which he graduated. During this time, he practiced writing essays on varying subjects to establish his style and voice in the written word. A short time later, he left on a two year ecclesiastical mission that lent greater insight and understanding to the subjects of his work. After returning, he began his college studies, married his wonderful wife, and took to writing with more focus and determination than ever before, completing several short stories and his first novel *Powers of Influence*.

WWW.JORDANAREY.COM
WWW.POWERSOFINFLUENCE.COM

HOMEBOUND PUBLICATIONS
Independent Publisher of Contemplative Titles

Going back to go forward is the philosophy of Homebound. We recognize the importance of going home to gather from the stores of old wisdom to help nourish our lives in this modern era. We choose to lend voice to those individuals who endeavor to translate the old truths into new context. Our titles introduce insights concerning mankind's present internal, social and ecological dilemmas.

It is the intention of those at Homebound to revive contemplative storytelling. We publish introspective full-length novels, parables, essay collections, epic verse, short story collections, journals and travel writing. In our fiction titles our intention is to introduce a new mythology that will directly aid mankind in the trials we face at present.

The stories humanity lives by give both context and perspective to our lives. Some older stories, while well-known to the generations, no longer resonate with the heart of the modern man nor do they address the present situation we face individually and as a global village. Homebound chooses titles that balance a reverence for the old wisdom; while at the same time presenting new perspectives by which to live.

WWW.HOMEBOUNDPUBLICATIONS.COM

CPSIA information can be obtained at www.ICGtesting.com
Printed in the USA
BVOW080210271112

306575BV00002B/98/P

9 781938 846021